DEEP-SPACE DESTROYERS!

The wing commander turned to the video screen. He saw, upper left, a globe of ships—what ships! Some were Service jobs, with extra turrets plastered on them. Some were orthodox freighters, with the same porcupine-bristle of weapons. Some were obviously home-made crates, hideously ugly—and as heavily armed as the others.

The interceptor squadron swam into the field—a sleek, deadly needle of vessels in perfect alignment. The contact was immediate and shocking. One of the rebel ships lumbered into the path of the interceptors, spraying fire from as many points as a man has pores. It rammed an interceptor with a crunch that must have killed every man before the first bulwark, and kept fighting . . .

> —*from* "The Only Thing We Learn"
> by Cyril M. Kornbluth

SPACE DREADNOUGHTS

EDITED BY
DAVID DRAKE
WITH CHARLES G. WAUGH
AND MARTIN HARRY GREENBERG

ACE BOOKS, NEW YORK

SPACE DREADNOUGHTS

An Ace Book / published by arrangement with
the editors

PRINTING HISTORY
Ace edition / July 1990

ISBN: 0-441-77735-X

CONTENTS

INTRODUCTION

A QUICK LOOK AT BATTLE FLEETS

One of the problems with figuring out how ships are going to fight in space (assuming that we have ships in space, which isn't as likely as I wish; and, that we're still fighting when we get there, which is unfortunately more probable) is that there are a lot of maritime models to choose from.

It's also true that some of the maritime models came from very specialized sets of circumstances; and a few of them weren't particularly good ideas even in their own time.

And it's also true that some of the writers applying the models have a better grasp of the essentials than others. That isn't limited to writers of fiction. For example, I recall two essays which were originally published about fifty years ago in *Astounding*.

In the first of the essays, Willy Ley, a very knowledgeable man who had been involved with the German rocket program, proved to my satisfaction that warships in space would carry guns, not missiles, because, over a certain small number of rounds, the weight of a gun and its ammunition was less than the weight of the same number of complete missiles. The essay was illustrated with graphs of pressure curves, and was based on the actual performance of nineteenth-century British rocket artillery ("the rockets' red glare" of Francis Scott Key).

As I say, the essay was perfectly convincing . . . until I read the paired piece by Malcolm Jameson.

Jameson's qualifications were relatively meager. Before throat cancer forced him to retire, he'd been a United States naval officer—but he was a mustang, risen from the ranks, rather than an officer with the benefit of an Annapolis education. For that matter, Jameson had been a submariner rather than a surface-ship sailor during much of his career. That was a dangerous specialty—certainly as dangerous a career track as any in the peacetime navy—but it had limited obvious bearing on war in vacuum.

Jameson's advantage was common sense. He pointed out (very gently) that at interplanetary velocities, a target would move something on the order of three miles between the time a gun was fired and the time the projectile reached the end of the barrel.

The rest of Jameson's essay discussed tactics for missile-launching spaceships—which were possible, as the laws of physics proved gun-laying spaceships were not. Ley could have done that math just as easily. It simply hadn't occurred to him to ask the necessary questions.

Light-swift beam weapons were a fictional staple in Jameson's day (he used them in his stories about Bullard of the Space Patrol) and a realistic possibility in ours. And the advent of the electrically-driven railgun has brought even projectile artillery back into the realm of space warfare.

Present realities don't prevent a writer from building any number of self-consistent constructs of how space war *will* work, however.

At one time, boarding and hand-to-hand combat were common notions in military science fiction (which, in the 1920s and 30s, was rather a lot of science fiction). Boarding has a long naval tradition as, at times, the heaviest available weapons were not by themselves sufficient to sink major warships. When oared warships grew sturdy enough to be equipped with rams, however, ramming replaced boarding as the tactic of choice . . .

Until sailing ships replaced oared warships. Sailing ships can't mount effective rams because their masts and rigging would come down with the shock. The guns available during the next five centuries weren't effective ship-killers, and boarding returned.

As guns became more powerful and ships were designed to mount large numbers of them along the sides, the sort of melees that characterized the Armada battles and the meeting engagements of the Anglo-Dutch Wars of the seventeenth century gave way to formal line-of-battle tactics. Opposing fleets were expected to sail along in parallel lines, firing all their guns at one another, until something happened.

Mostly, nothing much happened. A typical example is the action between the fleets of DeGrasse and Graves in 1781 in Chesapeake Bay. This was the crucial battle that decided the fate of the British army at Yorktown—and, thus, the Revolutionary War. It was a draw, with no ships lost on either side (which turned out to be good enough for the American rebels, of course).

Nelson changed matters by what amounted to assertiveness training for the British navy. *His* captains were expected to close with the enemy and board if necessary, instead of staying at a reasonable range and letting noise and smoke stand in the place of doing real damage. Nelson's opponents never beat him. In the end, they were able to kill him; but even dead he led his forces to victory.

The appearance of steam and armored warships in the nineteenth century gave rise to an amazing number of theories and some of the most outlandish warships ever built. What *didn't* emerge were major battles between the new vessels.

At Lissa in 1866, an Austrian fleet humiliated an Italian fleet of more modern and powerful ships, proving that competence and leadership had more to do with victory than equipment alone. (Nelson must have smiled from his grave.) Lissa proved little or nothing about the new hardware (theorists of the time thought otherwise; they were wrong), but it was as good a test as the century provided.

Ships generally mounted mixed armaments of large and mid-sized weapons, though there was a brief fad of equipping battleships with small numbers of very heavy guns. This was partly in the hope that a single huge shell could smash opposing armor (in the unlikely instance that such a shell hit its target); and partly because the planners wanted an easily quantifiable marker for their arms race. (The dangerous buffoons in the Pentagon and Kremlin with their "My throw weight is bigger than your throw weight" arguments had nineteenth century predecessors.)

Incidentally, as soon as steam removed the necessity for masts and rigging, rams returned as well. There were few successful examples of ramming in war, but in peacetime, rams sank almost as many friendly naval units as decomposing smokeless powder did.

The only real test of nineteenth century warships came in the twentieth century—1905—at the Strait of Tsu Shima, where a Russian fleet that did nothing whatsoever right met a Japanese fleet that did nothing important wrong. The Russians were massacred, and it was heavy gunfire alone that did the butchers' work.

An idiosyncratic genius named Jackie Cooper was running the British admiralty at the time. He came up with the first good idea in warship construction since Ericsson put a turret and screw propeller on the *Monitor:* Cooper built the *Dreadnought.*

The *Dreadnought* was big and fast and carried ten of the most powerful naval guns available, with none of the mid-sized weapons that had proved almost useless at Tsu Shima. Every battleship built after the *Dreadnought* is more similar to her than the *Dreadnought* was similar to anything that came before her.

Having had a brilliant idea, Cooper went on to have a lethally bad one: the battle cruiser. The battle cruiser was a dreadnought (the name became generic for all-big-gun warships) which had lighter armor and more powerful engines than a battleship, and was therefore faster. The theory was that "speed *is* armor." The reality was quite different, and thousands of sailors (mostly British) died in the two World Wars (the *Hood* was a battle cruiser) because a clever slogan can't repeal the laws of physics.

The dreadnought brought back the concept of the line of battle. It didn't work any better in the twentieth century than it had in the eighteenth, because both sides had to agree to play the game and the weaker side—the Germans, in this case—would inevitably lose. The German admirals of the World Wars were less than brilliant, but they weren't stupid.

Besides, the fleets of World War II were dominated by aircraft. The one major battleship-to-battleship fleet action of the war occurred at night in the Surigao Strait. It was a close copy of Tsu Shima, with the Japanese playing the part the Russians had forty years earlier.

There is enough in actual maritime history to provide models for almost any form of space warfare a writer wants to postulate. Because there *are* so many possibilities, writers can find a solidly-grounded situation that suits their story, rather than forcing the story into a narrow matrix.

And that, I think, makes for some very good stories.

Dave Drake,
Chapel Hill, North Carolina

SPACE DREADNOUGHTS

THE ONLY THING
WE LEARN

Cyril M. Kornbluth

The professor, though he did not know the actor's phrase for
it, was counting the house—peering through a spyhole in
the door through which he would in a moment appear before
the class. He was pleased with what he saw. Tier after tier
of young people, ready with notebooks and styli, chattering
tentatively, glancing at the door against which his nose was
flattened, waiting for the pleasant interlude known as
"Archaeo-Literature 203" to begin.

The professor stepped back, smoothed his tunic, crooked
four books on his left elbow, and made his entrance. Four
swift strides brought him to the lectern and, for the
thousandth-odd time, he impassively swept the lecture hall
with his gaze. Then he gave a wry little smile. Inside, for
the thousandth-odd time, he was nagged by the irritable
little thought that the lectern really ought to be a foot or so
higher.

The irritation did not show. He was out to win the
audience, and he did. A dead silence, the supreme tribute,
gratified him. Imperceptibly, the lights of the lecture hall
began to dim and the light on the lectern to brighten.

He spoke.

"Young gentlemen of the Empire, I ought to warn you that this and the succeeding lectures will be most subversive."

There was a little rustle of incomprehension from the audience—but by then the lectern light was strong enough to show the twinkling smile about his eyes that belied his stern mouth, and agreeable chuckles sounded in the gathering darkness of the tiered seats. Glow lights grew bright gradually at the students' tables, and they adjusted their notebooks in the narrow ribbons of illumination. He waited for the small commotion to subside.

"Subversive—" He gave them a link to cling to. "Subversive because I shall make every effort to tell both sides of our ancient beginnings with every resource of archaeology and with every clue my diligence has discovered in our epic literature.

"There *were* two sides, you know—difficult though it may be to believe that if we judge by the Old Epic alone—such epics as the noble and tempestuous *Chant of Remd*, the remaining fragments of *Krall's Voyage*, or the gory and rather out-of-date *Battle For the Ten Suns*." He paused while styli scribbled across the notebook pages.

"The Middle Epic is marked, however, by what I might call the rediscovered ethos." From his voice, every student knew that that phrase, surer than death and taxes, would appear on an examination paper. The styli scribbled. "By this I mean an awakening of fellow-feeling with the Home Suns People, which had once been filial loyalty to them when our ancestors were few and pioneers, but which turned into contempt when their numbers grew.

"The Middle Epic writers did not despise the Home Suns People, as did the bards of the Old Epic. Perhaps this was because they did not have to—since their long war against the Home Suns was drawing to a victorious close.

"Of the New Epic I shall have little to say. It was a literary fad, a pose, and a silly one. Written within historic times, the some two score pseudo-epics now moulder in their cylinders, where they belong. Our ripening civilization could not with integrity work in the epic form, and the artistic failures produced so indicate. Our genius turned to the lyric and to the unabashedly romantic novel.

"So much, for the moment, of literature. What contribution, you must wonder, have archaeological studies to make in an investigation of the wars from which our ancestry emerged?

"Archaeology offers—one—a check in historical matters in the epics—confirming or denying. Two—it provides evidence glossed over in the epics—for artistic or patriotic reasons. Three—it provides evidence which has been lost, owing to the fragmentary nature of some of the early epics."

All this he fired at them crisply, enjoying himself. Let them not think him a dreamy litterateur, or, worse, a flat precisionist, but let them be always a little off-balance before him, never knowing what came next, and often wondering, in class and out. The styli paused after heading Three.

"We shall examine first, by our archaeo-literary technique, the second book of the *Chant of Remd*. As the selected youth of the Empire, you know much about it, of course—much that is false, some that is true, and a great deal that is irrelevant. You know that Book One hurls us into the middle of things, aboard ship with Algan and his great captain, Remd, on their way from the triumph over a Home Suns stronghold, the planet Telse. We watch Remd on his diversionary action that splits the Ten Suns Fleet into two halves. But before we see the destruction of those halves by the Horde of Algan, we are told in Book Two of the battle for Telse."

He opened one of his books on the lectern, swept the amphitheater again, and read sonorously.

> "Then battle broke
> And high the blinding blast
> Sight-searing leaped
> While folk in fear below
> Cowered in caverns
> From the wrath of Remd—

"Or, in less sumptuous language, one fission bomb—or a stick of time-on-target bombs—was dropped. An unprepared and disorganized populace did not take the standard measure of dispersing, but huddled foolishly to await Algan's gunfighters and the death they brought.

"One of the things you believe because you have seen them in notes to elementary-school editions of *Remd* is that Telse was the fourth planet of the star, Sol. Archaeology denies it by establishing that the fourth planet—actually called Marse, by the way—was in those days weather-roofed at least, and possibly atmosphere-roofed as well. As potential warriors, you know that one does not waste fissionable material on a roof, and there is no mention of chemical explosives being used to crack the roof. Marse, therefore, was not the locale of *Remd*, Book Two.

"Which planet was? The answer to that has been established by X-radar, differential decay analyses, video-coring, and every other resource of those scientists still quaintly called 'diggers.' We know and can prove that Telse was the *third* planet of Sol. So much for the opening of the attack. Let us jump to Canto Three, the Storming of the Dynastic Palace.

> "Imperial purple wore they
> Fresh from the feast
> Grossly gorged
> They sought to slay—

"And so on. Now, as I warned you, Remd is of the Old Epic, and makes no pretense at fairness. The unorganized huddling of Telse's population was read as cowardice instead of poor A.R.P. The same is true of the Third Canto. Video-cores show on the site of the palace a hecatomb of dead in once-purple livery, but also shows impartially that they were not particularly gorged and that digestion of their last meals had been well advanced. They didn't give such a bad accounting of themselves, either. I hesitate to guess, but perhaps they accounted for one of our ancestors apiece and were simply outnumbered. The study is not complete.

"That much we know." The professor saw they were tiring of the terse scientist and shifted gears. "If but the veil of time were rent that shrouds the years between us and the Home Suns People, how much more would we learn? Would we despise the Home Suns People as our frontiersman ancestors did, or would we cry: '*This* is our spiritual home—this world of rank and order, this world of formal verse and exquisitely patterned arts'?"

If the veil of time were rent—?

We can try to rend it . . .

Wing Commander Arris heard the clear jangle of the radar net alarm as he was dreaming about a fish. Struggling out of his too-deep, too-soft bed, he stepped into a purple singlet, buckled on his Sam Browne belt with its holstered .45 automatic, and tried to read the radar screen. Whatever had set it off was either too small or too distant to register on the five-inch C.R.T.

He rang for his aide, and checked his appearance in a wall mirror while waiting. His space tan was beginning to fade, he saw, and made a mental note to get it renewed at the parlor. He stepped into the corridor as Evan, his aide, trotted up—younger, browner, thinner, but the same officer type that made the Service what it was, Arris thought with satisfaction.

Evan gave him a bone-cracking salute, which he returned. They set off for the elevator that whisked them down to a large, chilly, dark underground room where faces were greenly lit by radar screens and the lights of plotting tables. Somebody yelled "Attention!" and the tecks snapped. He gave them "At ease" and took the brisk salute of the senior teck, who reported to him in flat, machine-gun delivery:

"Object-becoming-visible-on-primary-screen-sir."

He studied the sixty-inch disk for several seconds before he spotted the intercepted particle. It was coming in fast from zenith, growing while he watched.

"Assuming it's now traveling at maximum, how long will it be before it's within striking range?" he asked the teck.

"Seven hours, sir."

"The interceptors at Idlewild alerted?"

"Yessir."

Arris turned on a phone that connected with Interception. The boy at Interception knew the face that appeared on its screen, and was already capped with a crash helmet.

"Go ahead and take him, Efrid," said the wing commander.

"Yessir!" and a punctilious salute, the boy's pleasure plain at being known by name and a great deal more at being on the way to a fight that might be first-class.

Arris cut him off before the boy could detect a smile that was forming on his face. He turned from the pale lunar glow of the sixty-incher to enjoy it. Those kids—when every meteor was an invading dreadnought, when every ragged scouting ship from the rebels was an armada!

He watched Efrid's squadron soar off on the screen and then he retreated to a darker corner. This was his post until the meteor or scout or whatever it was got taken care of. Evan joined him, and they silently studied the smooth, disciplined functioning of the plot room, Arris with satisfaction and Evan doubtless with the same. The aide broke silence, asking:

"Do you suppose it's a Frontier ship, sir?" He caught the wing commander's look and hastily corrected himself: "I mean rebel ship, sir, of course."

"Then you should have said so. Is that what the junior officers generally call those scoundrels?"

Evan conscientiously cast his mind back over the last few junior messes and reported unhappily: "I'm afraid we do, sir. We seem to have got into the habit."

"I shall write a memorandum about it. How do you account for that very peculiar habit?"

"Well, sir, they do have something like a fleet, and they did take over the Regulus Cluster, didn't they?"

What had got into this incredible fellow, Arris wondered in amazement. Why, the thing was self-evident! They had a few ships—accounts differed as to how many—and they had, doubtless by raw sedition, taken over some systems temporarily.

He turned from his aide, who sensibly became interested in a screen and left with a murmured excuse to study it very closely.

The brigands had certainly knocked together some ramshackle league or other, but— The wing commander wondered briefly if it could last, shut the horrid thought from his head, and set himself to composing mentally a stiff memorandum that would be posted in the junior officer's mess and put an end to this absurd talk.

His eyes wandered to the sixty-incher, where he saw the interceptor squadron climbing nicely toward the particle— which, he noticed, had become three particles. A low crooning distracted him. Was one of the tecks singing at work? It couldn't be!

It wasn't. An unsteady shape wandered up in the darkness, murmuring a song and exhaling alcohol. He recognized the Chief Archivist, Glen.

"This is Service country, mister," he told Glen.

"Hullo, Arris," the round little civilian said, peering at him. "I come down here regularly—regularly against regulations—to wear off my regular irregularities with the wine bottle. That's all right, isn't it?"

He was drunk and argumentative. Arris felt hemmed in. Glen couldn't be talked into leaving without loss of dignity to the wing commander, and he couldn't be chucked out because he was writing a biography of the chamberlain and could, for the time being, have any head in the palace for the asking. Arris sat down unhappily, and Glen plumped down beside him.

The little man asked him, "Is that a fleet from the Frontier League?" He pointed to the big screen. Arris didn't look at his face, but felt that Glen was grinning maliciously.

"I know of no organization called the Frontier League," Arris said. "If you are referring to the brigands who have recently been operating in Galactic East, you could at least call them by their proper names." Really, he thought— civilians!

"So sorry. But the brigands should have the Regulus Cluster by now, shouldn't they?" he asked, insinuatingly.

This was serious—a grave breach of security. Arris turned to the little man.

"Mister, I have no authority to command you," he said measuredly. "Furthermore, I understand you are enjoying a temporary eminence in the non-Service world which would make it very difficult for me to—ah—tangle with you. I shall therefore refer only to your altruism. How did you find out about the Regulus Cluster?"

"Eloquent!" murmured the little man, smiling happily. "I got it from Rome."

Arris searched his memory. "You mean Squadron Commander Romo broke security? I can't believe it!"

"No, commander. I mean Rome—a place—a time—a civilization. I got it also from Babylon, Assyria, the Mogul Raj—every one of them. You don't understand me, of course."

"I understand that you're trifling with Service security and that you're a fat, little, malevolent, worthless drone and scribbler!"

"Oh, commander!" protested the archivist. "I'm not so little!" He wandered away, chuckling.

Arris wished he had the shooting of him, and tried to explore the chain of secrecy for a weak link. He was tired and bored by this harping on the Fron—on the brigands.

His aide tentatively approached him. "Interceptors in striking range, sir," he murmured.

"Thank you," said the wing commander, genuinely grateful to be back in the clean, etched-line world of the Service and out of that blurred, water-color, civilian land where long-dead Syrians apparently retailed classified matter to nasty little drunken warts who had no business with it. Arris confronted the sixty-incher. The particle that had become three particles was now—he counted—eighteen particles. Big ones. Getting bigger.

He did not allow himself emotion, but turned to the plot on the interceptor squadron.

"Set up Lunar relay," he ordered.

"Yessir."

Half the plot room crew bustled silently and efficiently about the delicate job of applied relativistic physics that was 'lunar relay.' He knew that the palace power plant could take it for a few minutes, and he wanted to *see*. If he could not believe radar pips, he might believe a video screen.

On the great, green circle, the eighteen—now twenty-four—particles neared the thirty-six smaller particles that were interceptors, led by the eager young Efrid.

"Testing Lunar relay, sir," said the chief teck.

The wing commander turned to a twelve-inch screen. Unobtrusively, behind him, tecks jockeyed for position. The picture on the screen was something to see. The chief let mercury fill a thick-walled, ceramic tank. There was a sputtering and contact was made.

"Well done," said Arris. "Perfect seeing."

He saw, upper left, a globe of ships—what ships! Some were Service jobs, with extra turrets plastered on them wherever there was room. Some were orthodox freighters, with the same porcupine-bristle of weapons. Some were obviously home-made crates, hideously ugly—and as heavily armed as the others.

Next to him, Arris heard his aide murmur, "It's all wrong, sir. They haven't got any pick-up boats. They haven't got any hospital ships. What happens when one of them gets shot up?"

"Just what ought to happen, Evan," snapped the wing commander. "They float in space until they desiccate in their suits. Or if they get grappled inboard with a boat hook, they don't get any medical care. As I told you, they're brigands, without decency even to care of their own." He enlarged on the theme. "Their morale must be insignificant compared with our men's. When the Service goes into action, every rating and teck knows he'll be cared for if he's hurt. Why, if we didn't have pick-up boats and hospital ships the men wouldn't—" He almost finished it with "fight," but thought, and lamely ended,—"wouldn't like it."

Evan nodded, wonderingly, and crowded his chief a little as he craned his neck for a look at the screen.

"Get the hell away from here!" said the wing commander in a restrained yell, and Evan got.

The interceptor squadron swam into the field—a sleek, deadly needle of vessels in perfect alignment, with its little cloud of pick-ups trailing, and farther astern a white hospital ship with the ancient red cross.

The contact was immediate and shocking. One of the rebel ships lumbered into the path of the interceptors, spraying fire from what seemed to be as many points as a man has pores. The Service ships promptly riddled it and it should have drifted away—but it didn't. It kept on fighting. It rammed an interceptor with a crunch that must have killed every man before the first bulwark, but aft of the bulwark the ship kept fighting.

It took a torpedo portside and its plumbing drifted through space in a tangle. Still the starboard side kept squirting fire. Isolated weapon blisters fought on while they were obviously cut off from the rest of the ship. It was a pounded tangle of wreckage, and it had destroyed two interceptors, crippled two more, and kept fighting.

Finally, it drifted away, under feeble jets of power. Two more of the fantastic rebel fleet wandered into action, but the wing commander's horrified eyes were on the first pile of scrap. It was going *somewhere*—

The ship neared the thin-skinned, unarmored, gleaming hospital vessel, rammed it amidships, square in one of the red crosses, and then blew itself up, apparently with everything left in its powder magazine, taking the hospital ship with it.

The sickened wing commander would never have recognized what he had seen as it was told in a later version, thus:

> "The crushing course they took
> And nobly knew
> Their death undaunted
> By heroic blast
> The hospital's host

> They dragged to doom
> Hail! Men without mercy
> From the far frontier!"

Lunar relay flickered out as overloaded fuses flashed into vapor. Arris distractedly paced back to the dark corner and sank into a chair.

"I'm sorry," said the voice of Glen next to him, sounding quite sincere. "No doubt it was quite a shock to you."

"Not to you?" asked Arris bitterly.

"Not to me."

"Then how did they do it?" the wing commander asked the civilian in a low, desperate whisper. "They don't even wear .45's. Intelligence says their enlisted men have hit their officers and got away with it. They *elect* ship captains! Glen, what does it all mean?"

"It means," said the fat little man with a timbre of doom in his voice, "that they've returned. They always have. They always will. You see, commander, there is always somewhere a wealthy, powerful city, or nation, or world. In it are those whose blood is not right for a wealthy, powerful place. They must seek danger and overcome it. So they go out—on the marshes, in the desert, on the tundra, the planets, or the stars. Being strong, they grow stronger by fighting the tundra, the planets, or the stars. They—they change. They sing new songs. They know new heroes. And then, one day, they return to their old home.

"They return to the wealthy, powerful city, or nation or world. They fight its guardians as they fought the tundra, the planets, or the stars—a way that strikes terror to the heart. Then they sack the city, nation, or world and sing great, ringing sagas of their deeds. They always have. Doubtless they always will."

"But what shall we do?"

"We shall cower, I suppose, beneath the bombs they drop on us, and we shall die, some bravely, some not, defending the palace within a very few hours. But you will have your revenge."

"How?" asked the wing commander, with haunted eyes.

The fat little man giggled and whispered in the officer's ear. Arris irritably shrugged it off as a bad joke. He didn't believe it. As he died, drilled through the chest a few hours later by one of Algan's gunfighters, he believed it even less.

The professor's lecture was drawing to a close. There was time for only one more joke to send his students away happy. He was about to spring it when a messenger handed him two slips of paper. He raged inwardly at his ruined exit and poisonously read from them:

"I have been asked to make two announcements. One, a bulletin from General Sleg's force. He reports that the so-called Outland Insurrection is being brought under control and that there is no cause for alarm. Two, the gentlemen who are members of the S.O.T.C. will please report to the armory at 1375 hours—whatever that may mean—for blaster inspection. The class is dismissed."

Petulantly, he swept from the lectern and through the door.

C-CHUTE

Isaac Asimov

Even from the cabin into which he and the other passengers had been herded, Colonel Anthony Windham could still catch the essence of the battle's progress. For a while, there was silence, no jolting, which meant the spaceships were fighting at astronomical distance in a duel of energy blasts and powerful force-field defenses.

He knew that could have only one end. Their Earth ship was only an armed merchantman and his glimpse of the Kloro enemy just before he had been cleared off deck by the crew was sufficient to show it to be a light cruiser.

And in less than half an hour, there came those hard little shocks he was waiting for. The passengers swayed back and forth as the ship pitched and veered, as though it were an ocean liner in a storm. But space was calm and silent as ever. It was their pilot sending desperate bursts of steam through the steam-tubes, so that by reaction the ship would be sent rolling and tumbling. It could only mean that the inevitable had occurred. The Earth ship's screens had been drained and it no longer dared withstand a direct hit.

Colonel Windham tried to steady himself with his aluminum cane. He was thinking that he was an old man; that he had spent his life in the militia and had never seen a battle; but now, with a battle going on around him, he was old and fat and lame and had no men under his command.

They would be boarding soon, those Kloro monsters. It was their way of fighting. They would be handicapped by spacesuits and their casualties would be high, but they wanted the Earth ship. Windham considered the passengers. For a moment, he thought, *if they were armed and I could lead them—*

He abandoned the thought. Porter was in an obvious state of funk and the young boy, Leblanc, was hardly better. The Polyorketes brothers—dash it, he *couldn't* tell them apart—huddled in a corner speaking only to one another. Mullen was a different matter. He sat perfectly erect, with no signs of fear or any other emotion in his face. But the man was just about five feet tall and had undoubtedly never held a gun of any sort in his hands in all his life. He could do nothing.

And there was Stuart, with his frozen half-smile and the high-pitched sarcasm which saturated all he said. Windham looked sidelong at Stuart now as Stuart sat there, pushing his dead-white hands through his sandy hair. With those artificial hands he was useless, anyway.

Windham felt the shuddering vibration of ship-to-ship contact; and in five minutes, there was the noise of the fight through the corridors. One of the Polyorketes brothers screamed and dashed for the door. The other called, "Aristides! Wait!" and hurried after.

It happened so quickly. Aristides was out the door and into the corridor, running in brainless panic. A carbonizer glowed briefly and there was never even a scream. Windham, from the doorway, turned in horror at the blackened stump of what was left. Strange—a lifetime in uniform and he had never before seen a man killed in violence.

It took the combined force of the rest to carry the other brother back struggling into the room.

The noise of battle subsided.

Stuart said, "That's it. They'll put a prize crew of two

aboard and take us to one of their home planets. We're prisoners of war, naturally."

"Only two of the Kloros will stay aboard?" asked Windham, astonished.

Stuart said, "It is their custom. Why do you ask, Colonel? Thinking of leading a gallant raid to retake the ship?"

Windham flushed. "Simply a point of information, dash it." But the dignity and tone of authority he tried to assume failed him, he knew. He was simply an old man with a limp.

And Stuart was probably right. He had lived among the Kloros and knew their ways.

John Stuart had claimed from the beginning that the Kloros were gentlemen. Twenty-four hours of imprisonment had passed, and now he repeated the statement as he flexed the fingers of his hands and watched the crinkles come and go in the soft artiplasm.

He enjoyed the unpleasant reaction it aroused in the others. People were made to be punctured; windy bladders, all of them. And they had hands of the same stuff as their bodies.

There was Anthony Windham, in particular. Colonel Windham, he called himself, and Stuart was willing to believe it. A retired colonel who had probably drilled a home guard militia on a village green, forty years ago, with such lack of distinction that he was not called back to service in any capacity, even during the emergency of Earth's first interstellar war.

"Dashed unpleasant thing to be saying about the enemy, Stuart. Don't know that I like your attitude." Windham seemed to push the words through his clipped mustache. His head had been shaven, too, in imitation of the current military style, but now a gray stubble was beginning to show about a centered bald patch. His flabby cheeks dragged downward. That and the fine red lines on his thick nose gave him a somewhat undone appearance, as though he had been wakened too suddenly and too early in the morning.

Stuart said, "Nonsense. Just reverse the present situation. Suppose an Earth warship had taken a Kloro liner. What do you think would have happened to any Kloro civilians aboard?"

"I'm sure the Earth fleet would observe all the interstellar rules of war," Windham said stiffly.

"Except that there aren't any. If we landed a prize crew on one of their ships, do you think we'd take the trouble to maintain a chlorine atmosphere for the benefit of the survivors; allow them to keep their non-contraband possessions; give them the use of the most comfortable stateroom, etcetera, etcetera, etcetera?"

Ben Porter said, "Oh, shut up, for God's sake. If I hear your etcetera, etcetera once again, I'll go nuts."

Stuart said, "Sorry!" He wasn't.

Porter was scarcely responsible. His thin face and beaky nose glistened with perspiration, and he kept biting the inside of his cheek until he suddenly winced. He put his tongue against the sore spot, which made him look even more clownish.

Stuart was growing weary of baiting them. Windham was too flabby a target and Porter could do nothing but writhe. The rest were silent. Demetrios Polyorketes was off in a world of silent internal grief for the moment. He had not slept the night before, most probably. At least, whenever Stuart woke to change his position—he himself had been rather restless—there had been Polyorketes' thick mumble from the next cot. It said many things, but the moan to which it returned over and over again was, "Oh, my brother!"

He sat dumbly on his cot now, his red eyes rolling at the other prisoners out of his broad, swarthy, unshaven face. As Stuart watched, his face sank into calloused palms so that only his mop of crisp and curly black hair could be seen. He rocked gently, but now that they were all awake, he made no sound.

Claude Leblanc was trying, very unsuccessfully, to read a letter. He was the youngest of the six, scarcely out of college, returning to Earth to get married. Stuart had found him that morning weeping quietly, his pink and white face flushed and blotched as though it were a heartbroken child's. He was very fair, with almost a girl's beauty about his large blue eyes and full lips. Stuart wondered what kind of girl it was who had promised to be his wife. He had seen her picture. Who on the ship had not? She had the characterless prettiness that makes all pictures of fiancees indistinguishable. It seemed to Stuart that if he were a girl, however, he would want someone a little more pronouncedly masculine.

That left only Randolph Mullen. Stuart frankly did not have the least idea what to make of him. He was the only one of the six that had been on the Arcturian worlds for any length of time. Stuart himself, for instance, had been there only long enough to give a series of lectures on astronautical engineering at the provincial engineering institute. Colonel Windham had been on a Cook's tour; Porter was trying to buy concentrated alien vegetables for his canneries on Earth; and the Polyorketes brothers had attempted to establish themselves in Arcturus as truck farmers and, after two growing seasons, gave it up, had somehow unloaded at a profit, and were returning to Earth.

Randolph Mullen, however, had been in the Arcturian system for seventeen years. How did voyagers discover so much about one another so quickly? As far as Stuart knew, the little man had scarcely spoken aboard ship. He was unfailingly polite, always stepped to one side to allow another to pass, but his entire vocabulary appeared to consist only of "Thank you" and "Pardon me." Yet the word had gone around that this was his first trip to Earth in seventeen years.

He was a little man, very precise, almost irritatingly so. Upon awaking that morning, he had made his cot neatly, shaved, bathed and dressed. The habit of years seemed not in the least disturbed by the fact that he was a prisoner of the Kloros now. He was unobtrusive about it, it had to be admitted, and gave no impression of disapproving of the sloppiness of the others. He simply sat there, almost apologetic, trussed in his overconservative clothing, and hands loosely clasped in his lap. The thin line of hair on his upper lip, far from adding character to his face, absurdly increased its primness.

He looked like someone's idea of a caricature of a bookkeeper. And the queer thing about it all, Stuart thought, was that that was exactly what he was. He had noticed it on the registry—Randolph Fluellen Mullen; occupation, bookkeeper; employers, Prime Paper Box Co.; 27 Tobias Avenue, New Warsaw, Arcturus II.

"Mr. Stuart?"

Stuart looked up. It was Leblanc, his lower lip trembling slightly. Stuart tried to remember how one went about being gentle. He said, "What is it, Leblanc?"

"Tell me, when will they let us go?"

"How should I know?"

"Everyone says you lived on a Kloro planet, and just now you said they were gentlemen."

"Well, yes. But even gentlemen fight wars in order to win. Probably, we'll be interned for the duration."

"But that could be *years!* Margaret is waiting. She'll think I'm *dead!*"

"I suppose they'll allow messages to be sent through once we're on their planet."

Porter's hoarse voice sounded in agitation. "Look here, if you know so much about these devils, what will they do to us while we're interned? What will they feed us? Where will they get oxygen for us? They'll kill us, I tell you." And as an afterthought, "I've got a wife waiting for me, too," he added.

But Stuart had heard him speaking of his wife in the days before the attack. He wasn't impressed. Porter's nail-bitten fingers were pulling and plucking at Stuart's sleeve. Stuart drew away in sharp revulsion. He couldn't stand those ugly hands. It angered him to desperation that such monstrosities should be real while his own white and perfectly shaped hands were only mocking imitations grown out of an alien latex.

He said, "They won't kill us. If they were going to, they

would have done it before now. Look, we capture Kloros too, you know, and it's just a matter of common sense to treat your prisoners decently if you want the other side to be decent to your men. They'll do their best. The food may not be very good, but they're better chemists than we are. It's what they're best at. They'll know exactly what food factors we'll need and how many calories. We'll live. They'll see to that."

Windham rumbled, "You sound more and more like a blasted greenie sympathizer, Stuart. It turns my stomach to hear an Earthman speak well of the green fellas the way you've been doing. Burn it, man, where's your loyalty?"

"My loyalty's where it belongs. With honesty and decency, regardless of the shape of the being it appears in." Stuart held up his hands. "See these? Kloros made them. I lived on one of their planets for six months. My hands were mangled in the conditioning machinery of my own quarters. I thought the oxygen supply they gave me was a little poor—it wasn't, by the way—and I tried making the adjustments on my own. It was my fault. You should never trust yourself with the machines of another culture. By the time someone among the Kloros could put on an atmosphere suit and get to me, it was too late to save my hands.

"They grew these artiplasm things for me and operated. You know what that meant? It meant designing equipment and nutrient solutions that would work in oxygen atmosphere. It meant that their surgeons had to perform a delicate operation while dressed in atmosphere suits. And now I've got hands again." He laughed harshly, and clenched them into weak fists. "Hands—"

Windham said, "And you'd sell your loyalty to Earth for that?"

"Sell my loyalty? You're mad. For years, I hated the Kloros for this. I was a master pilot on the Trans-Galactic Spacelines before it happened. Now? Desk job. Or an occasional lecture. It took me a long time to pin the fault on myself and to realize that the only role played by the Kloros was a decent one. They have their code of ethics, and it's as good as ours. If it weren't for the stupidity of some of their people—and by God, of some of ours—we wouldn't be at war. And after its over—"

Polyorketes was on his feet. His thick fingers curved inward before him and his dark eyes glittered. "I don't like what you say, mister."

"Why don't you?"

"Because you talk too nice about these damned green bastards. The Kloros were good to you, eh? Well, they weren't good to my brother. They killed him. I think maybe I kill you, you damned greenie spy."

And he charged.

Stuart barely had time to raise his arms to meet the infuriated farmer. He gasped out, "What the hell—" as he caught one wrist and heaved a shoulder to block the other which groped toward his throat.

His artiplasm hand gave way. Polyorketes wrenched free with scarcely an effort.

Windham was bellowing incoherently, and Leblanc was calling out in his reedy voice, "Stop it! Stop it!" But it was little Mullen who threw his arms about the farmer's neck from behind and pulled with all his might. He was not very effective; Polyorketes seemed scarcely aware of the little man's weight upon his back. Mullen's feet left the floor so that he tossed helplessly to right and left. But he held his grip and it hampered Polyorketes sufficiently to allow Stuart to break free long enough to grasp Windham's aluminum cane.

He said, "Stay away, Polyorketes."

He was gasping for breath and fearful of another rush. The hollow aluminum cylinder was scarcely heavy enough to accomplish much, but it was better than having only his weak hands to defend himself with.

Mullen had loosed his hold and was now circling cautiously, his breathing roughened and his jacket in disarray.

Polyorketes, for a moment, did not move. He stood there, his shaggy head bent low. Then he said, "It is no use. I must kill Kloros. Just watch your tongue, Stuart. If it keeps on rattling too much, you're liable to get hurt. Really hurt, I mean."

Stuart passed a forearm over his forehead and thrust the cane back at Windham, who seized it with his left hand, while mopping his bald pate vigorously with a handkerchief in his right.

Windham said, "Gentlemen, we must avoid this. It lowers our prestige. We must remember the common enemy. We are Earthmen and we must act what we are—the ruling race of the Galaxy. We dare not demean ourselves before the lesser breeds."

"Yes, Colonel," said Stuart, wearily. "Give us the rest of the speech tomorrow."

He turned to Mullen. "I want to say thanks."

He was uncomfortable about it, but he had to. The little accountant had surprised him completely.

But Mullen said, in a dry voice that scarcely raised above a whisper, "Don't thank me, Mr. Stuart. It was the logical thing to do. If we are to be interned, we would need you as an interpreter, perhaps, one who would understand the Kloros."

Stuart stiffened. It was, he thought, too much of the bookkeeper type of reasoning, too logical, too dry of juice. Present risk and ultimate advantage. The assets and debits balanced neatly. He would have liked Mullen to leap to his defense out of—well, out of what? Out of pure, unselfish decency?

Stuart laughed silently at himself. He was beginning to expect idealism of human beings, rather than good, straight-forward, self-centered motivation.

Polyorketes was numb. His sorrow and rage were like acid inside him, but they had no words to get out. If he were Stuart, big-mouth, white-hands Stuart, he could talk and talk and maybe feel better. Instead, he had to sit there with half of him dead; with no brother, no Aristides—

It had happened so quickly. If he could only go back and have one second more warning, so that he might snatch Aristides, hold him, save him.

But mostly he hated the Kloros. Two months ago, he had

hardly ever heard of them, and now he hated them so hard, he would be glad to die if he could kill a few.

He said, without looking up, "What happened to start this war, eh?"

He was afraid Stuart's voice would answer. He hated Stuart's voice. But it was Windham, the bald one.

Windham said, "The immediate cause, sir, was a dispute over mining concessions in the Wyandotte system. The Kloros had poached on Earth property."

"Room for both, Colonel!"

Polyorketes looked up at that, snarling. Stuart could not be kept quiet for long. He was speaking again; the cripple-hand, wiseguy, Kloros-lover.

Stuart was saying, "Is that anything to fight over, Colonel? We can't use one another's worlds. Their chlorine planets are useless to us and our oxygen ones are useless to them. Chlorine is deadly to us and oxygen is deadly to them. There's no way we could maintain permanent hostility. Our races just don't coincide. Is there reason to fight then because both races want to dig iron out of the same airless planetoids when there are millions like them in the Galaxy?"

Windham said, "There is the question of planetary honor—"

"Planetary fertilizer. How can it excuse a ridiculous war like this one? It can only be fought on outposts. It has to come down to a series of holding actions and eventually be settled by negotiations that might just as easily have been worked out in the first place. Neither we nor the Kloros will gain a thing."

Grudgingly, Polyorketes found that he agreed with Stuart. What did he and Aristides care where Earth or the Kloros got their iron?

Was that something for Aristides to die over?

The little warning buzzer sounded.

Polyorketes' head shot up and he rose slowly, his lips drawing back. Only one thing could be at the door. He waited, arms tense, fists balled. Stuart was edging toward him. Polyorketes saw that and laughed to himself. Let the

Kloro come in, and Stuart, along with all the rest, could not stop him.

Wait, Aristides, wait just a moment, and a fraction of revenge will be paid back.

The door opened and a figure entered, completely swathed in a shapeless, billowing travesty of a spacesuit.

An odd, unnatural, but not entirely unpleasant voice began, "It is with some misgivings, Earthmen, that my companion and myself—"

It ended abruptly as Polyorketes, with a roar, charged once again. There was no science in the lunge. It was sheer bull-momentum. Dark head low, burly arms spread out with the hair-tufted fingers in choking position, he clumped on. Stuart was whirled to one side before he had a chance to intervene, and was spun tumbling across a cot.

The Kloro might have, without undue exertion, straight-armed Polyorketes to a halt, or stepped aside, allowing the whirlwind to pass. He did neither. With a rapid movement, a hand-weapon was up and a gentle pinkish line of radiance connected it with the plunging Earthman. Polyorketes stumbled and crashed down, his body maintaining its last curved position, one foot raised, as though a lightning paralysis had taken place. It toppled to one side and he lay there, eyes all alive and wild with rage.

The Kloro said, "He is not permanently hurt." He seemed not to resent the offered violence. Then he began again, "It is with some misgiving, Earthmen, that my companion and myself were made aware of a certain commotion in this room. Are you in any need which we can satisfy?"

Stuart was angrily nursing his knee which he had scraped in colliding with the cot. He said, "No, thank you, Kloro."

"Now, look here," puffed Windham, "this is a dashed outrage. We demand that our release be arranged."

The Kloro's tiny, insectlike head turned in the fat old man's direction. He was not a pleasant sight to anyone unused to him. He was about the height of an Earthman, but the top of him consisted of a thin stalk of a neck with a head that was the merest swelling. It consisted of a blunt triangular proboscis in front and two bulging eyes on either side. That was all. There was no brain pan and no brain. What corresponded to the brain in a Kloro was located in what would be an Earthly abdomen, leaving the head as a mere sensory organ. The Kloro's spacesuit followed the outlines of the head more or less faithfully, the two eyes being exposed by two clear semicircles of glass, which looked faintly green because of the chlorine atmosphere inside.

One of the eyes was now cocked squarely at Windham, who quivered uncomfortably under the glance, but insisted, "You have no right to hold us prisoner. We are noncombatants."

The Kloro's voice, sounding thoroughly artificial, came from a small attachment of chromium mesh on what served as its chest. The voice box was manipulated by compressed air under the control of one or two of the many delicate, forked tendrils that radiated from two circles about its upper body and were, mercifully enough, hidden by the suit.

The voice said, "Are you serious, Earthman? Surely you have heard of war and rules of war and prisoners of war?"

It looked about, shifting eyes with quick jerks of its head, staring at a particular object first with one, then with another. It was Stuart's understanding that each eye transferred a separate message to the abdominal brain, which had to coordinate the two to obtain full information.

Windham had nothing to say. No one had. The Kloro, its four main limbs, roughly arms and legs in pairs, had a vaguely human appearance under the masking of the suit, if you looked no higher than its chest, but there was no way of telling what it felt.

They watched it turn and leave.

Porter coughed and said in a strangled voice, "God, smell that chlorine. If they don't do something, we'll all die of rotted lungs."

Stuart said, "Shut up. There isn't enough chlorine in the air to make a mosquito sneeze, and what there is will be swept out in two minutes. Besides, a little chlorine is good for you. It may kill your cold virus."

Windham coughed and said, "Stuart, I feel that you might have said something to your Kloro friend about releasing us. You are scarcely as bold in their presence, dash it, as you are once they are gone."

"You heard what the creature said, Colonel. We're prisoners of war, and prisoner exchanges are negotiated by diplomats. We'll just have to wait."

Leblanc, who had turned pasty white at the entrance of the Kloro, rose and hurried into the privy. There was the sound of retching.

An uncomfortable silence fell while Stuart tried to think of something to say to cover the unpleasant sound. Mullen filled in. He had rummaged through a little box he had taken from under his pillow.

He said, "Perhaps Mr. Leblanc had better take a sedative before retiring. I have a few. I'd be glad to give him one." He explained his generosity immediately, "Otherwise he may keep the rest of us awake, you see."

"Very logical," said Stuart, dryly. "You'd better save one for Sir Launcelot here; save half a dozen." He walked to where Polyorketes still sprawled and knelt at his side. "Comfortable, baby?"

Windham said, "Deuced poor taste speaking like that, Stuart."

"Well, if you're so concerned about him, why don't you and Porter hoist him onto his cot?"

He helped them do so. Polyorketes' arms were trembling erratically now. From what Stuart knew of the Kloros' nerve weapons, the man should be in an agony of pins and needles about now.

Stuart said, "And don't be too gentle with him, either. The damned fool might have gotten us all killed. And for what?"

He pushed Polyorketes' stiff carcass to one side and sat at the edge of the cot. He said. "Can you hear me, Polyorketes?"

Polyorketes' eyes gleamed. An arm lifted abortively and fell back.

"Okay then, listen. Don't try anything like that again. The next time it may be the finish for all of us. If you had been a Kloro and he had been an Earthman, we'd be dead now. So just get one thing through your skull. We're sorry about your brother and it's a rotten shame, but it was his own fault."

Polyorketes tried to heave and Stuart pushed him back.

"No, you keep on listening," he said. "Maybe this is the only time I'll get to talk to you when you *have* to listen. Your brother had no right leaving passenger's quarters. There was no place for him to go. He just got in the way of our own men. We don't even know for certain that it was a Kloro gun that killed him. It might have been one of our own."

"Oh, I say, Stuart," objected Windham.

Stuart whirled at him. "Do you have proof it wasn't? Did you see the shot? Could you tell from what was left of the body whether it was Kloro energy or Earth energy?"

Polyorketes found his voice, driving his unwilling tongue into a fuzzy verbal snarl. "Damned stinking greenie bastard."

"Me?" said Stuart. "I know what's going on in your mind, Polyorketes. You think that when the paralysis wears off, you'll ease your feelings by slamming me around. Well, if you do, it will probably be curtains for all of us."

He rose, put his back against the wall. For the moment, he was fighting all of them. "None of you know the Kloros the way I do. The physical differences you see are not important. The differences in their temperament are. They don't understand our views on sex, for instance. To them, it's just a biological reflex like breathing. They attach no importance to it. But they *do* attach importance to social groupings. Remember, their evolutionary ancestors had lots in common with our insects. They always assume that any group of Earthmen they find together makes up a social unit.

"That means just about everything to them. I don't

understand exactly *what* it means. No Earthman can. But the result is that they never break up a group, just as we don't separate a mother and her children if we can help it. One of the reasons they may be treating us with kid gloves right now is that they imagine we're all broken up over the fact that they killed one of us, and they feel guilt about it.

"But this is what you'll have to remember. We're going to be interned together and *kept* together for duration. I don't like the thought. I wouldn't have picked any of you for co-internees and I'm pretty sure none of you would have picked me. But there it is. The Kloros could never understand that our being together on the ship is only accidental.

"That means we've got to get along somehow. That's not just goodie-goodie talk about birds in their little nest agreeing. What do you think would have happened if the Kloros had come in earlier and found Polyorketes and myself trying to kill each other? You don't know? Well, what do you suppose *you* would think of a mother you caught trying to kill her children?

"That's it, then. They would have killed every one of us as a bunch of Kloro-type perverts and monsters. Got that? How about you, Polyorketes? Have *you* got it? So let's call names if we have to, but let's keep our hands to ourselves. And now, if none of you mind, I'll massage my hands back into shape—these synthetic hands that I got from the Kloros and that one of my own kind tried to mangle again."

For Claude Leblanc, the worst was over. He had been sick enough; sick with many things; but sick most of all over having ever left Earth. It had been a great thing to go to college off Earth. It had been an adventure and had taken him away from his mother. Somehow, he had been sneakingly glad to make that escape after the first month of frightened adjustment.

And then on the summer holidays, he had been no longer Claude, the shy-spoken scholar, but Leblanc, space traveler. He had swaggered the fact for all it was worth. It made him feel such a man to talk of stars and Jumps and the customs and environments of other worlds; it had given him courage with Margaret. She had loved him for the dangers he had undergone—

Except that this had been the first one, really, and he had not done so well. He knew it and was ashamed and wished he were like Stuart.

He used the excuse of mealtime to approach. He said, "Mr. Stuart."

Stuart looked up and said shortly, "How do you feel?"

Leblanc felt himself blush. He blushed easily and the effort not to blush only made it worse. He said, "Much better, thank you. We are eating. I thought I'd bring you your ration."

Stuart took the offered can. It was standard space ration; thoroughly synthetic, concentrated, nourishing and, somehow, unsatisfying. It heated automatically when the can was opened, but could be eaten cold, if necessary. Though a combined fork-spoon utensil was enclosed, the ration was of a consistency that made the use of the fingers practical and not particularly messy.

Stuart said, "Did you hear my little speech?"

"Yes, sir. I want you to know you can count on me."

"Well, good. Now go and eat."

"May I eat here?"

"Suit yourself."

For a moment, they ate in silence, and then Leblanc burst out, "You are so sure of yourself, Mr. Stuart! It must be very wonderful to be like that!"

"Sure of myself? Thanks, but there's your self-assured one."

Leblanc followed the direction of the nod in surprise. "Mr. Mullen? That little man? Oh, no!"

"You don't think he's self-assured?"

Leblanc shook his head. He looked at Stuart intently to see if he could detect humor in his expression. "That one is just cold. He has no emotion in him. He's like a little machine. I find him repulsive. You're different, Mr. Stuart. You have it all inside, but you control it. I would like to be like that."

And as though attracted by the magnetism of the mention, even though unheard, of his name, Mullen joined them. His can of ration was barely touched. It was still steaming gently as he squatted opposite them.

His voice had its usual quality of furtively rustling underbrush. "How long, Mr. Stuart, do you think the trip will take?"

"Can't say, Mullen. They'll undoubtedly be avoiding the usual trade routes and they'll be making more Jumps through hyper-space than usual to throw off possible pursuit. I wouldn't be surprised if it took as long as a week. Why do you ask? I presume you have a very practical and logical reason?"

"Why, yes. Certainly." He seemed quite shellbacked to sarcasm. He said, "It occurred to me that it might be wise to ration the rations, so to speak."

"We've got enough food and water for a month. I checked on that first thing."

"I see. In that case, I will finish the can." He did, using the all-purpose utensil daintily and patting a handkerchief against his unstained lips from time to time.

Polyorketes struggled to his feet some two hours later. He swayed a bit, looking like the Spirit of Hangover. He did not try to come closer to Stuart, but spoke from where he stood.

He said, "You stinking greenie spy, you watch yourself."

"You heard what I said before, Polyorketes."

"I heard. But I also heard what you said about Aristides. I won't bother with you, because you're a bag of nothing but noisy air. But wait, someday you'll blow your air in one face too many and it will be let out of you."

"I'll wait," said Stuart.

Windham hobbled over, leaning heavily on his cane. "Now, now," he called with a wheezing joviality that overlaid his sweating anxiety so thinly as to emphasize it. "We're all Earthmen, dash it. Got to remember that; keep it as a glowing light of inspiration. Never let down before the blasted Kloros. We've got to forget private feuds and remember only that we are Earthmen united against alien blighters."

Stuart's comment was unprintable.

Porter was right behind Windham. He had been in a close conference with the shaven-headed colonel for an hour, and now he said with indignation, "It doesn't help to be a wiseguy, Stuart. You listen to the colonel. We've been doing some hard thinking about the situation."

He had washed some of the grease off his face, wet his hair and slicked it back. It did not remove the little tic on his right cheek just at the point where his lips ended, or make his hangnail hands more attractive in appearance.

"All right, Colonel," said Stuart. "What's on your mind?"

Windham said, "I'd prefer to have all the men together."

"Okay, call them."

Leblanc hurried over; Mullen approached with greater deliberation.

Stuart said, "You want that fellow?" He jerked his head at Polyorketes.

"Why, yes. Mr. Polyorketes, may we have you, old fella?"

"Ah, leave me alone."

"Go ahead," said Stuart, "leave him alone. I don't want him."

"No, no," said Windham. "This is a matter for all Earthmen. Mr. Polyorketes, we must have you."

Polyorketes rolled off one side of his cot. "I'm close enough, I can hear you."

Windham said to Stuart, "Would they—the Kloros, I mean—have this room wired?"

"No," said Stuart. "Why should they?"

"Are you sure?"

"Of course I'm sure. They didn't know what happened when Polyorketes jumped me. They just heard the thumping when it started rattling the ship."

"Maybe they were trying to give us the impression the room wasn't wired."

"Listen, Colonel, I've never known a Kloro to tell a deliberate lie—"

Polyorketes interrupted calmly, "That lump of noise just *loves* the Kloros."

Windham said hastily, "Let's not begin that. Look, Stuart, Porter and I have been discussing matters and we have decided that you know the Kloros well enough to think of some way of getting us back to Earth."

"It happens that you're wrong. I can't think of any way."

"Maybe there is some way we can take the ship back from the blasted green fellas," suggested Windham. "Some weakness they may have. Dash it, you know what I mean."

"Tell me, Colonel, what are you after? Your own skin or Earth's welfare?"

"I resent that question. I'll have you know that while I'm as careful of my own life as anyone has a right to be, I'm thinking of Earth primarily. And I think that's true of all of us."

"Damn right," said Porter, instantly. Leblanc looked anxious, Polyorketes resentful; and Mullen had no expression at all.

"Good," said Stuart. "Of course, I don't think we can take the ship. They're armed and we aren't. But there's this. You know why the Kloros took this ship intact. It's because they need ships. They may be better chemists than Earthmen are, but Earthmen are better astronautical engineers. We have bigger, better and more ships. In fact, if our crew had had a proper respect for military axioms in the first place, they would have blown the ship up as soon as it looked as though the Kloros were going to board."

Leblanc looked horrified. "And kill the passengers?"

"Why not? You heard what the good colonel said. Every one of us puts his own lousy little life after Earth's interests. What good are we to Earth alive right now? None at all. What harm will this ship do in Kloro hands? A hell of a lot, probably."

"Just why," asked Mullen, "did our men refuse to blow up the ship? They must have had a reason."

"They did. It's the firmest tradition of Earth's military

men that there must never be an unfavorable ratio of casualties. If we had blown ourselves up, twenty fighting men and seven civilians of Earth would be dead as compared with an enemy casualty total of zero. So what happens? We let them board, kill twenty-eight—I'm sure we killed at least that many—and let them have the ship."

"Talk, talk, talk," jeered Polyorketes.

"There's a moral to this," said Stuart. "We can't take the ship away from the Kloros. We *might* be able to rush them, though, and keep them busy long enough to allow one of us enough time to short the engines."

"What?" yelled Porter, and Windham shushed him in fright.

"Short the engines," Stuart repeated. "That would destroy the ship, of course, which is what we want to do, isn't it?"

Leblanc's lips were white. "I don't think that would work."

"We can't be sure till we try. But what have we to lose by trying?"

"Our lives, damn it!" cried Porter. "You insane maniac, you're crazy!"

"If I'm a maniac," said Stuart, "and insane to boot, then naturally I'm crazy. But just remember that if we lose our lives, which is overwhelmingly probable, we lose nothing of value to Earth; whereas if we destroy the ship, as we just barely might, we do Earth a lot of good. What patriot would hesitate? Who here would put himself ahead of his world?" He looked about in the silence. "Surely not you, Colonel Windham."

Windham coughed tremendously. "My dear man, that is not the question. There must be a way to save the ship for Earth *without* losing our lives, eh?"

"All right. You name it."

"Let's all think about it. Now there are only two of the Kloros aboard ship. If one of us could sneak up on them and—"

"How? The rest of the ship's all filled with chlorine. We'd have to wear a spacesuit. Gravity in their part of the ship is hopped up to Kloro level, so whoever is patsy in the deal would be clumping around, metal on metal, slow and heavy. Oh, he could sneak up on them, sure—like a skunk trying to sneak downwind."

"Then we'll drop it all," Porter's voice shook. "Listen, Windham, there's not going to be any destroying the ship. My life means plenty to me and if any of you try anything like that, I'll call the Kloros. I mean it."

"Well," said Stuart, "there's hero number one."

Leblanc said, "I want to go back to Earth, but I—"

Mullen interrupted, "I don't think our chances of destroying the ship are good enough unless—"

"Heroes number two and three. What about you, Polyorketes? You would have the chance of killing two Kloros."

"I want to kill them with my bare hands," growled the farmer, his heavy fists writhing. "On their planet, I will kill dozens."

"That's a nice safe promise for now. What about you, Colonel? Don't you want to march to death and glory with me?"

"Your attitude is very cynical and unbecoming, Stuart. It's obvious that if the rest are unwilling, then your plan will fall through."

"Unless I do it myself, huh?"

"You won't, do you hear?" said Porter, instantly.

"Damn right I won't," agreed Stuart. "I don't claim to be a hero. I'm just an average patriot, perfectly willing to head for any planet they take me to and sit out the war."

Mullen said, thoughtfully, "Of course, there *is* a way we could surprise the Kloros."

The statement would have dropped flat except for Polyorketes. He pointed a black-nailed, stubby forefinger and laughed harshly. "Mr. Bookkeeper!" he said. "Mr. Bookkeeper is a big shot talker like this damned greenie spy, Stuart. All right, Mr. Bookkeeper, go ahead. You make big speeches also. Let the words roll like an empty barrel."

He turned to Stuart and repeated venomously, "Empty

barrel! Cripple-hand empty barrel. No good for anything but talk."

Mullen's soft voice could make no headway until Polyorketes was through, but then he said, speaking directly to Stuart, "We might be able to reach them from outside. This room has a C-chute I'm sure."

"What's a C-chute?" asked Leblanc.

"Well—" began Mullen, and then stopped, at a loss.

Stuart said, mockingly, "It's a euphemism, my boy. Its full name is 'casualty chute.' It doesn't get talked about, but the main rooms on any ship would have them. They're just little airlocks down which you slide a corpse. Burial at space. Always lots of sentiment and bowed heads, with the captain making a rolling speech of the type Polyorketes here wouldn't like."

Leblanc's face twisted. "Use *that* to leave the ship?"

"Why not? Superstitious?—Go on, Mullen."

The little man had waited patiently. He said, "Once outside, one could re-enter the ship by the steam-tubes. It can be done—with luck. And then you would be an unexpected visitor in the control room."

Stuart stared at him curiously. "How do you figure this out? What do *you* know about steam-tubes?"

Mullen coughed. "You mean because I'm in the paper-box business? Well—" He grew pink, waited a moment, then made a new start in a colorless, unemotional voice. "My company, which manufactures fancy paper boxes and novelty containers, made a line of spaceship candy boxes for the juvenile trade some years ago. It was designed so that if a string were pulled, small pressure containers were punctured and jets of compressed air shot out through the mock steam-tubes, sailing the box across the room and scattering candy as it went. The sales theory was that the youngsters would find it exciting to play with the ship and fun to scramble for the candy.

"Actually, it was a complete failure. The ship would break dishes and sometimes hit another child in the eye. Worse still, the children would not only scramble for the candy but would fight over it. It was almost our worst failure. We lost thousands.

"Still, while the boxes were being designed, the entire office was extremely interested. It was like a game, very bad for efficiency and office morale. For a while, we all became steam-tube experts. I read quite a few books on ship construction. On my own time, however, not the company's."

Stuart was intrigued. He said, "You know it's a video sort of idea, but it might work if we had a hero to spare. Have we?"

"What about you?" demanded Porter, indignantly. "You go around sneering at us with your cheap wisecracks. I don't notice you volunteering for anything."

"That's because I'm no hero, Porter. I admit it. My object is to stay alive, and shinnying down steam-tubes is no way to go about staying alive. But the rest of you are noble patriots. The colonel says so. What about you, Colonel? You're the senior hero here."

Windham said, "If I were younger, blast it, and if you had your hands, I would take pleasure, sir, in trouncing you soundly."

"I've no doubt of it, but that's no answer."

"You know very well that at my time of life and with my leg—" he brought the flat of his hand down upon his stiff knee—"I am in no position to do anything of the sort, however much I should wish to."

"Ah, yes," said Stuart, "and I, myself, am crippled in the hands, as Polyorketes tells me. That saves us. And what unfortunate deformities do the rest of us have?"

"Listen," cried Porter, "I want to know what this is all about. How can anyone go down the steam-tubes? What if the Kloros use them while one of us is inside?"

"Why, Porter, that's part of the sporting chance. It's where the excitement comes in."

"But he'd be boiled in the shell like a lobster."

"A pretty image, but inaccurate. The steam wouldn't be on for more than a very short time, maybe a second or two, and the suit insulation would hold that long. Besides, the jet comes scooting out at several hundred miles a minute, so that you would be blown clear of the ship before the steam could even warm you. In fact, you'd be blown quite a few miles out into space, and after that you would be quite safe from the Kloros. Of course, you couldn't get back to the ship."

Porter was sweating freely. "You don't scare me for one minute, Stuart."

"I don't? Then you're offering to go? Are you sure you've thought out what being stranded in space means? You're all alone, you know; really all alone. The steam-jet will probably leave you turning or tumbling pretty rapidly. You won't feel that. You'll seem to be motionless. But all the stars will be going around and around so that they're just streaks in the sky. They won't ever stop. They won't even slow up. Then your heater will go off, your oxygen will give out, and you will die very slowly. You'll have lots of time to think. Or, if you are in a hurry, you could open your suit. That wouldn't be pleasant, either. I've seen faces of men who had a torn suit happen to them accidentally, and it's pretty awful. But it would be quicker. Then—"

Porter turned and walked unsteadily away.

Stuart said, lightly, "Another failure. One act of heroism still ready to be knocked down to the highest bidder with nothing offered yet."

Polyorketes spoke up and his harsh voice roughed the words. "You keep on talking, Mr. Big Mouth. You just keep banging that empty barrel. Pretty soon, we'll kick your teeth in. There's one boy I think would be willing to do it now, eh, Mr. Porter?"

Porter's look at Stuart confirmed the truth of Polyorketes' remarks, but he said nothing.

Stuart said, "Then what about you, Polyorketes? You're the barehand man with guts. Want me to help you into a suit?"

"I'll ask you when I want help."

"What about you, Leblanc?"

The young man shrank away.

"Not even to get back to Margaret?"

But Leblanc could only shake his head.

"Mullen?"

"Well—I'll try."

"You'll what?"

"I said, yes, I'll try. After all, it's my idea."

Stuart looked stunned. "You're serious? How come?"

Mullen's prim mouth pursed. "Because no one else will."

"But that's no reason. Especially for you."

Mullen shrugged.

There was a thump of a cane behind Stuart. Windham brushed past.

He said, "Do you really intend to go, Mullen?"

"Yes, Colonel."

"In that case, dash it, let me shake your hand. I like you. You're an—an Earthman, by heaven. Do this, and win or die, I'll bear witness for you."

Mullen withdrew his hand awkwardly from the deep and vibrating grasp of the other.

And Stuart just stood there. He was in a very unusual position. He was, in fact, in the particular position of all positions in which he most rarely found himself.

He had nothing to say.

The quality of tension had changed. The gloom and frustration had lifted a bit, and the excitement of conspiracy had replaced it. Even Polyorketes was fingering the space-suits and commenting briefly and hoarsely on which he considered preferable.

Mullen was having a certain amount of trouble. The suit hung rather limply upon him even though the adjustable joints had been tightened nearly to minimum. He stood there now with only the helmet to be screwed on. He wiggled his neck.

Stuart was holding the helmet with an effort. It was heavy, and his artiplasmic hands did not grip it well. He said, "Better scratch your nose if it itches. It's your last chance for a while." He didn't add, "Maybe forever," but he thought it.

Mullen said, tonelessly, "I think perhaps I had better have a spare oxygen cylinder."

"Good enough."

"With a reducing valve."

Stuart nodded. "I see what you're thinking of. If you do get blown clear of the ship, you could try to blow yourself back by using the cylinder as an action-reaction motor."

They clamped on the headpiece and buckled the spare cylinder to Mullen's waist. Polyorketes and Leblanc lifted him up to the yawning opening of the C-tube. It was ominously dark inside, the metal lining of the interior having been painted a mournful black. Stuart thought he could detect a musty odor about it, but that, he knew, was only imagination.

He stopped the proceedings when Mullen was half within the tube. He tapped upon the little man's faceplate.

"Can you hear me?"

Within, there was a nod.

"Air coming through all right? No last-minute troubles?"

Mullen lifted his armored arm in a gesture of reassurance.

"Then remember, don't use the suit-radio out there. The Kloros might pick up the signals."

Reluctantly, he stepped away. Polyorketes' brawny hands lowered Mullen until they could hear the thumping sound made by the steel-shod feet against the outer valve. The inner valve then swung shut with a dreadful finality, its beveled silicone gasket making a slight soughing noise as it crushed hard. They clamped it into place.

Stuart stood at the toggle-switch that controlled the outer valve. He threw it and the gauge that marked the air pressure within the tube fell to zero. A little pinpoint of red light warned that the outer valve was open. Then the light disappeared, the valve closed, and the gauge climbed slowly to fifteen pounds again.

They opened the inner valve again and found the tube empty.

Polyorketes spoke first. He said, "The little son-of-a-gun. He went!" He looked wonderingly at the others. "A little fellow with guts like that."

Stuart said, "Look, we'd better get ready in here. There's just a chance that the Kloros may have detected the valves opening and closing. If so, they'll be here to investigate and we'll have to cover up."

"How?" asked Windham.

"They won't see Mullen anywhere around. We'll say he's in the head. The Kloros know that it's one of the peculiar characteristics of Earthmen that they resent intrusion on their privacy in lavatories, and they'll make no effort to check. If we can hold them off—"

"What if they wait, or if they check the spacesuits?" asked Porter.

Stuart shrugged. "Let's hope they don't. And listen, Polyorketes, don't make any fuss when they come in."

Polyorketes grunted, "With that little guy out there? What do you think I am?" He stared at Stuart without animosity, then scratched his curly hair vigorously. "You know, I laughed at him. I thought he was an old woman. It makes me ashamed."

Stuart cleared his throat. He said, "Look, I've been saying some things that maybe weren't too funny after all, now that I come to think of it. I'd like to say I'm sorry if I have."

He turned away morosely and walked toward his cot. He heard the steps behind him, felt the touch on his sleeve. He turned; it was Leblanc.

The youngster said softly, "I keep thinking that Mr. Mullen is an old man."

"Well, he's not a kid. He's about forty-five or fifty, I think."

Leblanc said, "Do you think, Mr. Stuart, that *I* should have gone, instead? I'm the youngest here. I don't like the thought of having let an old man go in my place. It makes me feel like the devil."

"I know. If he dies, it will be too bad."

"But he volunteered. We didn't make him, did we?"

"Don't try to dodge responsibility, Leblanc. It won't make you feel better. There isn't one of us without a stronger motive to run the risk than he had." And Stuart sat there silently, thinking.

Mullen felt the obstruction beneath his feet yield and the walls about him slip away quickly, too quickly. He knew it was the puff of air escaping, carrying him with it, and he dug arms and legs frantically against the wall to brake himself. Corpses were supposed to be flung well clear of the ship, but he was no corpse—for the moment.

His feet swung free and threshed. He heard the *clunk* of one magnetic boot against the hull just as the rest of his body puffed out like a tight cork under air pressure. He teetered dangerously at the lip of the hole in the ship—he had changed orientation suddenly and was looking down on it—then took a step backward as its lid came down of itself and fitted smoothly against the hull.

A feeling of unreality overwhelmed him. Surely, it wasn't he standing on the outer surface of a ship. Not Randolph F. Mullen. So few human beings could ever say they had, even those who traveled in space constantly.

He was only gradually aware that he was in pain. Popping out of that hole with one foot clamped to the hull had nearly bent him in two. He tried moving, cautiously, and found his motions to be erratic and almost impossible to control. He *thought* nothing was broken, though the muscles of his left side were badly wrenched.

And then he came to himself and noticed that the wrist-lights of his suit were on. It was by their light that he had stared into the blackness of the C-chute. He stirred with the nervous thought that from within, the Kloros might see the twin spots of moving light just outside the hull. He flicked the switch upon the suit's midsection.

Mullen had never imagined that, standing on a ship, he would fail to see its hull. But it was dark, as dark below as above. There were the stars, hard and bright little nondimensional dots. Nothing more. Nothing more anywhere. Under his feet, not even the stars—*not even his feet*.

He bent back to look at the stars. His head swam. They were moving slowly. Or, rather, they were standing still and the ship was rotating, but he could not tell his eyes that. *They* moved. His eyes followed—down and behind the ship. New stars up and above from the other side. A black horizon. The ship existed only as a region where there were no stars.

No stars? Why, there was one almost at his feet. He nearly reached for it; then he realized that it was only a glittering reflection in the mirroring metal.

They were moving thousands of miles an hour. The stars were. The ship was. He was. But it meant nothing. To his senses, there was only silence and darkness and that slow wheeling of the stars. His eyes followed the wheeling—

And his head in its helmet hit the ship's hull with a soft bell-like ring.

He felt about in panic with his thick, insensitive, spun-silicate gloves. His feet were still firmly magnetized to the hull, that was true, but the rest of his body bent backward at the knees in a right angle. There was no gravity outside the ship. If he bent back, there was nothing to pull the upper part of his body down and tell his joints they were bending. His body stayed as he put it.

He pressed wildly against the hull and his torso shot upward and refused to stop when upright. He fell forward.

He tried more slowly, balancing with both hands against the hull, until he squatted evenly. Then upward. Very slowly. Straight up. Arms out to balance.

He was straight now, aware of his nausea and lightheadedness.

He looked about. My God, where were the steam-tubes? He couldn't see them. They were black on black, nothing on nothing.

Quickly, he turned on the wrist-lights. In space, there were no beams, only elliptical, sharply defined spots of blue steel, winking light back at him. Where they struck a rivet, a shadow was cast, knife-sharp and as black as space, the lighted region illuminated abruptly and without diffusion.

He moved his arms, his body swaying gently in the opposite direction; action and reaction. The vision of a steam-tube with its smooth cylindrical sides sprang at him.

He tried to move toward it. His foot held firmly to the hull. He pulled and it slogged upward, straining against quicksand that eased quickly. Three inches up and it had almost sucked free; six inches up and he thought it would fly away.

He advanced it and let it down, felt it enter the quicksand. When the sole was within two inches of the hull, it snapped down; out of control, hitting the hull ringingly. His space-suit carried the vibrations, amplifying them in his ears.

He stopped in absolute terror. The dehydrators that dried the atmosphere within his suit could not handle the sudden gush of perspiration that drenched his forehead and armpits.

He waited, then tried lifting his foot again—a bare inch, holding it there by main force and moving it horizontally. Horizontal motion involved no effort at all; it was motion perpendicular to the lines of magnetic force. But he had to keep the foot from snapping down as he did so, and then lower it slowly.

He puffed with the effort. Each step was agony. The tendons of his knees were cracking, and there were knives in his side.

Mullen stopped to let the perspiration dry. It wouldn't do to steam up the inside of his faceplate. He flashed his wrist-lights, and the steam-cylinder was right ahead.

The ship had four of them, at ninety degree intervals, thrusting out at an angle from the midgirdle. They were the "fine adjustment" of the ship's course. The coarse adjustment was the powerful thrusters back and front which fixed final velocity by their accelerative and the decelerative force, and the hyperatomics that took care of the space-swallowing Jumps.

But occasionally the direction of flight had to be adjusted slightly and then the steam-cylinders took over. Singly, they could drive the ship up, down, right, left. By twos, in appropriate ratios of thrust, the ship could be turned in any desired direction.

The device had been unimproved in centuries, being too simple to improve. The atomic pile heated the water content of a closed container into steam, driving it, in less than a second, up to temperatures where it would have broken down into a mixture of hydrogen and oxygen, and then into a mixture of electrons and ions. Perhaps the breakdown actually took place. No one ever bothered testing; it worked, so there was no need to.

At the critical point, a needle valve gave way and the steam thrust madly out in a short but incredible blast. And the ship, inevitably and majestically, moved in the opposite direction, veering about its own center of gravity. When the degrees of turn were sufficient, an equal and opposite blast would take place and the turning would be canceled. The ship would be moving at its original velocity, but in a new direction.

Mullen had dragged himself out to the lip of the steam-cylinder. He had a picture of himself—a small speck teetering at the extreme end of a structure thrusting out of an ovoid that was tearing through space at ten thousand miles an hour.

But there was no air-stream to whip him off the hull, and his magnetic soles held him more firmly than he liked.

With lights on, he bent down to peer into the tube and the ship dropped down precipitously as his orientation changed. He reached out to steady himself, but he was not falling. There was no up or down in space except for what his confused mind chose to consider up or down.

The cylinder was just large enough to hold a man, so that it might be entered for repair purposes. His light caught the rungs almost directly opposite his position at the lip. He puffed a sigh of relief with what breath he could muster. Some ships didn't have ladders.

He made his way to it, the ship appearing to slip and twist beneath him as he moved. He lifted an arm over the lip of the tube, feeling for the rung, loosened each foot, and drew himself within.

The knot in his stomach that had been there from the first was a convulsed agony now. If they should choose to manipulate the ship, if the steam should whistle out now—

He would never hear it; never know it. One instant he

would be holding a rung, feeling slowly for the next with a groping arm. The next moment he would be alone in space, the ship a dark, dark nothingness lost forever among the stars. There would be, perhaps, a brief glory of swirling ice crystals drifting with him, shining in his wrist-lights and slowly approaching and rotating about him, attracted by his mass like infinitesimal planets to an absurdly tiny Sun.

He was trickling sweat again, and now he was also conscious of thirst. He put it out of his mind. There would be no drinking until he was out of his suit—if ever.

Up a rung; up another; and another. How many were there? His hand slipped and he stared in disbelief at the glitter that showed under his light.

Ice?

Why not? The steam, incredibly hot as it was, would strike metal that was at nearly absolute zero. In the few split-seconds of thrust, there would not be time for the metal to warm above the freezing point of water. A sheet of ice would condense that would sublime slowly into the vacuum. It was the speed of all that happened that prevented the fusion of the tubes and of the original water-container itself.

His groping hand reached the end. Again the wrist-lights. He stared with crawling horror at the steam nozzle, half an inch in diameter. It looked dead, harmless. But it always would, right up to the micro-second before—

Around it was the outer steam lock. It pivoted on a central hub that was springed on the portion toward space, screwed on the part toward the ship. The springs allowed it to give under the first wild thrust of steam pressure before the ship's mighty inertia could be overcome. The steam was bled into the inner chamber, breaking the force of the thrust, leaving the total energy unchanged, but spreading it over time so that the hull itself was in that much less danger of being staved in.

Mullen braced himself firmly against a rung and pressed against the outer lock so that it gave a little. It was stiff, but it didn't have to give much, just enough to catch on the screw. He felt it catch.

He strained against it and turned it, feeling his body twist in the opposite direction. It held tight, the screw taking up the strain as he carefully adjusted the small control switch that allowed the springs to fall free. How well he remembered the books he had read!

He was in the interlock space now, which was large enough to hold a man comfortably, again for convenience in repairs. He could no longer be blown away from the ship. If the steam blast were turned on now, it would merely drive him against the inner lock—hard enough to crush him to a pulp. A quick death he would never feel, at least.

Slowly, he unhooked his spare oxygen cylinder. There was only an inner lock between himself and the control room now. This lock opened outward into space so that the steam blast could only close it tighter, rather than blow it open. And it fitted tightly and smoothly. There was absolutely no way to open it from without.

He lifted himself above the lock, forcing his bent back against the inner surface of the interlock area. It made breathing difficult. The spare oxygen cylinder dangled at a queer angle. He held its metal-mesh hose and straightened it, forcing it against the inner lock so that vibration thudded. Again—again—

It would *have* to attract the attention of the Kloros. They would *have* to investigate.

He would have no way of telling when they were about to do so. Ordinarily, they would first let air into the interlock to force the outer lock shut. But now the outer lock was on the central screw, well away from its rim. Air would suck about it ineffectually, dragging out into space.

Mullen kept on thumping. Would the Kloros look at the air-gauge, note that it scarcely lifted from zero, or would they take its proper working for granted?

Porter said, "He's been gone an hour and a half."

"I know," said Stuart.

They were all restless, jumpy, but the tension among themselves had disappeared. It was as though all the threads of emotion extended to the hull of the ship.

Porter was bothered. His philosophy of life had always been simple—take care of yourself because no one will take care of you for you. It upset him to see it shaken.

He said, "Do you suppose they've caught him?"

"If they had, we'd hear about it," replied Stuart, briefly.

Porter felt, with a miserable twinge, that there was little interest on the part of the others in speaking to him. He could understand it; he had not exactly earned their respect. For the moment, a torrent of self-excuse poured through his mind. The others had been frightened, too. A man had a right to be afraid. No one likes to die. At least, he hadn't broken like Aristides Polyorketes. He hadn't wept like Leblanc. He—

But there was Mullen, out there on the hull.

"Listen," he cried, "why did he do it?" They turned to look at him, not understanding, but Porter didn't care. It bothered him to the point where it had to come out. "I want to know why Mullen is risking his life."

"The man," said Windham, "is a patriot—"

"No, none of that!" Porter was almost hysterical. "That little fellow has no emotions at all. He just has reasons and I want to know what those reasons are, because—"

He didn't finish the sentence. Could he say that if those reasons applied to a little middle-aged bookkeeper, they might apply even more forcibly to himself?

Polyorketes said, "He's one brave damn little fellow."

Porter got to his feet. "Listen," he said, "he may be stuck out there. Whatever he's doing, he may not be able to finish it alone. I—I volunteer to go out after him."

He was shaking as he said it and he waited in fear for the sarcastic lash of Stuart's tongue. Stuart was staring at him, probably with surprise, but Porter dared not meet his eyes to make certain.

Stuart said, mildly, "Let's give him another half-hour."

Porter looked up, startled. There was no sneer on Stuart's face. It was even friendly. They *all* looked friendly.

He said, "And then—"

"And then all those who do volunteer will draw straws or

something equally democratic. Who volunteers, besides Porter?"

They all raised their hands; Stuart did, too.

But Porter was happy. He had volunteered first. He was anxious for the half-hour to pass.

It caught Mullen by surprise. The outer lock flew open and the long, thin, snakelike, almost headless neck of a Kloro sucked out, unable to fight the blast of escaping air.

Mullen's cylinder flew away, almost tore free. After one wild moment of frozen panic, he fought for it, dragging it above the airstream, waiting as long as he dared to let the first fury die down as the air of the control room thinned out, then bringing it down with force.

It caught the sinewy neck squarely, crushing it. Mullen, curled above the lock, almost entirely protected from the stream, raised the cylinder again and plunging it down again striking the head, mashing the staring eyes to liquid ruin. In the near-vacuum, green blood was pumping out of what was left of the neck.

Mullen dared not vomit, but he wanted to.

With eyes averted, he backed away, caught the outer lock with one hand and imparted a whirl. For several seconds, it maintained that whirl. At the end of the screw, the springs engaged automatically and pulled it shut. What was left of the atmosphere tightened it and the laboring pumps could now begin to fill the control room once again.

Mullen crawled over the mangled Kloro and into the room. It was empty.

He had barely time to notice that when he found himself on his knees. He rose with difficulty. The transition from non-gravity to gravity had taken him entirely by surprise. It was Klorian gravity, too, which meant that with this suit, he carried a fifty percent overload for his small frame. At least, though, his heavy metal clogs no longer clung so exasperatingly to the metal underneath. Within the ship, floors and wall were of cork-covered aluminum alloy.

He circled slowly. The neckless Kloro had collapsed and lay with only an occasional twitch to show it had once been a living organism. He stepped over it, distastefully, and drew the steam-tube lock shut.

The room had a depressing bilious cast and the lights shone yellow-green. It was the Kloro atmosphere, of course.

Mullen felt a twinge of surprise and reluctant admiration. The Kloros obviously had some way of treating materials so that they were impervious to the oxidizing effect of chlorine. Even the map of Earth on the wall, printed on glossy plastic-backed paper, seemed fresh and untouched. He approached, drawn by the familiar outlines of the continents—

There was a flash of motion caught in the corner of his eyes. As quickly as he could in his heavy suit, he turned, then screamed. The Kloro he had thought dead was rising to its feet.

Its neck hung limp, an oozing mass of tissue mash, but its arms reached out blindly, and the tentacles about its chest vibrated rapidly like innumerable snakes' tongues.

It was blind, of course. The destruction of its neck-stalk had deprived it of all sensory equipment, and partial asphyxiation had disorganized it. But the brain remained whole and safe in the abdomen. It still lived.

Mullen backed away. He circled, trying clumsily and unsuccessfully to tiptoe, though he knew that what was left of the Kloro was also deaf. It blundered on its way, struck a wall, felt to the base and began sidling along it.

Mullen cast about desperately for a weapon, found nothing. There was the Kloro's holster, but he dared not reach for it. Why hadn't he snatched it at the very first? Fool!

The door to the control room opened. It made almost no noise. Mullen turned, quivering.

The other Kloro entered, unharmed, entire. It stood in the doorway for a moment, chest-tendrils stiff and unmoving; its neck-stalk stretched forward; its horrible eyes flickering first at him and then at its nearly dead comrade.

And then its hand moved quickly to its side.

Mullen, without awareness, moved as quickly in pure

reflex. He stretched out the hose of the spare oxygen cylinder, which, since entering the control room, he had replaced in its suit-clamp, and cracked the valve. He didn't bother reducing the pressure. He let it gush out unchecked so that he nearly staggered under the backward push.

He could *see* the oxygen stream. It was a pale puff, billowing out amid the chlorine-green. It caught the Kloro with one hand on the weapon's holster.

The Kloro threw its hands up. The little beak on its head-nodule opened alarmingly but noiselessly. It staggered and fell, writhed for a moment, then lay still. Mullen approached and played the oxygen-stream upon its body as though he were extinguishing a fire. And then he raised his heavy foot and brought it down upon the center of the neck-stalk and crushed it on the floor.

He turned to the first. It was sprawled, rigid.

The whole room was pale with oxygen, enough to kill whole legions of Kloros, and his cylinder was empty.

Mullen stepped over the dead Kloro, out of the control room and along the main corridor toward the prisoners' room.

Reaction had set in. He was whimpering in blind, incoherent fright.

Stuart was tired. False hands and all, he was at the controls of a ship once again. Two light cruisers of Earth were on the way. For better than twenty-four hours he had handled the controls virtually alone. He had discarded the chlorinating equipment, rerigged the old atmospherics, located the ship's position in space, tried to plot a course, and sent out carefully guarded signals—which had worked.

So when the door of the control room opened, he was a little annoyed. He was too tired to play conversational handball. Then he turned, and it was Mullen stepping inside.

Stuart said, "For God's sake, get back into bed, Mullen!"

Mullen said, "I'm tired of sleeping, even though I never thought I would be a while ago."

"How do you feel?"

"I'm stiff all over. Especially my side." He grimaced and stared involuntarily around.

"Don't look for the Kloros," Stuart said. "We dumped the poor devils." He shook his head. "I was sorry for them. To themselves, *they're* the human beings, you know, and *we're* the aliens. Not that I'd rather they'd killed you, you understand."

"I understand."

Stuart turned a sidelong glance upon the little man who sat looking at the map of Earth and went on, "I owe you a particular and personal apology, Mullen. I didn't think much of you."

"It was your privilege," said Mullen in his dry voice. There was no feeling in it.

"No, it wasn't. It is no one's privilege to despise another. It is only a hard-won right after long experience."

"Have you been thinking about this?"

"Yes, all day. Maybe I can't explain. It's these hands." He held them up before him, spread out. "It was hard knowing that other people had hands of their own. I had to hate them for it. I always had to do my best to investigate and belittle their motives, point up their deficiencies, expose their stupidities. I had to do anything that would prove to myself that they weren't worth envying."

Mullen moved restlessly. "This explanation is not necessary."

"It is. It is!" Stuart felt his thought intently, strained to put them into words. "For years I've abandoned hope of finding any decency in human beings. Then you climbed into the C-chute."

"You had better understand," said Mullen, "that I was motivated by practical and selfish considerations. I will not have you present me to myself as a hero."

"I wasn't intending to. I know that you would do nothing without a reason. It was what your action did to the rest of us. It turned a collection of phonies and fools into decent people. And not by magic either. They were decent all along. It was just that they needed something to live up to and you supplied it. And—I'm one of them. I'll have to live up to you, too. For the rest of my life, probably."

Mullen turned away uncomfortably. His hand straightened his sleeves, which were not in the least twisted. His finger rested on the map.

He said, "I was born in Richmond, Virginia, you know. Here it is. I'll be going there first. Where were you born?"

"Toronto," said Stuart.

"That's right here. Not very far apart on the map, is it?"

Stuart said, "Would you tell me something?"

"If I can."

"Just why *did* you go out there?"

Mullen's precise mouth pursed. He said, dryly, "Wouldn't my rather prosaic reason ruin the inspirational effect?"

"Call it intellectual curiosity. Each of the rest of us had such obvious motives. Porter was scared to death of being interned; Leblanc wanted to get back to his sweetheart; Polyorketes wanted to kill Kloros; and Windham was a patriot according to his lights. As for me, I thought of myself as a noble idealist, I'm afraid. Yet in none of us was the motivation strong enough to get us into a spacesuit and out the C-chute. Then what made *you* do it, *you* of all people?"

"Why the phrase, 'of all people'?"

"Don't be offended, but you seem devoid of all emotion."

"Do I?" Mullen's voice did not change. It remained precise and soft, yet somehow a tightness had entered it. "That's only training, Mr. Stuart, and self-discipline; not nature. A small man can have no respectable emotions. Is there anything more ridiculous than a man like myself in a state of rage? I'm five feet one-half inch tall, and one hundred and two pounds in weight, if you care for exact figures. I insist on the half inch and the two pounds.

"Can I be dignified? Proud? Draw myself to my full height without inducing laughter? Where can I meet a woman who will not dismiss me instantly with a giggle?

Naturally, I've had to learn to dispense with external display of emotion.

"*You* talk about deformities. No one would notice your hands or know they were different, if you weren't so eager to tell people all about it the instant you meet them. Do you think that the eight inches of height I do not have can be hidden? That it is not the first and, in most cases, the only thing about me that a person will notice?"

Stuart was ashamed. He had invaded a privacy he ought not have. He said, "I'm sorry."

"Why?"

"I should not have forced you to speak of this. I should have seen for myself that you—that you—"

"That I what? Tried to prove myself? Tried to show that while I might be small in body, I held within it a giant's heart?"

"I would not have put it mockingly."

"Why not? It's a foolish idea, and nothing like it is the reason I did what I did. What would I have accomplished if that's what was in my mind? Will they take me to Earth now and put me up before the television cameras—pitching them low, of course, to catch my face, or standing me on a chair—and pin medals on me?"

"They are quite likely to do exactly that."

"And what good would it do me? They would say, 'Gee, and he's such a little guy.' And afterward, what? Shall I tell each man I meet, 'You know, I'm the fellow they decorated for incredible valor last month?' How many medals, Mr. Stuart, do you suppose it would take to put eight inches and sixty pounds on me?"

Stuart said, "Put that way, I see your point."

Mullen was speaking a trifle more quickly now; a controlled heat had entered his words, warming them to just a tepid room temperature. "There *were* days when I thought I would show them, the mysterious 'them' that includes all the world. I was going to leave Earth and carve out worlds for myself. I would be a new and even smaller Napoleon. So I left Earth and went to Arcturus. And what could I do on Arcturus that I could not have done on Earth? Nothing.

I balance books. So I am past the vanity, Mr. Stuart, of trying to stand on tiptoe."

"Then why *did* you do it?"

"I left Earth when I was twenty-eight and came to the Arcturian System. I've been there ever since. This trip was to be my first vacation, my first visit back to Earth in all that time. I was going to stay on Earth for six months. The Kloros instead captured us and would have kept us interned indefinitely. But I couldn't—I *couldn't* let them stop me from traveling to Earth. No matter what the risk, I had to prevent their interference. It wasn't love of woman, or fear, or hate, or idealism of any sort. It was stronger than any of those."

He stopped, and stretched out a hand as though to caress the map on the wall.

"Mr. Stuart," Mullen asked quietly, "haven't you ever been homesick?"

ALLAMAGOOSA

Eric Frank Russell

It was a long time since the *Bustler* had been so silent. She lay in the Sirian spaceport, her tubes cold, her shell particle-scarred, her air that of a long-distance runner exhausted at the end of a marathon. There was good reason for this: she had returned from a lengthy trip by no means devoid of troubles.

Now, in port, well-deserved rest had been gained if only temporarily. Peace, sweet peace. No more bothers, no more crises, no more major upsets, no more dire predicaments such as crop up in free flight at least twice a day. Just peace.

Hah!

Captain McNaught reposed in his cabin, feet up on desk, and enjoyed the relaxation to the utmost. The engines were dead, their hellish pounding absent for the first time in months. Out there in the big city four hundred of his crew were making whoopee under a brilliant sun. This evening, when First Officer Gregory returned to take charge, he was going to go into the fragrant twilight and make the rounds of neon-lit civilization.

That was the beauty of making landfall at long last. Men

55

could give way to themselves, blow off surplus steam, each according to his fashion. No duties, no worries, no dangers, no responsibilities in spaceport. A haven of safety and comfort for tired rovers.

Again, hah!

Burman, the chief radio officer, entered the cabin. He was one of the half-dozen remaining on duty and bore the expression of a man who can think of twenty better things to do.

"Relayed signal just come in, sir." Handing the paper across, he waited for the other to look at it and perhaps dictate a reply.

Taking the sheet, McNaught removed the feet from his desk, sat erect and read the message aloud.

Terran Headquarters to BUSTLER. Remain Siriport pending further orders. Rear Admiral Vane W. Cassidy due there seventeenth. Feldman. Navy Op. Command. Sirisec.

He looked up, all happiness gone from his leathery features. "Oh, Lord!" he groaned.

"Something wrong?" asked Burman, vaguely alarmed.

McNaught pointed at three thin books on his desk. "The middle one. Page twenty."

Leafing through it, Burman found an item that said:

Vane W. Cassidy, R-Ad. Head Inspector Ships and Stores.

Burman swallowed hard. "Does that mean—?"

"Yes, it does," said McNaught without pleasure. "Back to training-college and all its rigmarole. Paint and soap, spit and polish." He put on an officious expression, adopted a voice to match it. "Captain, you have only seven ninety-nine emergency rations. Your allocation is eight hundred. Nothing in your logbook accounts for the missing one. Where is it? What happened to it? How is it that one of the men's kits lacks an officially issued pair of suspenders? Did you report his loss?"

"Why does he pick on us?" asked Burman, appalled. "He's never chivvied us before."

"That's why," informed McNaught, scowling at the wall. "It's our turn to be stretched across the barrel." His gaze found the calendar. "We have three days—and we'll need 'em! Tell Second Officer Pike to come here at once."

Burman departed gloomily. In short time Pike entered. His face reaffirmed the old adage that bad news travels fast.

"Make out an indent," ordered McNaught, "for one hundred gallons of plastic paint, Navy-gray, approved quality. Make out another for thirty gallons of interior white enamel. Take them to spaceport stores right away. Tell them to deliver by six this evening along with our correct issue of brushes and sprayers. Grab up any cleaning material that's going for free."

"The men won't like this," remarked Pike, feebly.

"They're going to love it," McNaught asserted. "A bright and shiny ship, all spic and span, is good for morale. It says so in that book. Get moving and put those indents in. When you come back, find the stores and equipment sheets and bring them here. We've got to check stocks before Cassidy arrives. Once he's here we'll have no chance to make up shortages or smuggle out any extra items we happened to find in our hands."

"Very well, sir." Pike went out wearing the same expression as Burman.

Lying back in his chair McNaught muttered to himself. There was a feeling in his bones that something was sure to cause a last-minute ruckus. A shortage of any item would be serious enough unless covered by a previous report. A surplus would be bad, very bad. The former implied carelessness or misfortune. The latter suggested barefaced theft of government property in circumstances condoned by the commander.

For instance, there was that recent case of Williams of the heavy cruiser *Swift*. He'd heard of it over the spacevine when out around Bootes. Williams had been found in unwitting command of eleven reels of electric-fence wire when his official issue was ten. It had taken a court-martial to decide that the extra reel—which had formidable barter-value on a certain planet—had not been stolen from space stores or, in sailor jargon, "teleportated aboard." But Williams had been reprimanded. And that did not help promotion.

He was still rumbling discontentedly when Pike returned bearing a folder of foolscap sheets.

"Going to start right away, sir?"

"We'll have to." He heaved himself erect, mentally bidding goodbye to time off and a taste of the bright lights. "It'll take long enough to work right through from bow to tail. I'll leave the men's kit inspection to the last."

Marching out of the cabin, he set forth toward the bow, Pike following with broody reluctance.

As they passed the open main lock Peaslake observed them, bounded eagerly up the gangway and joined behind. A pukka member of the crew, he was a large dog whose ancestors had been more enthusiastic than selective. He wore with pride a big collar inscribed: *Peaslake—Property of S.S. Bustler*. His chief duties, ably performed, were to keep alien rodents off the ship and, on rare occasions, smell out dangers not visible to human eyes.

The three paraded forward, McNaught and Pike in the manner of men grimly sacrificing pleasure for the sake of duty, Peaslake with the panting willingness of one ready for any new game no matter what.

Reaching the bow-cabin, McNaught dumped himself in the pilot's seat, took the folder from the other. "You know this stuff better than me—the chart-room is where I shine. So I'll read them out while you look them over." He opened the folder, started on the first page. "K1. Beam compass, type D, one of."

"Check," said Pike.

"K2. Distance and direction indicator, electronic, type JJ, one of."

"Check."

Peaslake planted his head in McNaught's lap, blinked soulfully and whined. He was beginning to get the others' viewpoint. This tedious itemizing and checking was a hell of a game. McNaught consolingly lowered a hand and played with Peaslake's ears while he plowed his way down the list.

"K187. Foam rubber cushions, pilot and co-pilot, one pair."

"Check."

By the time First Officer Gregory appeared they had reached the tiny intercom cubby and poked around it in semi-darkness. Peaslake had long departed in disgust.

"M24. Spare minispeakers, three-inch, type T2, one set of six."

"Check."

Looking in, Gregory popped his eyes and said, "What the devil is going on?"

"Major inspection due soon." McNaught glanced at his watch. "Go see if stores has delivered a load and if not why not. Then you'd better give me a hand and let Pike take a few hours off."

"Does this mean land-leave is cancelled?"

"You bet it does—until after Hizonner has been and gone." He glanced at Pike. "When you get into the city search around and send back any of the crew you can find. No arguments or excuses. It's an order."

Pike registered unhappiness. Gregory glowered at him, went away, came back and said, "Stores will have the stuff here in twenty minutes' time." With bad grace he watched Pike depart.

"M47. Intercom cable, woven-wire protected, three drums."

"Check," said Gregory, mentally kicking himself for returning at the wrong time.

The task continued until late in the evening, was resumed early next morning. By that time three-quarters of the men were hard at work inside and outside the vessel, doing their jobs as though sentenced to them for crimes contemplated but not yet committed.

Moving around the ship's corridors and catwalks had to be done crab-fashion, with a nervous sideways edging. Once again it was being demonstrated that the Terran lifeform suffers from ye fear of wette paynt. The first smearer would have ten years willed off his unfortunate life.

It was in these conditions, in mid-afternoon of the second day, that McNaught's bones proved their feelings had been prophetic. He recited the ninth page while Jean Blanchard confirmed the presence and actual existence of all items enumerated. Two-thirds of the way down they hit the rocks, metaphorically speaking, and commenced to sink fast.

McNaught said boredly, "V1097. Drinking-bowl, enamel, one of."

"Is zis," said Blanchard, tapping it.

"V1098. Offog, one."

"*Quoi?*" asked Blanchard, staring.

"V1098. Offog, one," repeated McNaught. "Well, why are you looking thunderstruck? This is the ship's galley. You're the head cook. You know what's supposed to be in the galley, don't you? Where's this offog?"

"Never hear of heem," stated Blanchard, flatly.

"You must have done. It's on the equipment-sheet in plain, clear type. Offog, one, it says. It was here when we were fitted out four years ago. We checked it ourselves and signed for it."

"I signed for nossings called offog," Blanchard denied. "In zee cuisine zere is no such sing."

"Look!" McNaught scowled and showed him the sheet.

Blanchard looked and sniffed disdainfully. "I have here zee electronic oven, one of. I have jacketed boilers, graduated capacities, one set. I have bain marie pans, seex of. But no offog. Never heard of heem. I do not know of heem." He spread his hands and shrugged.

"There's got to be," McNaught insisted. "What's more, when Cassidy arrives there'll be hell to pay if there isn't."

"You find heem," Blanchard suggested.

"You got a certificate from the International Hotels School of Cookery. You got a certificate from the Cordon

Bleu College of Cuisine. You got a certificate with three credits from the Space-Navy Feeding Center," McNaught pointed out. "All that—and you don't know what an offog is."

"*Nom d'un chien!*" ejaculated Blanchard, waving his arms around. "I tell you ten t'ousand time zere is no offog. Zere never was an offog. Escoffier heemself could not find zee offog of vich zere is none. Am I a magician perhaps?"

"It's part of the culinary equipment," McNaught maintained. "It must be because it's on page nine. And page nine means its proper home is in the galley, care of the head cook."

"Like hail it does," Blanchard retorted. He pointed at a metal box on the wall. "Intercom booster. Is zat mine?"

McNaught thought it over, conceded, "No, it's Burman's. His stuff rambles all over the ship."

"Zen ask heem for zis bloody offog," said Blanchard, triumphantly.

"I will. If it's not yours it must be his. Let's finish this checking first. If I'm not systematic and thorough Cassidy will jerk down my pants along with my insignia." His eyes sought the list. "V1099. Inscribed collar, leather, brass studded, dog, for the use of. No need to look for that. I saw it myself five minutes ago." He ticked the item, continued, "V1100. Sleeping basket, woven reed, one of."

"Is zis," said Blanchard, kicking it into a corner.

"V1101. Cushion, foam rubber, to fit sleeping basket, one of."

"Half of," Blanchard contradicted. "In four years he have chewed away other half."

"Maybe Cassidy will let us indent for a new one. It doesn't matter. We're okay so long as we can produce the half we've got." McNaught stood up, closed the folder. "That's the lot for here, I'll go see Burman about this missing item."

Burman switched off a UHF receiver, removed his earplugs and raised a questioning eyebrow.

"In the galley we're short an offog," explained Mc-Naught. "Where is it?"

"Why ask me? The galley is Blanchard's bailiwick."

"Not entirely. A lot of your cables run through it. You've two terminal boxes in there, also an automatic switch and an intercom booster. Where's the offog?"

"Never heard of it," said Burman, baffled.

McNaught shouted, "Don't tell me that! I'm already fed up hearing Blanchard saying it. Four years back we had an offog. It says so here. This is our copy of what we checked and signed for. It says we signed for an offog. Therefore we must have one. It's got to be found before Cassidy gets here."

"Sorry, sir," sympathized Burman. "I can't help you."

"You can think again," advised McNaught. "Up in the bow there's a direction and distance indicator. What do *you* call it?"

"A didin," said Burman, mystified.

"And," McNaught went on, pointed at the pulse transmitter, "what do you call *that?*"

"The opper-popper."

"Baby names, see? Didin and opper-popper. Now rack your brains and remember what you called an offog four years ago."

"Nothing," asserted Burman, "has ever been called an offog to my knowledge."

"Then," demanded McNaught, "why the blue blazes did we sign for one?"

"I didn't sign for anything. You did all the signing."

"While you and others did the checking. Four years ago, presumably in the galley, I said, 'Offog, one,' and either you or Blanchard pointed to it and said, 'Check.' I took somebody's word for it. I have to take other specialists' words for it. I am an expert navigator, familiar with all the latest navigational gadgets but not with other stuff. So I'm compelled to rely on people who know what an offog is—or ought to."

Burman had a bright thought. "All kinds of oddments were dumped in the main lock, the corridors and the galley

when we were fitted out. We had to sort through a deal of
stuff and stash it where it prope·ly belonged, remember?
This offog-thing might be anyplace today. It isn't necessarily my responsibility or Blanchard's."

"I'll see what the other officers say," agreed McNaught,
conceding the point. "Gregory, Worth, Sanderson, or one
of the others may be coddling the item. Wherever it is, it's
got to be found."

He went out. Burman pulled a face, inserted his earplugs,
resumed fiddling with his apparatus. An hour later Mc-
Naught came back wearing a scowl.

"Positively," he announced with ire, "there is no such
thing on the ship. Nobody knows of it. Nobody can so much
as guess at it."

"Cross it off and report it lost," Burman suggested.

"What, when we're hard aground? You know as well as
I do that loss and damage must be signaled at time of
occurrence. If I tell Cassidy the offog went west in space,
he'll want to know when, where, how and why it wasn't
signaled. There'll be a real ruckus if the contraption
happens to be valued at half a million credits. I can't dismiss
it with an airy wave of the hand."

"What's the answer then?" inquired Burman, innocently
ambling straight into the trap.

"There's one and only one," McNaught announced. "*You*
will manufacture an offog."

"Who? *Me?*" said Burman, twitching his scalp.

"You and no other. I'm fairly sure the thing is your
pigeon, anyway."

"Why?"

"Because it's typical of the baby-names used for your
kind of stuff. I'll bet a month's pay that an offog is some
sort of scientific allamagoosa. Something to do with fog,
perhaps. Maybe a blind-approach gadget."

"The blind-approach transceiver is called 'the fumbly,' "
Burman informed.

"There you are!" said McNaught as if that clinched it.
"So you will make an offog. It will be completed by six

tomorrow evening and ready for my inspection then. It had better be convincing, in fact pleasing."

Burman stood up, let his hands dangle, and said in hoarse tones, "How the devil can I make an offog when I don't even know what it is?"

"Neither does Cassidy know," McNaught pointed out, leering at him. "He's more of a quantity surveyor than anything else. As such he counts things, looks at things, certifies that they exist, accepts advice on whether they are functionally satisfactory or worn out. All we need do is concoct an imposing allamagoosa and tell him it's the offog."

"Holy Moses!" said Burman, fervently.

"Let us not rely on the dubious assistance of Biblical characters," McNaught reproved. "Let us use the brains that God has given us. Get a grip on your soldering-iron and make a topnotch offog by six tomorrow evening. That's an order!"

He departed, satisfied with this solution. Behind him, Burman gloomed at the wall and licked his lips once, twice.

Rear Admiral Vane W. Cassidy arrived dead on time. He was a short, paunchy character with a florid complexion and eyes like those of a long-dead fish. His gait was an important strut.

"Ah, Captain, I trust that you have everything ship-shape."

"Everything usually is," assured McNaught, glibly. "I see to that."

"Good!" approved Cassidy. "I like a commander who takes his responsibilities seriously. Much as I regret saying so, there are a few who do not." He marched through the main lock, his cod-eyes taking note of the fresh white enamel. "Where do you prefer to start, bow or tail?"

"My equipment-sheets run from bow backward. We may as well deal with them the way they're set."

"Very well." He trotted officiously toward the nose, paused on the way to pat Peaslake and examine his collar. "Well cared for, I see. Has the animal proved useful?"

"He saved five lives on Mardia by barking a warning."

"The details have been entered in your log, I suppose?"

"Yes, sir. The log is in the chart-room awaiting your inspection."

"We'll get to it in due time." Reaching the bow-cabin, Cassidy took a seat, accepted the folder from McNaught, started off at businesslike pace. "K1. Beam compass, type D, one of."

"This is it, sir," said McNaught, showing him.

"Still working properly?"

"Yes, sir."

They carried on, reached the intercom-cubby, the computer-room, a succession of other places back to the galley. Here, Blanchard posed in freshly laundered white clothes and eyed the newcomer warily.

"V147. Electronic oven, one of."

"Is zis," said Blanchard, pointing with disdain.

"Satisfactory?" inquired Cassidy, giving him the fishy eye.

"Not beeg enough," declared Blanchard. He encompassed the entire galley with an expressive gesture. "Nossings beeg enough. Place too small. Everysings too small. I am chef de cuisine an' she is a cuisine like an attic."

"This is a warship, not a luxury liner," Cassidy snapped. He frowned at the equipment-sheet. "V148. Timing device, electronic oven, attachment thereto, one of."

"Is zis," spat Blanchard, ready to sling it through the nearest port if Cassidy would first donate the two pins.

Working his way down the sheet, Cassidy got nearer and nearer while nervous tension built up. Then he reached the critical point and said, "V1098. Offog, one."

"*Morbleau!*" said Blanchard, shooting sparks from his eyes, "I have say before an' I say again, zere never was—"

"The offog is in the radio-room, sir," McNaught chipped in hurriedly.

"Indeed?" Cassidy took another look at the sheet. "Then why is it recorded along with galley equipment?"

"It was placed in the galley at the time of fitting out , sir.

It's one of those portable instruments left to us to fix up where most suitable."

"H'm! Then it should have been transferred to the radio-room list. Why didn't you transfer it?"

"I thought it better to wait for your authority to do so, sir."

The fish-eyes registered gratification. "Yes, that is quite proper of you, Captain. I will transfer it now." He crossed the item from sheet nine, initialed it, entered it on sheet sixteen, initialed that. "V1099. Inscribed collar, leather . . . oh, yes, I've seen that. The dog was wearing it."

He ticked it. An hour later he strutted into the radio-room. Burman stood up, squared his shoulders but could not keep his feet or hands from fidgeting. His eyes protruded slightly and kept straying toward McNaught in silent appeal. He was like a man wearing a porcupine in his breeches.

"V1098. Offog, one," said Cassidy in his usual tone of brooking no nonsense.

Moving with the jerkiness of a slightly uncoordinated robot, Burman pawed a small box fronted with dials, switches and colored lights. It looked like a radio ham's idea of a fruit machine. He knocked down a couple of switches. The lights came on, played around in intriguing combinations.

"This is it, sir," he informed with difficulty.

"Ah!" Cassidy left his chair and moved across for a closer look. "I don't recall having seen this item before. But there are so many different models of the same things. Is it still operating efficiently?"

"Yes, sir."

"It's one of the most useful things in the ship," contributed McNaught for good measure.

"What does it *do?*" inquired Cassidy, inviting Burman to cast a pearl of wisdom before him.

Burman paled.

Hastily, McNaught said, "A full explanation would be rather involved and technical but, to put it as simply as possible, it enables us to strike a balance between opposing gravitational fields. Variations in lights indicate the extent and degree of imbalance at any given time."

"It's a clever idea," added Burman, made suddenly reckless by this news, "based upon Finagle's Constant."

"I see," said Cassidy, not seeing at all. He resumed his seat, ticked the offog and carried on. "Z44. Switchboard, automatic, forty-line intercom, one of."

"Here it is, sir."

Cassidy glanced at it, returned his gaze to the sheet. The others used his momentary distraction to mop perspiration from their foreheads.

Victory had been gained.

All was well.

For the third time, hah!

Rear Admiral Vane W. Cassidy departed pleased and complimentary. Within one hour the crew bolted to town. McNaught took turns with Gregory at enjoying the gay lights. For the next five days all was peace and pleasure.

On the sixth day Burman brought in a signal, dumped it upon McNaught's desk and waited for the reaction. He had an air of gratification, the pleasure of one whose virtue is about to be rewarded.

> *Terran Headquarters to BUSTLER. Return here immediately for overhaul and refitting. Improved powerplant to be installed. Feldman. Navy Op. Command. Sirisec.*

"Back to Terra," commented McNaught, happily. "And an overhaul will mean at least one month's leave." He eyed Burman. "Tell all officers on duty to go to town at once and order the crew aboard. The men will come running when they know why."

"Yes, sir," said Burman, grinning.

Everyone was still grinning two weeks later, when the Siriport had receded far behind and Sol had grown to a vague speck in the sparkling mist of the bow starfield.

Eleven weeks still to go, but it was worth it. Back to Terra. Hurrah!

In the captain's cabin the grins abruptly vanished one evening when Burman suddenly developed the willies. He marched in, chewed his bottom lip while waiting for McNaught to finish writing in the log.

Finally, McNaught pushed the book away, glanced up, frowned. "What's the matter with you? Got a bellyache or something?"

"No, sir. I've been thinking."

"Does it hurt that much?"

"I've been thinking," persisted Burman in funereal tones. "We're going back for overhaul. You know what that means. We'll walk off the ship and a horde of experts will walk onto it." He stared tragically at the other. "Experts, I said."

"Naturally they'll be experts," McNaught agreed. "Equipment cannot be tested and brought up to scratch by a bunch of dopes."

"It will require more than a mere expert to bring the offog up to scratch," Burman pointed out. "It'll need a genius."

McNaught rocked back, swapped expressions like changing masks. "Jumping Judas! I'd forgotten all about that thing. When we get to Terra we won't blind *those* boys with science."

"No, sir, we won't," endorsed Burman. He did not add any more but his face shouted aloud, "You got me into this. You get me out of it." He waited quite a time while McNaught did some intense thinking, then prompted, "What do you suggest, sir?"

Slowly the satisfied smile returned to McNaught's features as he answered, "Break up the contraption and feed it into the disintegrator."

"That doesn't solve the problem," said Burman. "We'll still be short an offog."

"No we won't. Because I'm going to signal its loss owing to the hazards of space service." He closed one eye in an emphatic wink. "We're in free flight right now." He reached for a message pad and scribbled on it while Burman stood by, vastly relieved.

> BUSTLER to Terran Headquarters. Item V1098, Offog, one, came apart under gravitational stress while passing through twin-sun field Hector Major-Minor. Material used as fuel. McNaught, Commander. BUSTLER.

Burman took it to the radio-room and beamed it Earthward. All was peace and progress for another two days. The next time he went to the captain's cabin he went running.

"General call, sir," he announced breathlessly and thrust the message into the other's hands.

> Terran Headquarters for relay all sectors. Urgent and Important. All ships grounded forthwith. Vessels in flight under official orders will make for nearest spaceport pending further instructions. Welling. Alarm and Rescue Command. Terra.

"Something's gone bust," commented McNaught, undisturbed. He traipsed to the chart room, Burman following. Consulting the charts, he dialed the intercom phone, got Pike in the bow and ordered, "There's a panic. All ships grounded. We've got to make for Zaxted-port, about three days' run away. Change course at once. Starboard seventeen degrees, declination ten." Then he cut off, griped, "Bang goes that sweet month on Terra. I never did like Zaxted, either. It stinks. The crew will feel murderous about this and I don't blame them."

"What d'you think has happened, sir?" asked Burman.

"Heaven alone knows. The last general call was seven years ago, when the *Starider* exploded halfway along the Mars run. They grounded every ship in existence while they investigated the cause." He rubbed his chin, pondered, went on, "And the call before that one was when the entire crew of the *Blowgun* went nuts. Whatever it is this time, you can bet it's serious."

"It wouldn't be the start of a space war?"

"Against whom?" McNaught made a gesture of contempt. "Nobody has the ships with which to oppose us. No, it's something technical. We'll learn of it eventually. They'll tell us before we reach Zaxted or soon afterward."

They did tell him. Within six hours. Burman rushed in with face full of horror.

"What's eating you now?" demanded McNaught, staring at him.

"The offog," stuttered Burman. He made motions as though brushing off invisible spiders.

"What of it?

"It's a typographical error. In your copy it should read 'off. dog.'"

"Off. dog?" echoed McNaught, making it sound like foul language.

"See for yourself." Dumping the signal on the desk, Burman bolted out, left the door swinging. McNaught scowled after him, picked up the message.

Terran Headquarters to BUSTLER. Your report V1098, ship's official dog Peaslake. Detail fully circumstances and manner in which animal came apart under gravitational stress. Cross-examine crew and signal all coincidental symptoms experienced by them. Urgent and Important. Welling. Alarm and Rescue Command. Terra.

In the privacy of his cabin McNaught commenced to eat his nails. Every now and again he went a little cross-eyed as he examined them for nearness to the flesh.

A QUESTION
OF COURAGE

J. F. Bone

I smelled the trouble the moment I stepped on the lift and took the long ride up the side of the *Lachesis*. There was something wrong. I couldn't put my finger on it but five years in the Navy gives a man a feeling for these things. From the outside the ship was beautiful, a gleaming shaft of duralloy, polished until she shone. Her paint and brightwork glistened. The antiradiation shields on the gun turrets and launchers were folded back exactly according to regulations. The shore uniform of the liftman was spotless and he stood at his station precisely as he should. As the lift moved slowly up past no-man's country to the life section, I noted a work party hanging precariously from a scaffolding smoothing out meteorite pits in the gleaming hull, while on the catwalk of the gantry standing beside the main cargo hatch a steady stream of supplies disappeared into the ship's belly.

I returned the crisp salute of the white-gloved sideboys, saluted the colors, and shook hands with an immaculate ensign with an O.D. badge on his tunic.

"Glad to have you aboard, sir," the ensign said.

"I'm Marsden," I said. "Lieutenant Thomas Marsden. I have orders posting me to this ship as executive."

"Yes, sir. We have been expecting you. I'm Ensign Halloran."

"Glad to meet you, Halloran."

"Skipper's orders, sir. You are to report to him as soon as you come aboard."

Then I got it. Everything was SOP. The ship wasn't taut, she was tight! And she wasn't happy. There was none of the devilmaycare spirit that marks crews in the Scouting Force and separates them from the stodgy mass of the Line. Every face I saw on my trip to the skipper's cabin was blank, hard-eyed, and unsmiling. There was none of the human noise that normally echoes through a ship, no laughter, no clatter of equipment, no deviations from the order and precision so dear to admirals' hearts. This crew was G.I. right down to the last seam tab on their uniforms. Whoever the skipper was, he was either bucking for another cluster or a cold feeling automaton to whom the Navy Code was father, mother, and Bible.

The O.D. stopped before the closed door, executed a mechanical right face, knocked the prescribed three times and opened the door smartly on the heels of the word "Come" that erupted from the inside. I stepped in followed by the O.D.

"Commander Chase," the O.D. said. "Lieutenant Marsden."

Chase! Not Cautious Charley Chase! I could hardly look at the man behind the command desk. But look I did—and my heart did a ninety degree dive straight to the thick soles of my space boots. No wonder this ship was sour. What else could happen with Lieutenant Commander Charles Augustus Chase in command! He was three classes up on me, but even though he was a First Classman at the time I crawled out of Beast Barracks, I knew him well. Every Midshipman in the Academy knew him—Rule-Book Charley—By-The-Numbers Chase—his nicknames were legion and not one of them was friendly. "Lieutenant Thomas Marsden reporting for duty," I said.

He looked at the O.D. "That'll be all, Mr. Halloran," he said.

"Aye, sir," Halloran said woodenly. He stepped backward, saluted, executed a precise about face and closed the hatch softly behind him.

"Sit down, Marsden," Chase said. "Have a cigarette."

He didn't say, "Glad to have you aboard." But other than that he was Navy right down to the last parenthesis. His voice was the same dry schoolmaster's voice I remembered from the Academy. And his face was the same dry gray with the same fishy blue eyes and rat trap jaw. His hair was thinner, but other than that he hadn't changed. Neither the war nor the responsibilities of command appeared to have left their mark upon him. He was still the same lean, undersized square-shouldered blob of nastiness.

I took the cigarette, sat down, puffed it into a glow, and looked around the drab 6 × 8 foot cubicle called the Captain's cabin by ship designers who must have laughed as they laid out the plans. It had about the room of a good-sized coffin. A copy of the Navy Code was lying on the desk. Chase had obviously been reading his bible.

"You are three minutes late, Marsden," Chase said. "Your orders direct you to report at 0900. Do you have any explanation?"

"No, sir," I said.

"Don't let it happen again. On this ship we are prompt."

"Aye, sir," I muttered.

He smiled, a thin quirk of thin lips. "Now let me outline your duties, Marsden. You are posted to my ship as Executive Officer. An Executive Officer is the Captain's right hand."

"So I have heard," I said drily.

"Belay that, Mr. Marsden. I do not appreciate humor during duty hours."

You wouldn't, I thought.

"As I was saying, Marsden, Executive Officer, you will be responsible for—" He went on and on, covering the Code-chapter, book and verse on the duties of an Executive

Officer. It made no difference that I had been Exec under Andy Royce, the skipper of the *Clotho*, the ship with the biggest confirmed kill in the entire Fleet Scouting Force. I was still a new Exec, and the book said I must be briefed on my duties. So "briefed" I was—for a solid hour.

Feeling angry and tired, I finally managed to get away from Rule Book Charley and find my quarters which I shared with the Engineer. I knew him casually, a glum reservist named Allyn. I had wondered why he always seemed to have a chip on his shoulder. Now I knew.

He was lying in his shock-couch as I came in. "Welcome, sucker," he greeted me. "Glad to have you aboard."

"The feeling's not mutual," I snapped.

"What's the matter? Has the Lieutenant Commander been rolling you out on the red carpet?"

"You could call it that," I said. "I've just been told the duties of an Exec. Funny—no?"

He shook his head. "Not funny. I feel for you. He told me how to be an engineer six months ago." Allyn's thin face looked glummer than usual.

"Did I ever tell you about our skip—captain?" Allyn went on. "Or do I have to tell you? I see you're wearing an Academy ring."

"You can't tell me much I haven't already heard," I said coldly. I don't like wardroom gossips as a matter of policy. A few disgruntled men on a ship can shoot morale to hell, and on a ship this size the exec is the morale officer. But I was torn between the two desires. I wanted Allyn to go on, but I didn't want to hear what Allyn had to say. I was like the proverbial hungry mule standing halfway between two haystacks of equal size and attractiveness. And like the mule I would stand there turning my head one way and the other until I starved to death.

But Allyn solved my problem for me. "You haven't heard *this*," he said bitterly. "The whole crew applied for transfer when we came back to base after our last cruise. Of course, they didn't get it, but you get the idea. Us reservists and draftees get about the same consideration as the Admiral's dog—No! dammit!—Less than the dog. They wouldn't let a mangy cur ship out with Gutless Gus."

Gutless Gus! That was a new one. I wondered how Chase had managed to acquire that sobriquet.

"It was on our last patrol," Allyn went on, answering my question before I asked it. "We were out at maximum radius when the detectors showed a disturbance in normal space. Chase ordered us down from Cth for a quick look—and so help me, God, we broke out right in the middle of a Rebel supply convoy—big, fat, sitting ducks all around us. We got off about twenty mark VII torpedoes before Chase passed the word to change over. We scooted back into Cth so fast we hardly knew we were gone. And then he raises hell with Detector section for not identifying every class of ship in that convoy!

"And when Bancroft, that's the exec whom you've relieved, asked for a quick check to confirm our kills, Chase sat on him like a ton of brick. 'I'm not interested in how many poor devils we blew apart back there,' our Captain says. 'Our mission is to scout, to obtain information about enemy movements and get that information back to Base. We cannot transmit information from a vaporized ship, and that convoy had a naval escort. Our mission cannot be jeopardized merely to satisfy morbid curiosity. Request denied. And, Mr. Bancroft, have Communications contact Fleet. This information should be in as soon as possible.' And then he turned away leaving Bancroft biting his fingernails. He wouldn't even push out a probe—scooted right back into the blue where we'd be safe!

"You know, we haven't had one confirmed kill posted on the list since we've been in space. It's getting so we don't want to come in any more. Like the time—the *Atropos* came in just after we touched down. She was battered—looked like she'd been through a meatgrinder, but she had ten confirmed and six probable, and four of them were escorts! Hell! Our boys couldn't hold their heads up. The *Lachesis* didn't have a mark on her and all we had was a few possible hits. You know how it goes—someone asks where you're from. You say the *Lachesis* and they say 'Oh, yes, the cruise ship.' And that's that. It's so true you don't even feel like resenting it."

I didn't like the bitter note in Allyn's voice. He was a reservist, which made it all the worse. Reservists have ten times the outside contacts we regulars do. In general when a regular and reservist tangle, the Academy men close ranks like musk-oxen and meet the challenge with an unbroken ring of horns. But somehow I didn't feel like ringing up.

I kept hoping there was another side to the story. I'd check around and find out as soon as I got settled. And if there was another side, I was going to take Allyn apart as a malicious trouble-maker. I felt sick to my stomach.

We spent the next three days taking on stores and munitions, and I was too busy supervising the stowage and checking manifests to bother about running down Allyn's story. I met the other officers—Lt. Pollard the gunnery officer, Ensign Esterhazy the astrogator, and Ensign Blakiston. Nice enough guys, but all wearing that cowed, frustrated look that seemed to be a *Lachesis* trademark. Chase, meanwhile, was up in Flag Officer's Country picking up the dope on our next mission. I hoped that Allyn was wrong but the evidence all seemed to be in his favor. Even more than the officers, the crew was a mess underneath their clean uniforms. From Communications Chief CPO Haskins to Spaceman Zelinski there was about as much spirit in them as you'd find in a punishment detail polishing brightwork in Base Headquarters. I'm a cheerful soul, and usually I find no trouble getting along with a new command, but this one was different. They were efficient enough, but one could see that their hearts weren't in their work. Most crews preparing to go out are nervous and high tempered. There was none of that here. The men went through the motions with a mechanical indifference that was frightening. I had the feeling that they didn't give a damn whether they went or not—or came back or not. The indifference was so thick you could cut it with a knife. Yet there was nothing you could put your hand on. You can't touch people who don't care.

Four hours after Chase came back, we lifted gravs from Earth. Chase was sitting in the control chair, and to give him credit, we lifted as smooth as a silk scarf slipping through the fingers of a pretty woman. We hypered at eight miles and swept up through the monochromes of Cth until we hit middle blue, when Chase slipped off the helmet, unfastened his webbing, and stood up.

"Take over, Mr. Marsden," he said. "Lay a course for Parth."

"Aye, sir," I replied, slipping into the chair and fastening the web. I slipped the helmet on my head and instantly I was a part of the ship. It's a strange feeling, this synthesis of man and metal that makes a fighting ship the metallic extension of the Commander's will. I was conscious of every man on duty. What they saw I saw, what they heard I heard, through the magic of modern electronics. The only thing missing was that I couldn't feel what they felt, which perhaps was a mercy considering the condition of the crew. Using the sensor circuits in the command helmet, I let my perception roam through the ship, checking the engines, the gun crews, the navigation board, the galley—all the manifold stations of a fighting ship. Everything was secure, the ship was clean and trimmed, the generators were producing their megawatts of power without a hitch, and the converters were humming contentedly, keeping us in the blue as our speed built to fantastic levels.

I checked the course, noted it was true, set the controls on standby and relaxed, half dozing in the chair as Lume after Lume dropped astern with monotonous regularity.

An hour passed and Halloran came up to relieve me. With a sigh of relief I surrendered the chair and headset. The unconscious strain of being in rapport with ship and crew didn't hit me until I was out of the chair. But when it did, I felt like something was crushing me flat. Not that I didn't expect it, but the *Lachesis* was worse than the *Clotho* had ever been.

I had barely hit my couch when General Quarters

sounded. I smothered a curse as I pounded up the companionway to my station at the bridge. Chase was there, stopwatch in hand, counting the seconds.

"Set!" Halloran barked.

"Fourteen seconds," Chase said. "Not bad. Tell the crew well done." He put the watch in his pocket and walked away.

I picked up the annunciator mike and pushed the button. "Skipper says well done," I said.

"He got ten seconds out of us once last trip," Halloran said. "And he's been trying to repeat that fluke ever since. Bet you a munit to an "F" ration that he'll be down with the section chief trying to shave off another second or two. Hey!—what's that—oh . . ." He looked at me. "Disturbance in Cth yellow, straight down—shall we go?"

"Stop ship," I ordered. "Sound general quarters." There was no deceleration. We merely swapped ends as the alarm sounded, applied full power and stopped. That was the advantage of Cth—no inertia. We backtracked for three seconds and held in middle blue.

"What's going on?" Chase demanded as he came up from below. His eyes raked the instruments. "Why are we stopped?"

"Disturbance in Cth yellow, sir," I said. "We're positioned above it."

"Very good, Mr. Marsden." He took the spare helmet from the Exec's chair, clapped it on, fiddled with the controls for a moment, nodded, and took the helmet off. "Secure and resume course," he said. "That's the *Amphitrite*—fleet supply and maintenance. One of our people."

"You sure, sir?" I asked, and then looked at the smug grin on Halloran's face and wished I hadn't asked.

"Of course," Chase said. "She's a three converter job running at full output. Since the Rebels have no three converter ships, she had to be one of ours. And since she's running at full output and only in Cth yellow, it means she's big, heavy, and awkward—which means a maintenance or an ammunition supply ship. There's an off phase beat in her number two converter that gives a twenty cycle pulse to her pattern. And the only heavy ship in the fleet with this pattern is *Amphitrite*. You see?"

I saw—with respect. "You know all the heavies like that, sir?" I asked.

"Not all of them—but I'd like to. It's as much a part of a scoutship commander's work to know our own ships as those of the enemy."

"Could that trace be a Rebel ruse?"

"Not likely—travelling in the yellow. A ship would be cold meat this far inside our perimeter. And besides, there's no Rebel alive who can tune a converter like a Navy mechanic."

"You sure?" I persisted.

"I'm sure. But take her down if you wish."

I did. And it was the *Amphitrite*.

"I served on her for six months," Chase said drily as we went back through the components. I understood his certainty now. A man has a feeling for ships if he's a good officer. But it was a trait I'd never expected in Chase. I gave the orders and we resumed our band and speed. Chase looked at me.

"You acted correctly, Mr. Marsden," he said. "Something I would hardly expect, but something I was glad to see."

"I served under Andy Royce," I reminded him.

"I know," Chase replied. "That's why I'm surprised." He turned away before I could think of an answer that would combine insolence and respect for his rank. "Keep her on course, Mr. Halloran," he tossed over his shoulder as he went out.

We kept on course—high and hard despite a couple of disturbances that lumbered by underneath us. Once I made a motion to stop ship and check, but Halloran shook his head.

"Don't do it, sir," he warned.

"Why not?"

"You heard the Captain's orders. He's a heller for having them obeyed. Besides, they might be Rebs—and we might get hurt shooting at them. We'll just report their position and approximate course—and keep on travelling. Haskins is on the Dirac right now." Halloran's voice was sarcastic.

I didn't like the sound of it, and said so.

"Well, sir—we won't lose them entirely," Halloran said comfortably. "Some cruiser will investigate them. Chances are they're ours anyway—and if they aren't there's no sense in us risking our nice shiny skin stopping them—even though we could take them like Lundy took Koromaja. Since the book doesn't say we have to investigate, we won't." His voice was bitter again.

At 0840 hours on the fourth day out, my annunciator buzzed. "Sir," the talker's voice came over the intercom, "Lieutenants Marsden and Allyn are wanted in the Captain's quarters."

Chase was there—toying with the seals of a thin, brown envelope. "I have to open this in the presence of at least two officers," he said nodding at Allyn who came in behind me. "You two are senior on the ship and have the first right to know." He slid a finger through the flap.

"Effective 12, Eightmonth, GY2964," he read, "USN *Lachesis* will proceed on offensive mission against enemy vessels as part of advance covering screen Fleet Four for major effort against enemy via sectors YD 274, YD 275, and YD 276. Entire scouting Force IV quadrant will be grouped as Fleet Four Screen Unit under command Rear Admiral SIMMS. Initial station *Lachesis* coordinates X 06042 Y 1327 Betelgeuse-Rigel baseline. ETA Rendezvous point 0830 plus or minus 30, 13/8/64.

A. Evars, Fleet Admiral USN
Commanding"

There it was! I could see Allyn stiffen as a peculiar sick look crossed Chase's dry face. And suddenly I heard all the ugly little nicknames—Subspace Chase, Gutless Gus, Cautious Charley—and the dozen others. For Chase was afraid. It was so obvious that not even the gray mask of his face could cover it.

Yet his voice when he spoke was the same dry, pedantic

voice of old. "You have the rendezvous point, Mr. Marsden. Have Mr. Esterhazy set the course and speed to arrive on time." He dismissed us with the traditional "That's all, gentlemen," and we went out separate ways. I didn't want to look at the triumphant smile on Allyn's face.

We hit rendezvous at 0850, picked up a message from the Admiral at 0853, and at 0855 were on our way. We were part of a broad hemispherical screen surrounding the Cruiser Force which englobed the Line and supply train —the heavies that are the backbone of any fleet. We were headed roughly in the direction of the Rebel's fourth sector, the one topheavy with metals industries. Our exact course was known only to the brass and the computers that planned our interlock. But where we were headed wasn't important. The *Lachesis* was finally going to war! I could feel the change in the crew, the nervousness, the anticipation, the adrenal responses of fear and excitement. After a year in the doldrums, Fleet was going to try to smash the Rebels again. We hadn't done so well last time, getting ambushed in the Fifty Suns group and damn near losing our shirts before we managed to get out. The Rebs weren't as good as we were, but they were trickier, and they could fight. After all, why shouldn't they be able to. They were human, just as we were, and any one of a dozen extinct intelligent races could testify to our fighting ability, as could others not-quite-extinct. Man ruled this section of the galaxy, and someday if he didn't kill himself off in the process he'd rule all of it. He wasn't the smartest race but he was the hungriest, the fiercest, the most adaptable, and the most unrelenting. Qualities which, by the way, were exactly the ones needed to conquer a hostile universe.

But mankind was slow to learn the greatest lesson, that they *had* to cooperate if they were to go further. We were already living on borrowed time. Before the War, ten of eleven exploration ships sent into the galactic center had disappeared without a trace. Somewhere, buried deep in the billions of stars that formed the galactic hub, was a race that was as tough and tricky as we were—maybe even tougher.

This was common knowledge, for the eleventh ship had returned with the news of the aliens, a story of hairbreadth escape from destruction, and a pattern of their culture which was enough like ours to frighten any thinking man. The worlds near the center of humanity's sphere realized the situation at once and quickly traded their independence for a Federal Union to pool their strength against the threat that might come any day.

But as the Union Space Navy began to take shape on the dockyards of Earth and a hundred other worlds, the independent worlds of the periphery began to eye the Union with suspicion. They had never believed the exploration report and didn't want to unite with the worlds of the center. They thought that the Union was a trick to deprive them of their fiercely cherished independence, and when the Union sent embassies to invite them into the common effort, they rejected them. And when we suggested that in the interests of racial safety they abandon their haphazard colonization efforts that resulted in an uncontrolled series of jumps into the dark, punctuated by minor wars and clashes when colonists from separate origins landed, more or less simultaneously, on a promising planet, they were certain we were up to no good.

Although we explained and showed them copies of the exploration ship's report, they were not convinced. Demagogues among them screamed about manifest destiny, independence, interference in internal affairs, and a thousand other things that made the diplomatic climate between Center and Periphery unbearably hot. And their colonists kept moving outward.

Of course the Union was not about to cooperate in this potential race suicide. We simply couldn't allow them to give that other race knowledge of our whereabouts until we were ready for them. So we informed each of the outer worlds that we would consider any further efforts at colonizing an unfriendly act, and would take steps to discourage it.

That did it.

• • •

We halted a few colonizing ships and sent them home under guard. We uprooted a few advance groups and returned them to their homeworlds. We established a series of observation posts to check further expansion—and six months later we were at war.

The outer worlds formed what they called a defensive league and with characteristic human rationality promptly attacked us. Naturally, they didn't get far. We had a bigger and better fleet and we were organized while they were not. And so they were utterly defeated at the Battle of Ophiuchus.

It was then that we had two choices. We could either move in and take over their defenseless worlds, or we could let them rebuild and get strong, and with their strength acquire a knowledge of cooperation—and take the chance that they would ultimately beat us. Knowing this, we wisely chose the second course and set about teaching our fellow men a lesson that was now fifteen years along and not ended yet.

By applying pressure at the right places we turned their attention inward to us rather than to the outside, and by making carefully timed sorties here and there about the periphery we forced them through sheer military necessity to gradually tighten their loosely organized League into tightly centralized authority, with the power to demand and obtain—to meet our force with counterforce. By desperate measures and straining of all their youthful resources they managed to hold us off. And with every strain they were welded more tightly together. And slowly they were learning through war what we could not teach through peace.

Curiously enough, they wouldn't believe our aims even when captured crews told them. They thought it was some sort of tricky mental conditioning designed to frustrate their lie detectors. Even while they tightened their organization and built new fleets, they would not believe that we were forcing them into the paths they must travel to avoid future annihilation.

It was one of the ironies of this war that it was fought and would be fought with the best of intentions. For it was obvious now that we could never win—nor could they. The Rebels, as we called them, were every whit as strong as we, and while we enjoyed the advantages of superior position and technology, they had the advantage of superior numbers. It was stalemate—the longest, fiercest stalemate in man's bloody history. But it was stalemate with a purpose. It was a crazy war—a period of constant hostilities mingled with sporadic offensive actions like the one we were now engaged in—but to us, at least, it was war with a purpose— the best and noblest of human purposes—the preservation of the race.

The day was coming, not too many years away, when the first of the aliens would strike the Outer worlds. Then we would unite—on the League's terms if need be—to crush the invaders and establish mankind as the supreme race in the galaxy.

But this wasn't important right now. Right now I was the executive officer of a scout ship commanded by a man I didn't trust. He smelled too much like a stinking coward. I shook my head. Having Chase running the ship was like putting a moron in a jet car on one of the super-highways— and then sabotaging the automatics. Just one fearful mistake and a whole squadron could be loused up. But Chase was the commander—the ultimate authority on this ship. All I could do was pray that things were going to come out all right.

We moved out in the lower red. Battles weren't fought in Cth. There was no way to locate a unit at firing range in that monochromatic madness. Normal physical laws simply didn't apply. A ship had to come out into threespace to do any damage. All Cth was was a convenient road to the battlefront.

With one exception.

By hanging in the infra band, on the ragged edge of threespace, a scout ship could remain concealed until a critical moment, breakout into threespace—discharge her weapons—and flick back into Cth before an enemy could get a fix on her. Scouts, with their high capacity converters, could perform this maneuver, but the ponderous battlewagons and cruisers with their tremendous weight of armor, screens, and munitions couldn't maneuver like this. They simply didn't have the agility. Yet only they had the ability to penetrate defensive screens and kill the Rebel heavies. So space battle was conducted on the classic pattern—the Lines slugging it out at medium range while the screen of scouts buzzed around and through the battle trying to add their weight of metal against some overstrained enemy and ensure his destruction. A major battle could go on for days—and it often did. In the Fifty Suns action the battle had lasted nearly two weeks subjective before we withdrew to lick our wounds.

For nearly a day we ran into nothing, and such are the distances that separate units of a fleet, we had the impression that we were alone. We moved quietly, detectors out, scanning the area for a light-day around as we moved forward at less than one Lume through Cth. More would have been fatal for had we been forced to resort to a quick breakout to avoid enemy action, and if were travelling above one Lume when we hit threespace, we'd simply disappear, leaving a small spatial vortex in our wake.

On the "morning" of the third day the ships at the apex of Quadrant One ran into a flight of Rebel scouts. There was a brief flurry of action, the Rebels were englobed, a couple of cruisers drove in, latched onto the helplessly straining Rebel scouts and ragged them into threespace. The Rebs kept broadcasting right up to the end—after which they surrendered before the cruisers could annihilate them. Smart boys.

But the Rebels were warned. We couldn't catch all their scouts and the disturbance our Line was making in Cth would register on any detector within twenty parsecs. So they would be waiting to meet us. But that was to be expected. There is no such thing as surprise in a major action.

We went on until we began to run into major opposition. Half a dozen scouts were caught in englobements at half a dozen different places along the periphery as they came in contact with the Rebels' covering forces. And that was that. The advance halted waiting for the Line to come up, and a host of small actions took place as the forward screening forces collided. Chase was in the control chair, hanging in the blackness of the infra band on the edge of normal space. But we weren't flicking in and out of threespace like some of the others. We had a probe out and the main buffeting was taken by the duralloy tube with its tiny converter at its bulbous tip. With consummate pilotage Chase was holding us in infra. It was a queasy sensation, hanging halfway between normalcy and chaos, and I had to admire his skill. The infra band was black as ink and hot as the hinges of hell—and since the edges of threespace and Cth are not as knife sharp as they are further up in the Cth components, we bucked and shuddered on the border, but avoided the bone-crushing slams and gut-wrenching twists that less skillful skippers were giving their ships as they flicked back and forth between threespace and Cth. Our scouting line must have been a peculiar sight to a threespace observer with the thousand or so scouts flickering in and out of sight across a huge hemisphere of space.

And then we saw them. Our probe picked up the flicker of enemy scouts.

"Action imminent," Chase said drily. "Stand by."

I clapped the other control helmet over my head and dropped into the exec's chair. A quick check showed the crew at their stations, the torpedo hatches clear, the antiradiation shields up and the ship in fighting trim. I stole a quick glance at Chase. Sweat stood out on his gray forehead. His lips were drawn back into a thin line, showing his teeth. His face was tense, but whether with fear or excitement I didn't know.

"Stand by," he said, and then we hit threespace, just as the enormous cone of the Rebel Line flicked into sight. The enemy line had taken the field, and under the comparatively slow speeds of threespace was rushing forward to meet our Line which had emerged a few minutes ago. Our launchers flamed as we sent a salvo of torpedoes whistling toward the Rebel fleet marking perhaps the opening shots of the main battle. We twisted back into Cth as one of the scanner men doubled over with agony, heaving his guts out into a disposal cone. I felt sorry for him. The tension, the racking agony of our motion, and the fact that he was probably in his first major battle had all combined to take him for the count. He grinned greenly at me and turned back to his dials and instruments. Good man!

"Target—range one eight zero four. Azimuth two four oh, elevation one oh seven," the rangefinder reported. "Mass four." Mass four:—a cruiser.

"Stand by," Chase said. "All turrets prepare to fire." And he took us down. We slammed into threespace and our turrets flamed. To our left rear and above hung the mass of an enemy cruiser, her screens glowing on standby as she drove forward to her place in the line. We had caught her by surprise, a thousand to one shot, and our torpedoes were on their way before her detectors spotted us. We didn't stay to see what happened, but the probe showed an enormous fireball which blazed briefly in the blackness, shooting out globs of scintillating molten metal that cooled and disappeared as we watched.

"Scratch one cruiser," someone in fire control yelped.

The effect on morale was electric. In that instant all doubts of Chase's ability disappeared. All except mine. One lucky shot isn't a battle, and I guess Chase figured the same way because his hands were shaking as he jockeyed us along on the edge of Cth. He looked like he wanted to vomit.

"Take it easy, skipper," I said.

"Mind your own business, Marsden—and I'll mind mine," Chase snapped. "Stand by," he ordered, and we dove into threespace again—loosed another salvo at another Reb, and flicked out of sight. And that was the way it went for hour after hour until we pulled out, our last torpedo fired and the crew on the ragged edge of exhaustion. Somehow, by some miracle compounded of luck and good pilotage, we were unmarked. And Chase, despite his twitching face and shaking hands, was one hell of a combat skipper! I didn't wonder about him any more. He had the guts all right. But it was a different sort of courage from the icy contempt for danger that marked Andy Royce. Even so, I couldn't help thinking that I was glad to be riding with Chase. We drove to the rear, heading for the supply train, our ammunition expended, while behind us the battlewagons and cruisers were hammering each other to metal pulp.

In the quiet of the rear area it was hardly believable that a major battle was going on ahead of us. We raised the *Amphitrite,* identified ourselves, and put in a request for supply.

"Lay aboard," *Amphitrite* signaled back. "How's the war going?"

"Don't know. We've been too busy," our signalman replied.

"I'll bet—you're *Lachesis* aren't you?"

"Affirmative."

"How'd you lose your ammo? Jettison it?"

"Stow that, you unprintable obscenity," Haskins replied. "We're a fighting ship."

Amphitrite chuckled nastily. "That I'll believe when I see it!"

"Communications," Chase snapped. "This isn't a social call. Get our heading and approach instructions." He sounded as schoolmasterish as ever, but there was a sickly smile on his face, and the gray-green look was gone.

"Morale seems a little better, doesn't it, Marsden?" he said to me as the *Amphitrite* flicked out into threespace and we followed.

I nodded. "Yes, sir," I agreed. "Quite a little."

Our cargo hatches snapped open and we cuddled up against *Amphitrite*'s bulging belly while our crew and the supply echelon worked like demons to transfer ammunition. We had fifty torpedoes aboard when the IFF detector shrilled alarm.

Three hundred feet above us the *Amphitrite*'s main battery let loose a salvo at three Rebel scouts that had flickered into being less than fifty miles away. Their launchers flared with a glow that lighted the blackness of space.

"Stand by!" Chase yelled as he threw the convertor on.

"Hatches!" I screamed as we shimmered and vanished.

Somehow we got most of them closed, losing only the crew on number two port turret which was still buttoning up as we slipped over into the infra band. I ordered the turret sealed. Cth had already ruined the unshielded sighting mechanisms and I had already seen what happened to men caught in Cth unprotected. I had no desire to see it again—or let our crew see it if it could be avoided. A human body turned inside out isn't the most wholesome of sights.

"How did *they* get through?" Chase muttered as we put out our probe.

"I don't know—maybe someone wasn't looking."

"What's it like down there?" Chase asked. "See anything?"

"*Amphitrite*'s still there," I said.

"She's *what?*"

"Still there," I repeated. "And she's in trouble."

"She's big. She can take it—but—"

"Here, you look," I said, flipping the probe switch.

"My God!" Chase muttered—as he took one look at the supply ship lying dead in space, her protective batteries flaming. She had gotten one of the Rebel scouts but the other two had her bracketed and were pouring fire against her dim screens.

"She can't keep this up," I said. "She's been hulled—and it looks like her power's taken it."

"Action imminent," Chase ordered, and the rangefinder took up his chant.

We came storming out of Cth right on top of one of the Rebel scouts. A violent shock raced through the ship, slamming me against my web. The rebound sent us a good two miles away before our starboard battery flamed. The enemy scout, disabled by the shock, stunned and unable to maneuver took the entire salvo amidships and disappeared in a puff of flame.

The second Rebel disappeared and we did too. She was back in Cth looking for a better chance at the *Amphitrite*. The big ship was wallowing like a wounded whale, half of one section torn away, her armor dented, and her tubes firing erratically.

We took one long look and jumped back into Cth. But not before Haskins beamed a message to the supply ship. "Now you've seen it, you damned storekeeper," he gloated. "What do you think?" *Amphitrite* didn't answer.

"Probe out," Chase ordered, neglecting, I noticed, to comment on the signalman's act.

I pushed the proper buttons but nothing happened. I pushed again and then turned on the scanners. The one aft of the probe was half covered with a twisted mass of metal tubing that had once been our probe. We must have smashed it when we rammed. Quickly I shifted to the auxiliary probe, but the crumpled mass had jammed the hatch. It wouldn't open.

"No probes, sir," I announced.

"Damn," Chase said. "Well, we'll have to do without them. Hold tight, we're going down."

We flicked into threespace just in time to see a volcano of fire erupt from *Amphitrite*'s side and the metallic flick of the Rebel scout slipping back into Cth.

"What's your situation, *Amphitrite*?" our signal asked.

"Not good," the faint answer came back. "They've got us in the power room and our accumulators aren't going to stand this load very long. That last salvo went through our screens, but our armor stopped it. But if the screens go down—"

Our batteries flared at the Rebel as he again came into sight. He didn't wait, but flicked right back into Cth without firing a shot. Pollard was on the ball.

"Brave lad, that Reb," Chase said. There was a sneer in his voice.

For the moment it was stalemate. The Reb wasn't going to come into close range with a warship of equal power to his own adding her metal to the *Amphitrite*'s, but he could play cat and mouse with us, drawing our fire until we had used up our torpedoes, and then come in to finish the supply ship. Or he could harass us with long range fire. Or he could go away.

It was certain he wouldn't do the last, and he'd be a fool if he did the second. *Amphitrite* could set up a mine screen that would take care of any long range stuff,—and we could dodge it. His probe was still working and he had undoubtedly seen ours crushed against our hull. If he hadn't he was blind—and that wasn't a Rebel characteristic. We could hyper, of course, but we were blind up there in Cth. His best bet was to keep needling us, and take the chance that we'd run out of torps.

"What's our munition?" Chase asked almost as an echo to my thought. I switched over to Pollard.

"Thirty mark sevens," Pollard said, "and a little small arms."

"One good salvo," Chase said, thoughtfully.

The Rebel flashed in and out again, and we let go a burst.

"Twenty, now," I said.

Chase didn't hear me. He was busy talking to Allyn on damage control. "You can't cut it, hey?—All right—disengage the convertor on the auxiliary probe and break out that roll of duralloy cable in the stores—Pollard! Don't fire over one torp at a time when that lad shows up. Load the other launchers with blanks. Make him think we're shooting. We have to keep him hopping. Now listen to me—Yes, Allyn, I mean you. Fasten that converter onto the cable and stand by. We're going to make a probe." Chase turned to me.

"You were exec with Royce," he said. "You should know how to fight a ship."

"What are you planning to do?" I asked.

"We can't hold that Rebel off. Maybe with ammunition we could, but there's less than a salvo aboard and he has the advantage of position. We can't be sure he won't try to take us in spite of *Amphitrite*'s support and if he does finish us, *Amphitrite*'s a dead duck." The *Lachesis* quivered as the port turrets belched flame. "That leaves nineteen torpedoes," he said. "In Cth we're safe enough but we're helpless without a probe. Yet we can only get into attack position from Cth. That leaves us only one thing to do—improvise a probe."

"And how do you do that?" I asked.

"Put a man out on a line—with the converter from the auxiliary. Give him a command helmet and have him talk the ship in."

"But that's suicide!"

"No, Marsden, not suicide—just something necessary. A necessary sacrifice, like this whole damned war! I don't believe in killing men. It makes me sick. But I kill if I have to, and sacrifice if I must." His face twisted and the gray green look came back. "There are over a thousand men on the *Amphitrite*, and a vital cargo of munitions. One life, I think, is fair trade for a thousand, just as a few hundred thousand is fair trade for a race." The words were school-masterish and would have been dead wrong coming from anyone except Chase. But he gave them an air of reasonable inevitability. And for a moment I forgot that he was coldbloodedly planning someone's death. For a moment I felt the spirit of sacrifice that made heroes out of ordinary people.

"Look, skipper," I said. "How about letting me do it?" I could have kicked myself a moment later, but the words were out before I could stop them. He had me acting noble, and that trait isn't one of my strong suits.

He smiled. "You know, Marsden," he said, "I was expecting that." His voice was oddly soft. "Thanks." Then it became dry and impersonal. "Request denied," he said, "This is my party."

I shivered inside. While I'm no coward, I didn't relish the thought of slamming around at the end of a duralloy cable stretching into a nowhere where there was no inertia. A hair too heavy a hand on the throttle in Cth would crush the man on the end to a pulp. But he shouldn't go either. It was his responsibility to command the ship.

"Who else is qualified?" Chase said answering the look

on my face. "I know more about maneuver than any man aboard, and I'll be controlling the ship until the last moment. Once I order the attack I'll cut free, and you can pick me up later."

"You won't have time," I protested.

"Just in case I don't make it," Chase continued, making the understatement of the war with a perfectly straight face, "Take care of the crew. They're a good bunch—just a bit too eager for the *real* Navy—but good. I've tried to make them into spacemen and they've resented me for it. I've tried to protect them and they've hated me—"

"They won't now—" I interrupted.

"I've tried to make them a unit." He went on as though I hadn't said a thing. "Maybe I've tried too hard, but I'm responsible for every life aboard this ship." He picked up his helmet. "Take command of the ship, Mr. Marsden," he said, and strode out of the room. The *Lachesis* shuddered to the recoil from the port turrets. Eighteen torpedoes left, I thought.

We lowered Chase a full hundred feet on the thin strand of duralloy. He dangled under the ship, using his converter to keep the line taut.

"You hear me, skipper?" I asked.

"Clearly—and you?"

"Four-four. Hang on now—we're going up." I eased the *Lachesis* into Cth and hung like glue to the border. "How's it going, skipper?"

"A bit rough but otherwise all right. Now steer right—easy now—aagh!"

"Skipper!"

"Okay, Marsden. You nearly pulled me in half—that's all. You did fine. We're in good position in relation to 'Amphitrite.' Now let's get our signals straight. Front is the way we're going now—base all my directions on that—got it?"

"Aye, sir."

"Good, Marsden, throttle back and hang on your converters."

I did as I was told.

"Ah—there she is—bear left a little. Hmm—she's looking for us—looks suspicious. Now she's turning toward *Amphitrite*. Guess she figures we are gone. She's in position preparing to fire. *Now!* Drop out and fire—elevation zero, aximuth three sixty—*Move!*"

I moved. The *Lachesis* dropped like a stone. Chase was dead now. Nothing made of flesh could survive the punishment but we—we came out right on top of them, just like Chase had done to the other—except that we fired before we collided. And as with the other Rebel we gained complete surprise. Our eighteen torpedoes crashed home, her magazines exploded, and into that hell of molten and vaporized metal that had once been a Rebel scout we crashed a split second later. Two thousand miles per second relative is too fast for even an explosion to hurt much if there isn't any solid material in the way, and we passed through only the outer edges of the blast, but even so, the vaporized metal scoured our starboard plating down to the insulation. It was like a giant emery wheel had passed across our flank. The shock slammed us out of control and we went tumbling in crazy gyrations across space for several minutes before I could flip the *Lachesis* into Cth, check the speed and motion, and get back into threespace.

Chase was gone—and *Lachesis* was done. A week in drydock and she'd be as good as new, but she was no longer a fighting ship. She was a wreck. For us the battle was over—but somehow it didn't make me happy. The *Amphitrite* hung off our port bow, a tiny silver dot in the distance, and as I watched two more silver dots winked into being beside her. Haskins reported the I.F.F. readings.

"They're ours," he said. "A couple of cruisers."

"They should have been here ten minutes ago," I replied bitterly. I couldn't see very well. You can't when emotion clogs your tubes. Chase—coward?—not him. He was man clear through—a better one than I'd ever be even if I lived out my two hundred years. I wondered if the crew knew what sort of man their skipper was. I turned up the command helmet. "Men—" I began, but I didn't finish.

"We know," the blended thoughts and voices came back at me. Sure they knew! Chase had been on command circuit too. It was enough to make you cry—the mixture of pride, sadness and shame that rang through the helmet. It seemed to echo and reecho for a long time before I shut it off.

I sat there, thinking. I wasn't mad at the Rebels. I wasn't anything. All I could think was that we were paying a pretty grim price for survival. Those aliens had better show up pretty soon—and they'd better be as nasty as their reputation. There was a score—a big score—and I wanted to be there when it was added up and settled.

SUPERIORITY

Arthur C. Clarke

In making this statement—which I do of my own free will—I wish first to make it perfectly clear that I am not in any way trying to gain sympathy, nor do I expect any mitigation of whatever sentence the Court may pronounce. I am writing this in an attempt to refute some of the lying reports broadcast over the prison radio and published in the papers I have been allowed to see. These have given an entirely false picture of the true cause of our defeat, and as the leader of my race's armed forces at the cessation of hostilities I feel it my duty to protest against such libels upon those who served under me.

I also hope that this statement may explain the reasons for the application I have twice made to the Court, and will now induce it to grant a favor for which I can see no possible grounds of refusal.

The ultimate cause of our failure was a simple one: despite all statements to the contrary, it was not due to lack of bravery on the part of our men, or to any fault of the Fleet's. We were defeated by one thing only—by the inferior science of our enemies. I repeat—by the *inferior* science of our enemies.

When the war opened we had no doubt of our ultimate victory. The combined fleets of our allies greatly exceeded in number and armament those which the enemy could muster against us, and in almost all branches of military science we were their superiors. We were sure that we could maintain this superiority. Our belief proved, alas, to be only too well founded.

At the opening of the war our main weapons were the long-range homing torpedo, dirigible ball-lightning and the various modifications of the Klydon beam. Every unit of the Fleet was equipped with these and though the enemy possessed similar weapons their installations were generally of lesser power. Moreover, we had behind us a far greater military Research Organization, and with this initial advantage we could not possibly lose.

The campaign proceeded according to plan until the Battle of the Five Suns. We won this, of course, but the opposition proved stronger than we had expected. It was realized that victory might be more difficult, and more delayed, than had first been imagined. A conference of supreme commanders was therefore called to discuss our future strategy.

Present for the first time at one of our war conferences was Professor-General Norden, the new Chief of the Research Staff, who had just been appointed to fill the gap left by the death of Malvar, our greatest scientist. Malvar's leadership had been responsible, more than any other single factor, for the efficiency and power of our weapons. His loss was a very serious blow, but no one doubted the brilliance of his successor—though many of us disputed the wisdom of appointing a theoretical scientist to fill a post of such vital importance. But we had been overruled.

I can well remember the impression Norden made at that conference. The military advisers were worried, and as usual turned to the scientists for help. Would it be possible to improve our existing weapons, they asked, so that our present advantage could be increased still further?

Norden's reply was quite unexpected. Malvar had often been asked such a question—and he had always done what we requested.

"Frankly, gentlemen," said Norden, "I doubt it. Our existing weapons have practically reached finality. I don't wish to criticize my predecessor, or the excellent work done by the Research Staff in the last few generations, but do you realize that there has been no basic change in armaments for over a century? It is, I am afraid, the result of a tradition that has become conservative. For too long, the Research Staff has devoted itself to perfecting old weapons instead of developing new ones. It is fortunate for us that our opponents have been no wiser: we cannot assume that this will always be so."

Norden's words left an uncomfortable impression, as he had no doubt intended. He quickly pressed home the attack.

"What we want are *new* weapons—weapons totally different from any that have been employed before. Such weapons can be made: it will take time, of course, but since assuming charge I have replaced some of the older scientists by young men and have directed research into several unexplored fields which show great promise. I believe, in fact, that a revolution in warfare may soon be upon us."

We were skeptical. There was a bombastic tone in Norden's voice that made us suspicious of his claims. We did not know, then, that he never promised anything that he had not already almost perfected in the laboratory. *In the laboratory*—that was the operative phrase.

Norden proved his case less than a month later, when he demonstrated the Sphere of Annihilation, which produced complete disintegration of matter over a radius of several hundred meters. We were intoxicated by the power of the new weapon, and were quite prepared to overlook one fundamental defect—the fact that it *was* a sphere and hence destroyed its rather complicated generating equipment at the instant of formation. This meant, of course, that it could not be used on warships but only on guided missiles, and a great program was started to convert all homing torpedoes to carry the new weapon. For the time being all further offensives were suspended.

We realize now that this was our first mistake. I still think that it was a natural one, for it seemed to us then that all our existing weapons had become obsolete overnight, and we already regarded them as almost primitive survivals. What we did not appreciate was the magnitude of the task we were attempting, and the length of time it would take to get the revolutionary super-weapon into battle. Nothing like this had happened for a hundred years and we had no previous experience to guide us.

The conversion problem proved far more difficult than anticipated. A new class of torpedo had to be designed, as the standard model was too small. This meant in turn that only the larger ships could launch the weapon, but we were prepared to accept this penalty. After six months, the heavy units of the Fleet were being equipped with the Sphere. Training maneuvers and tests had shown that it was operating satisfactorily and we were ready to take it into action. Norden was already being hailed as the architect of victory, and had half promised even more spectacular weapons.

Then two things happened. One of our battleships disappeared completely on a training flight, and an investigation showed that under certain conditions the ship's long-range radar could trigger the Sphere immediately after it had been launched. The modification needed to overcome this defect was trivial, but it caused a delay of another month and was the source of much bad feeling between the naval staff and the scientists. We were ready for action again—when Norden announced that the radius of effectiveness of the Sphere had now been increased by ten, thus multiplying by a thousand the chances of destroying an enemy ship.

So the modifications started all over again, but everyone agreed that the delay would be worth it. Meanwhile, however, the enemy had been emboldened by the absence of further attacks and had made an unexpected onslaught. Our ships were short of torpedoes, since none had been coming from the factories, and were forced to retire. So we lost the systems of Kyrane and Floranus, and the planetary fortress of Rhamsandron.

It was an annoying but not a serious blow, for the recaptured systems had been unfriendly, and difficult to administer. We had no doubt that we could restore the position in the near future, as soon as the new weapon became operational.

These hopes were only partially fulfilled. When we renewed our offensive, we had to do so with fewer of the Spheres of Annihilation than had been planned, and this was one reason for our limited success. The other reason was more serious.

While we had been equipping as many of our ships as we could with the irresistible weapon, the enemy had been building feverishly. His ships were of the old pattern with the old weapons—but they now outnumbered ours. When we went into action, we found that the numbers ranged against us were often 100 per cent greater than expected, causing target confusion among the automatic weapons and resulting in higher losses than anticipated. The enemy losses were higher still, for once a Sphere had reached its objective, destruction was certain, but the balance had not swung as far in our favor as we had hoped.

Moreover, while the main fleets had been engaged, the enemy had launched a daring attack on the lightly held systems of Eriston, Duranus, Carmanidora and Pharanidon—recapturing them all. We were thus faced with a threat only fifty light-years from our home planets.

There was much recrimination at the next meeting of the supreme commanders. Most of the complaints were addressed to Norden—Grand Admiral Taxaris in particular maintaining that thanks to our admittedly irresistible weapon we were now considerably worse off than before. We should, he claimed, have continued to build conventional ships, thus preventing the loss of our numerical superiority.

Norden was equally angry and called the naval staff ungrateful bunglers. But I could tell that he was worried— as indeed we all were—by the unexpected turn of events.

He hinted that there might be a speedy way of remedying the situation.

We now know that Research had been working on the Battle Analyzer for many years, but at the time it came as a revelation to us and perhaps we were too easily swept off our feet. Norden's argument, also, was seductively convincing. What did it matter, he said, if the enemy had twice as many ships as we—if the efficiency of ours could be doubled or even trebled? For decades the limiting factor in warfare had been not mechanical but biological—it had become more and more difficult for any single mind, or group of minds, to cope with the rapidly changing complexities of battle in three-dimensional space. Norden's mathematicians had analyzed some of the classic engagements of the past, and had shown that even when we had been victorious we had often operated our units at much less than half of their theoretical efficiency.

The Battle Analyzer would change all this by replacing the operations staff with electronic calculators. The idea was not new, in theory, but until now it had been no more than a utopian dream. Many of us found it difficult to believe that it was still anything but a dream: after we had run through several very complex dummy battles, however, we were convinced.

It was decided to install the Analyzer in four of our heaviest ships, so that each of the main fleets could be equipped with one. At this stage, the trouble began— though we did not know it until later.

The Analyzer contained just short of a million vacuum tubes and needed a team of five hundred technicians to maintain and operate it. It was quite impossible to accommodate the extra staff aboard a battleship, so each of the four units had to be accompanied by a converted liner to carry the technicians not on duty. Installation was also a very slow and tedious business, but by gigantic efforts it was completed in six months.

Then, to our dismay, we were confronted by another crisis. Nearly five thousand highly skilled men had been selected to serve the Analyzers and had been given an intensive course at the Technical Training Schools. At the end of seven months, 10 per cent of them had had nervous breakdowns and only 40 per cent had qualified.

Once again, everyone started to blame everyone else. Norden, of course, said that the Research Staff could not be held responsible, and so incurred the enmity of the Personnel and Training Commands. It was finally decided that the only thing to do was to use two instead of four Analyzers and to bring the others into action as soon as men could be trained. There was little time to lose, for the enemy was still on the offensive and his morale was rising.

The first Analyzer fleet was ordered to recapture the system of Eriston. On the way, by one of the hazards of war, the liner carrying the technicians was struck by a roving mine. A warship would have survived, but the liner with its irreplaceable cargo was totally destroyed. So the operation had to be abandoned.

The other expedition was, at first, more successful. There was no doubt at all that the Analyzer fulfilled its designers' claims, and the enemy was heavily defeated in the first engagements. He withdrew, leaving us in possession of Saphran, Leucon and Hexanerax. But his Intelligence Staff must have noted the change in our tactics and the inexplicable presence of a liner in the heart of our battle-fleet. It must have noted, also, that our first fleet had been accompanied by a similar ship—and had withdrawn when it had been destroyed.

In the next engagement, the enemy used his superior numbers to launch an overwhelming attack on the Analyzer ship and its unarmed consort. The attack was made without regard to losses—both ships were, of course, very heavily protected—and it succeeded. The result was the virtual decapitation of the Fleet, since an effectual transfer to the old operational methods proved impossible. We disengaged under heavy fire, and so lost all our gains and also the systems of Lormyia, Ismarnus, Beronis, Alphanidon and Sideneus.

At this stage, Grand Admiral Taxaris expressed his

disapproval of Norden by committing suicide, and I assumed supreme command.

The situation was now both serious and infuriating. With stubborn conservatism and complete lack of imagination, the enemy continued to advance with his old-fashioned and inefficient but now vastly more numerous ships. It was galling to realize that if we had only continued building, without seeking new weapons, we would have been in a far more advantageous position. There were many acrimonious conferences at which Norden defended the scientists while everyone else blamed them for all that had happened. The difficulty was that Norden had proved every one of his claims: he had a perfect excuse for all the disasters that had occurred. And we could not now turn back—the search for an irresistible weapon must go on. At first it had been a luxury that would shorten the war. Now it was a necessity if we were to end it victoriously.

We were on the defensive, and so was Norden. He was more than ever determined to re-establish his prestige and that of the Research Staff. But we had been twice disappointed, and would not make the same mistake again. No doubt Norden's twenty thousand scientists would produce many further weapons: we would remain unimpressed.

We were wrong. The final weapon was something so fantastic that even now it seems difficult to believe that it ever existed. Its innocent, noncommittal name—The Exponential Field—gave no hint of its real potentialities. Some of Norden's mathematicians had discovered it during a piece of entirely theoretical research into the properties of space, and to everyone's great surprise their results were found to be physically realizable.

It seems very difficult to explain the operation of the Field to the layman. According to the technical description, it "produces an exponential condition of space, so that a finite distance in normal, linear space may become infinite in pseudo-space." Norden gave an analogy which some of us found useful. It was as if one took a flat disk of rubber—representing a region of normal space—and then pulled its center out to infinity. The circumference of the disk would be unaltered—but its "diameter" would be infinite. That was the sort of thing the generator of the Field did to the space around it.

As an example, suppose that a ship carrying the generator was surrounded by a ring of hostile machines. If it switched on the Field, *each* of the enemy ships would think that it—and the ships on the far side of the circle—had suddenly receded into nothingness. Yet the circumference of the circle would be the same as before: only the journey to the center would be of infinite duration, for as one proceeded, distances would appear to become greater and greater as the "scale" of space altered.

It was a nightmare condition, but a very useful one. Nothing could reach a ship carrying the Field: it might be englobed by an enemy fleet yet would be as inaccessible as if it were at the other side of the Universe. Against this, of course, it could not fight back without switching off the Field, but this still left it at a very great advantage, not only in defense but in offense. For a ship fitted with the Field could approach an enemy fleet undetected and suddenly appear in its midst.

This time there seemed to be no flaws in the new weapon. Needless to say, we looked for all the possible objections before we committed ourselves again. Fortunately the equipment was fairly simple and did not require a large operating staff. After much debate, we decided to rush it into production, for we realized that time was running short and the war was going against us. We had now lost about the whole of our initial gains and enemy forces had made several raids into our own solar system.

We managed to hold off the enemy while the Fleet was re-equipped and the new battle techniques were worked out. To use the Field operationally it was necessary to locate an enemy formation, set a course that would intercept it, and then switch on the generator for the calculated period of time. On releasing the Field again—if the calculations had been accurate—one would be in the enemy's midst and could do great damage during the resulting confusion, retreating by the same route when necessary.

The first trial maneuvers proved satisfactory and the equipment seemed quite reliable. Numerous mock attacks were made and the crews became accustomed to the new technique. I was on one of the test flights and can vividly remember my impressions as the Field was switched on. The ships around us seemed to dwindle as if on the surface of an expanding bubble: in an instant they had vanished completely. So had the stars—but presently we could see that the Galaxy was still visible as a faint band of light around the ship. The virtual radius of our pseudo-space was not really infinite, but some hundred thousand light-years, and so the distance to the farthest stars of our system had not been greatly increased—though the nearest had of course totally disappeared.

These training maneuvers, however, had to be cancelled before they were complete owing to a whole flock of minor technical troubles in various pieces of equipment, notably the communications circuits. These were annoying, but not important, though it was thought best to return to Base to clear them up.

At that moment the enemy made what was obviously intended to be a decisive attack against the fortress planet of Iton at the limits of our solar system. The Fleet had to go into battle before repairs could be made.

The enemy must have believed that we had mastered the secret of invisibility—as in a sense we had. Our ships appeared suddenly out of nowhere and inflicted tremendous damage—for a while. And then something quite baffling and inexplicable happened.

I was in command of the flagship *Hircania* when the trouble started. We had been operating as independent units, each against assigned objectives. Our detectors observed an enemy formation at medium range and the navigating officers measured its distance with great accuracy. We set course and switched on the generator.

The Exponential Field was released at the moment when we should have been passing through the center of the enemy group. To our consternation, we emerged into normal space at a distance of many hundred miles—and when we found the enemy, he had already found us. We retreated, and tried again. This time we were so far away from the enemy that he located us first.

Obviously, something was seriously wrong. We broke communicator silence and tried to contact the other ships of the Fleet to see if they had experienced the same trouble. Once again we failed—and this time the failure was beyond all reason, for the communication equipment appeared to be working perfectly. We could only assume, fantastic though it seemed, that the rest of the Fleet had been destroyed.

I do not wish to describe the scenes when the scattered units of the Fleet struggled back to Base. Our casualties had actually been negligible, but the ships were completely demoralized. Almost all had lost touch with one another and had found that their ranging equipment showed inexplicable errors. It was obvious that the Exponential Field was the cause of the troubles, despite the fact that they were only apparent when it was switched off.

The explanation came too late to do us any good, and Norden's final discomfiture was small consolation for the virtual loss of the war. As I have explained, the Field generators produced a radial distortion of space, distances appearing greater and greater as one approached the center of the artificial pseudo-space. When the Field was switched off, conditions returned to normal.

But not quite. It was never possible to restore the initial state *exactly*. Switching the Field on and off was equivalent to an elongation and contraction of the ship carrying the generator, but there was an hysteretic effect, as it were, and the initial condition was never quite reproducible, owing to all the thousands of electrical changes and movements of mass aboard the ship while the Field was on. These asymmetries and distortions were cumulative, and though they seldom amounted to more than a fraction of one per cent, that was quite enough. It meant that the precision ranging equipment and the tuned circuits in the communication apparatus were thrown completely out of adjustment. Any single ship could never detect the change—only when it compared its equipment with that of another vessel, or tried to communicate with it, could it tell what had happened.

It is impossible to describe the resultant chaos. Not a single component of one ship could be expected with certainty to work aboard another. The very nuts and bolts were no longer interchangeable, and the supply position became quite impossible. Given time, we might even have overcome these difficulties, but the enemy ships were already attacking in thousands with weapons which now seemed centuries behind those that we had invented. Our magnificent Fleet, crippled by our own science, fought on as best it could until it was overwhelmed and forced to surrender. The ships fitted with the Field were still invulnerable, but as fighting units they were almost helpless. Every time they switched on their generators to escape from enemy attack, the permanent distortion of their equipment increased. In a month, it was all over.

This is the true story of our defeat, which I give without prejudice to my defense before this Court. I make it, as I have said, to counteract the libels that have been circulating against the men who fought under me, and to show where the true blame for our misfortunes lay.

Finally, my request, which as the Court will now realize, I make in no frivolous manner and which I hope will therefore be granted.

The Court will be aware that the conditions under which we are housed and the constant surveillance to which we are subjected night and day are somewhat distressing. Yet I am not complaining of this: nor do I complain of the fact that shortage of accommodation has made it necessary to house us in pairs.

But I cannot be held responsible for my future actions if I am compelled any longer to share my cell with Professor Norden, late Chief of the Research Staff of my armed forces.

HINDSIGHT

Jack Williamson

Something was wrong with the cigar.

But Brek Veronar didn't throw it away. Earth-grown tobacco was precious, here on Ceres. He took another bite off the end, and pressed the lighter cone again. This time, imperfectly, the cigar drew—with an acrid, puzzling odor of scorching paper.

Brek Veronar—born William Webster, Earthman—was sitting in his big, well-furnished office, adjoining the arsenal laboratory. Beyond the perdurite windows, magnified in the crystalline clarity of the asteroid's synthetic atmosphere, loomed a row of the immense squat turret forts that guarded the Astrophon base—their mighty twenty-four-inch rifles, coupled to the Veronar autosight, covered with their theoretical range everything within Jupiter's orbit. A squadron of the fleet lay on the field beyond, seven tremendous dead-black cigar shapes. Far off, above the rugged red palisades of a second plateau, stood the many-colored domes and towers of Astrophon itself, the Astrarch's capital.

A tall, gaunt man, Brek Veronar wore the bright,

close-fitting silks of the Astrarchy. Dyed to conceal the increasing streaks of gray, his hair was perfumed and curled. In abrupt contrast to the force of his gray, wide-set eyes, his face was white and smooth from cosmetic treatments. Only the cigar could have betrayed him as a native of Earth, and Brek Veronar never smoked except here in his own locked laboratory.

He didn't like to be called the Renegade.

Curiously, that whiff of burning paper swept his mind away from the intricate drawing of a new rocket-torpedo gyropilot pinned to a board on the desk before him, and back across twenty years of time. It returned him to the university campus, on the low yellow hills beside the ancient Martian city of Toran—to the fateful day when Bill Webster had renounced allegiance to his native Earth, for the Astrarch.

Tony Grimm and Elora Ronee had both objected. Tony was the freckled, irresponsible redhead who had come out from Earth with him six years before, on the other of the two annual engineering scholarships. Elora Ronee was the lovely dark-eyed Martian girl—daughter of the professor of geodesics, and a proud descendant of the first colonists—whom they both loved.

He walked with them, that dry, bright afternoon, out from the yellow adobe buildings, across the rolling, stony, ocher-colored desert. Tony's sunburned, blue-eyed face was grave for once, as he protested.

"You can't do it, Bill. No Earthman could."

"No use talking," said Bill Webster, shortly. "The Astrarch wants a military engineer. His agents offered me twenty thousand eagles a year, with raises and bonuses—ten times what any research scientist could hope to get, back on Earth."

The tanned, vivid face of Elora Ronee looked hurt. "Bill—what about your own research?" the slender girl cried. "Your new reaction tube! You promised you were going to break the Astrarch's monopoly on space transport. Have you forgotten?"

"The tube was just a dream," Bill Webster told her, "but

probably it's the reason he offered the contract to me, and not Tony. Such jobs don't go begging."

Tony caught his arm. "You can't turn against your own world, Bill," he insisted. "You can't give up everything that means anything to an Earthman. Just remember what the Astrarch is—a superpirate."

Bill Webster's toe kicked up a puff of yellow dust. "I know history," he said. "I know that the Astrarchy had its beginnings from the space pirates who established their bases in the asteroids, and gradually turned to commerce instead of raiding."

His voice was injured and defiant. "But, so far as I'm concerned, the Astrarchy is just as respectable as such planet nations as Earth and Mars and the Jovian Federation. And it's a good deal more wealthy and powerful than any of them."

Tense-faced, the Martian girl shook her dark head. "Don't blind yourself, Bill," she begged urgently. "Can't you see that the Astrarch really is no different from any of the old pirates? His fleets still seize any independent vessel, or make the owners ransom it with his space-patrol tax."

She caught an indignant breath. "Everywhere—even here on Mars—the agents and residents and traders of the Astrarchy have brought graft and corruption and oppression. The Astrarch is using his wealth and his space power to undermine the government of every independent planet. He's planning to conquer the system!"

Her brown eyes flashed. "You won't aid him, Bill. You—couldn't!"

Bill Webster looked into the tanned, intent loveliness of her face—he wanted suddenly to kiss the smudge of yellow dust on her impudent little nose. He had loved Elora Ronee, had once hoped to take her back to Earth. Perhaps he still loved her. But now it was clear that she had always wanted Tony Grimm.

Half angrily, he kicked an iron-reddened pebble. "If things had been different, Elora, it might have been—" With an abrupt little shrug, he looked back at Tony.

"Anyhow," he said flatly, "I'm leaving for Astrophon tonight."

That evening, after they had helped him pack, he made a bonfire of his old books and papers. They burned palely in the thin air of Mars, with a cloud of acrid smoke.

That sharp odor was the line that had drawn Brek Veronar back across the years, when his nostrils stung to the scorched-paper scent. The cigar came from a box that had just arrived from Cuba, Earth—made to his special order.

He could afford such luxuries. Sometimes, in fact, he almost regretted the high place he had earned in the Astrarch's favor. The space officers, and even his own jealous subordinates in the arsenal laboratory, could never forget that he was an Earthman—the Renegade.

The cigar's odor puzzled him.

Deliberately, he crushed out the smoldering tip, peeled off the brown wrapper leaves. He found a tightly rolled paper cylinder. Slipping off the rubber bands, he opened it. A glimpse of the writing set his heart to thudding.

It was the hand of Elora Ronee!

Brek Veronar knew that fine graceful script. For once Bill Webster had treasured a little note that she had written him, when they were friends at school. He read it eagerly:

DEAR BILL: This is the only way we can hope to get word to you, past the Astrarch's spies. Your old name, Bill, may seem strange to you. But we—Tony and I—want you to remember that you are an Earthman.

You can't know the oppression that Earth now is suffering, under the Astrarch's heel. But independence is almost gone. Weakened and corrupted, the government yields everywhere. Every Earthman's life is choked with taxes and unjust penalties and the unfair competition of the Astrarch traders.

But Earth, Bill, has not completely yielded. We are going to strike for liberty. Many years of our lives—Tony's and mine—have gone into the plan. And the toil and the sacrifices of millions of our fellow Earthmen. We have at least a chance to recover our lost freedom.

But we need you, Bill—desperately.

For your own world's sake, come back. Ask for a vacation trip to Mars. The Astrarch will not deny you that. On April 8th, a ship will be waiting for you in the desert outside Toran—where we walked the day you left.

Whatever your decision, Bill, we trust you to destroy this letter and keep its contents secret. But we believe that you will come back. For Earth's sake, and for your old friends,

TONY AND ELORA.

Brek Veronar sat for a long time at his desk, staring at the charred, wrinkled sheet. His eyes blurred a little, and he saw the tanned vital face of the Martian girl, her brown eyes imploring. At last he sighed and reached slowly for the lighter cone. He held the letter until the flame had consumed it.

Next day four space officers came to the laboratory. They were insolent in the gaudy gold and crimson of the Astrarch, and the voice of the captain was suave with a triumphant hate:

"Earthman, you are under technical arrest, by the Astrarch's order. You will accompany us at once to his quarters aboard the *Warrior Queen*."

Brek Veronar knew that he was deeply disliked, but very seldom had the feeling been so openly shown. Alarmed, he locked his office and went with the four.

Flagship of the Astrarch's space fleets, the *Warrior Queen* lay on her cradle, at the side of the great field beyond the low gray forts. A thousand feet and a quarter of a million tons of fighting metal, with sixty-four twenty-inch rifles mounted in eight bulging spherical turrets, she was the most powerful engine of destruction the system had ever seen.

Brek Veronar's concern was almost forgotten in a silent

pride, as a swift electric car carried them across the field. It was his autosight—otherwise the Veronar achronic field detector geodesic achron-integration self-calculating range finder—that directed the fire of those mighty guns. It was the very fighting brain of the ship—of all the Astrarch's fleet.

No wonder these men were jealous.

"Come, Renegade!" The bleak-faced captain's tone was ominous. "The Astrarch is waiting."

Bright-uniformed guards let them into the Astrarch's compact but luxurious suite, just aft the console room and forward of the autosight installation, deep in the ship's armored bowels. The Astrarch turned from a chart projector, and crisply ordered the two officers to wait outside.

"Well, Veronar?"

A short, heavy, compact man, the dictator of the Astrarchy was vibrant with a ruthless energy. His hair was waved and perfumed, his face a rouged and powdered mask, his silk-swathed figure loaded with jewels. But nothing could hide the power of his hawklike nose and his burning black eyes.

The Astrarch had never yielded to the constant pressure of jealousy against Brek Veronar. The feeling between them had grown almost to friendship. But now the Earthman sensed, from the cold inquiry of those first words, and the probing flash of the ruler's eyes, that his position was gravely dangerous.

Apprehension strained his voice. "I'm under arrest?"

The Astrarch smiled, gripped his hand. "My men are overzealous, Veronar." The voice was warm, yet Brek Veronar could not escape the sense of something sharply critical, deadly. "I merely wish to talk with you, and the impending movements of the fleet allowed little time."

Behind that smiling mask, the Astrarch studied him. "Veronar, you have served me loyally. I am leaving Astrophon for a cruise with the fleet, and I feel that you, also, have earned a holiday. Do you want a vacation from your duties here—let us say, to Mars?"

Beneath those thrusting eyes, Brek Veronar flinched.

"Thank you, Gorro," he gulped—he was among the few privileged to call the Astrarch by name. "Later, perhaps. But the torpedo guide isn't finished. And I've several ideas for improving the autosight. I'd much prefer to stay in the laboratory."

For an instant, the short man's smile seemed genuine. "The Astrarchy is indebted to you for the autosight. The increased accuracy of fire has in effect quadrupled our fleets." His eyes were sharp again, doubtful. "Are further improvements possible?"

Brek Veronar caught his breath. His knees felt a little weak. He knew that he was talking for his life. He swallowed, and his words came at first unsteadily.

"Geodesic analysis and integration is a completely new science," he said desperately. "It would be foolish to limit the possibilities. With a sufficiently delicate pick-up, the achronic detector fields ought to be able to trace the world lines of any object almost indefinitely. Into the future—"

He paused for emphasis. "Or into the past!"

An eager interest flashed in the Astrarch's eyes. Brek felt confidence returning. His breathless voice grew smoother.

"Remember, the principle is totally new. The achronic field can be made a thousand times more sensitive than any telescope—I believe, a million times! And the achronic beam eliminates the time lag of all electromagnetic methods of observation. Timeless, paradoxically it facilitates the exploration of time."

"Exploration?" questioned the dictator. "Aren't you speaking rather wildly, Veronar?"

"Any range finder, in a sense, explores time," Brek assured him urgently. "It analyzes the past to predict the future—so that a shell fired from a moving ship and deflected by the gravitational fields of space may move thousands of miles to meet another moving ship, minutes in the future.

"Instruments depending on visual observation and electromagnetic transmission of data were not very successful. One hit in a thousand used to be good gunnery. But the autosight has solved the problem—now you reprimand gunners for failing to score two hits in a hundred."

Brek caught his breath. "Even the newest autosight is just a rough beginning. Good enough, for a range finder. But the detector fields can be made infinitely more sensitive, the geodesic integration infinitely more certain.

"It ought to be possible to unravel the past for years, instead of minutes. It ought to be possible to foretell the position of a ship for weeks ahead—to anticipate every maneuver, and even watch the captain eating his breakfast!"

The Earthman was breathless again, his eyes almost feverish. "From geodesic analysis," he whispered, "there is one more daring step—control. You are aware of the modern view that there is no absolute fact, but only probability. I can prove it! And probability can be manipulated, through pressure of the achronic field.

"It is possible, even, I tell you—"

Brek's rushing voice faltered. He saw that doubt had drowned the flash of interest in the Astrarch's eyes. The dictator made an impatient gesture for silence. In a flat, abrupt voice he stated: "Veronar, you are an Earthman."

"Once I was an Earthman."

The black, flashing eyes probed into him. "Veronar," the Astrarch said, "trouble is coming with Earth. My agents have uncovered a dangerous plot. The leader of it is an engineer named Grimm, who has a Martian wife. The fleet is moving to crush the rebellion." He paused. "Now, do you want the vacation?"

Before those ruthless eyes, Brek Veronar stood silent. Life, he was now certain, depended on his answer. He drew a long, unsteady breath. "No," he said.

Still the Astrarch's searching tension did not relax. "My officers," he said, "have protested against serving with you, against Earth. They are suspicious."

Brek Veronar swallowed. "Grimm and his wife," he whispered hoarsely, "once were friends of mine. I had hoped that it would not be necessary to betray them. But I have received a message from them."

He gulped again, caught his breath. "To prove to your

men that I am no longer an Earthman—a ship that they have sent for me will be waiting, on April 8th, Earth calendar, in the desert south of the Martian city of Toran."

The white, lax mask of the Astrarch smiled. "I'm glad you told me, Veronar," he said. "You have been very useful—and I like you. Now I can tell you that my agents read the letter in the cigar. The rebel ship was overtaken and destroyed by the space patrol, just a few hours ago."

Brek Veronar swayed to a giddy weakness.

"Entertain no further apprehensions." The Astrarch touched his arm. "You will accompany the fleet, in charge of the autosight. We take off in five hours."

The long black hull of the *Warrior Queen* lifted on flaring reaction tubes, leading the squadron. Other squadrons moved from the bases on Pallas, Vesta, Thule, and Eros. The Second Fleet came plunging Sunward from its bases on the Trojan planets. Four weeks later, at the rendezvous just within the orbit of Mars, twenty-nine great vessels had come together.

The armada of the Astrarchy moved down upon Earth.

Joining the dictator in his chartroom, Brek was puzzled. "Still I don't see the reason for such a show of strength," he said. "Why have you gathered three fourths of your space forces, to crush a handful of plotters?"

"We have to deal with more than a handful of plotters." Behind the pale mask of the Astrarch's face, Brek could sense a tension of worry. "Millions of Earthmen have labored for years to prepare for this rebellion. Earth has built a space fleet."

Brek was astonished. "A fleet?"

"The parts were manufactured secretly, mostly in underground mills," the Astrarch told him. "The ships were assembled by divers, under the surface of fresh-water lakes. Your old friend, Grimm, is clever and dangerous. We shall have to destroy his fleet, before we can bomb the planet into submission."

Steadily, Brek met the Astrarch's eyes. "How many ships?" he asked.

"Six."

"Then we outnumber them five to one." Brek managed a confident smile. "Without considering the further advantage of the autosight. It will be no battle at all."

"Perhaps not," said the Astrarch, "but Grimm is an able man. He has invented a new type reaction tube, in some regards superior to our own." His dark eyes were somber. "It is Earthman against Earthman," he said softly. "And one of you shall perish."

Day after day, the armada dropped Earthward.

The autosight served also as the eyes of the fleet, as well as the fighting brain. In order to give longer base lines for the automatic triangulations, additional achronic-field pick-ups had been installed upon half a dozen ships. Tight achronic beams brought their data to the immense main instrument, on the *Warrior Queen*. The autosight steered every ship, by achronic beam control, and directed the fire of its guns.

The *Warrior Queen* led the fleet. The autosight held the other vessels in accurate line behind her, so that only one circular cross section might be visible to the telescopes of Earth.

The rebel planet was still twenty million miles ahead, and fifty hours at normal deceleration, when the autosight discovered the enemy fleet.

Brek Veronar sat at the curving control table.

Behind him, in the dim-lit vastness of the armored room, bulked the main instrument. Banked thousands of green-painted cases—the intricate cells of the mechanical brain—whirred with geodesic analyzers and integrators. The achronic field pick-ups—sense organs of the brain—were housed in insignificant black boxes. And the web of achronic transmission beams—instantaneous, ultrashort, nonelectromagnetic waves of the sub-electronic order—the nerve fibers that joined the busy cells—was quite invisible.

Before Brek stood the twenty-foot cube of the stereo-screen, through which the brain communicated its findings. The cube was black, now, with the crystal blackness of space. Earth, in it, made a long misty crescent of wavering crimson splendor. The Moon was a smaller scimitar, blue with the dazzle of its artificial atmosphere.

Brek touched intricate controls. The Moon slipped out of the cube. Earth grew—and turned. So far had the autosight conquered time and space. It showed the planet's Sunward side.

Earth filled the cube, incredibly real. The vast white disk of one low-pressure area lay upon the Pacific's glinting blue. Another, blotting out the winter brown of North America, reached to the bright gray cap of the arctic.

Softly, in the dim room, a gong clanged. Numerals of white fire flickered against the image in the cube. An arrow of red flame pointed. At its point was a tiny fleck of black.

The gong throbbed again, and another black mote came up out of the clouds. A third followed. Presently there were six. Watching, Brek Veronar felt a little stir of involuntary pride, a dim numbness of regret.

Those six vessels were the mighty children of Tony Grimm and Elora, the fighting strength of Earth. Brek felt an aching tenseness in his throat, and tears stung his eyes. It was too bad that they had to be destroyed.

Tony would be aboard one of those ships. Brek wondered how he would look, after twenty years. Did his freckles still show? Had he grown stout? Did concentration still plow little furrows between his blue eyes?

Elora—would she be with him? Brek knew she would. His mind saw the Martian girl, slim and vivid and intense as ever. He tried to thrust away the image. Time must have changed her. Probably she looked worn from the years of toil and danger; her dark eyes must have lost their sparkle.

Brek had to forget that those six little blots represented the lives of Tony and Elora, and the independence of the Earth. They were only six little lumps of matter, six targets for the autosight.

He watched them, rising, swinging around the huge, luminous curve of the planet. They were only six mathematical points, tracing world lines through the continuum, making a geodesic pattern for the analyzers to unravel and the integrators to project against the future—

The gong throbbed again.

Tense with abrupt apprehension, Brek caught up a telephone.

"Give me the Astrarch. . . . An urgent report. . . . No, the admiral won't do. . . . Gorro, the autosight has picked up the Earth fleet . . . Yes, only six ships, just taking off from the Sunward face. But there is one alarming thing."

Brek Veronar was hoarse, breathless. "Already, behind the planet, they have formed a cruising line. The axis extends exactly in our direction. That means that they know our precise position, before they have come into telescopic view. That suggests that Tony Grimm has invented an autosight of his own!"

Strained hours dragged by. The Astrarch's fleet decelerated, to circle and bombard the mother world, after the battle was done. The Earth ships came out at full normal acceleration.

"They must stop," the Astrarch said. "That is our advantage. If they go by us at any great velocity, we'll have the planet bombed into submission before they can return. They must turn back—and then we'll pick them off."

Puzzlingly, however, the Earth fleet kept up acceleration, and a slow apprehension grew in the heart of Brek Veronar. There was but one explanation. The Earthmen were staking the life of their planet on one brief encounter.

As if certain of victory!

The hour of battle neared. Tight achronic beams relayed telephoned orders from the Astrarch's chartroom, and the fleet deployed into battle formation—into the shape of an immense shallow bowl, so that every possible gun could be trained upon the enemy.

The hour—and the instant!

Startling in the huge dim space that housed the autosight, crackling out above the whirring of the achron-integrator, the speaker that was the great brain's voice counted off the minutes.

"Minus four—"

The autosight was set, the pick-ups tuned, the director relays tested, a thousand details checked. Behind the control table, Brek Veronar tried to relax. His part was done.

A space battle was a conflict of machines. Human beings were too puny, too slow, even to comprehend the play of the titanic forces they had set loose. Brek tried to remember that he was the autosight's inventor; he fought an oppression of helpless dread.

"Minus three—"

Sodium bombs filled the void ahead with vast silver plumes and streamers—for the autosight removed the need of telescopic eyes, and enabled ships to fight from deep smoke screens.

"Minus two—"

The two fleets came together at a relative velocity of twelve hundred thousand miles an hour. Maximum useful range of twenty-inch guns, even with the autosight, was only twenty thousand miles in free space.

Which meant, Brek realized, that the battle could last just two minutes. In that brief time lay the destinies of Astrarchy and Earth—and Tony Grimm's and Elora's and his own.

"Minus one—"

The sodium screens made little puffs and trails of silver in the great black cube. The six Earth ships were visible behind them, through the magic of the achronic field pick-ups, now spaced in a close ring, ready for action.

Brek Veronar looked down at the jeweled chronometer on his wrist—a gift from the Astrarch. Listening to the rising hum of the achron-integrators, he caught his breath, tensed instinctively.

"Zero!"

The *Warrior Queen* began quivering to her great guns, a salvo of four firing every half-second. Brek breathed again, watching the chronometer. That was all he had to do. And in two minutes—

The vessel shuddered, and the lights went out. Sirens wailed, and air valves clanged. The lights came on, went off again. And abruptly the cube of the stereo screen was dark. The achron-integrators clattered and stopped.

The guns ceased to thud.

"Power!" Brek gasped into a telephone. "Give me power! Emergency! The autosight has stopped and—"

But the telephone was dead.

There were no more hits. Smothered in darkness, the great room remained very silent. After an eternal time, feeble emergency lights came on. Brek looked again at his chronometer, and knew that the battle was ended.

But who the victor?

He tried to hope that the battle had been won before some last chance broadside crippled the flagship—until the Astrarch came stumbling into the room, looking dazed and pale.

"Crushed," he muttered. "You failed me, Veronar."

"What are the losses?" whispered Brek.

"Everything." The shaken ruler dropped wearily at the control table. "Your achronic beams are dead. Five ships remain able to report defeat by radio. Two of them hope to make repairs.

"The *Queen* is disabled. Reaction batteries shot away, and main power plant dead. Repair is hopeless. And our present orbit will carry us far too close to the Sun. None of our ships able to undertake rescue. We'll be baked alive."

His perfumed dark head sank hopelessly. "In those two minutes, the Astrarchy was destroyed." His hollow, smoldering eyes lifted resentfully to Brek. "Just two minutes!" He crushed a soft white fist against the table. "If time could be recaptured—"

"How were we beaten?" demanded Brek. "I can't understand!"

"Marksmanship," said the tired Astrarch. "Tony Grimm has something better than your autosight. He shot us to pieces before we could find the range." His face was a pale mask of bitterness. "If my agents had employed him, twenty years ago, instead of you—" He bit blood from his lip. "But the past cannot be changed."

Brek was staring at the huge, silent bulk of the autosight. "Perhaps"—he whispered—"it can be!"

Trembling, the Astrarch rose to clutch his arm. "You spoke of that before," gasped the agitated ruler. "Then I wouldn't listen. But now—try anything you can, Veronar. To save us from roasting alive, at perihelion. Do you really think—"

The Astrarch shook his pale head. "I'm the madman," he whispered. "To speak of changing even two minutes of the past!" His hollow eyes clung to Brek. "Though you have done amazing things, Veronar."

The Earthman continued to stare at his huge creation. "The autosight itself brought me one clue, before the battle," he breathed slowly. "The detector fields caught a beam of Tony Grimm's, and analyzed the frequencies. He's using achronic radiation a whole octave higher than anything I've tried. That must be the way to the sensitivity and penetration I have hoped for."

Hope flickered in the Astrarch's eyes. "You believe you can save us? How?"

"If the high-frequency beam can search out the determiner factors," Brek told him, "it might be possible to alter them, with a sufficiently powerful field. Remember that we deal with probabilities, not with absolutes. And that small factors can determine vast results.

"The pick-ups will have to be rebuilt. And we'll have to have power. Power to project the tracer fields. And a river of power—if we can trace out a decisive factor and attempt to change it. But the power plants are dead."

"Rebuild your pick-ups," the Astrarch told him. "And you'll have power—if I have to march every man aboard into the conversion furnaces, for fuel."

Calm again, and confident, the short man surveyed the tall, gaunt Earthman with wondering eyes.

"You're a strange individual, Veronar," he said. "Fighting time and destiny to crush the planet of your birth! It isn't strange that men call you the Renegade."

Silent for a moment, Brek shook his haggard head. "I

don't want to be baked alive," he said at last. "Give me power—and we'll fight that battle again."

The wreck dropped Sunward. A score of expert technicians toiled, under Brek's expert direction, to reconstruct the achronic pick-ups. And a hundred men labored, beneath the ruthless eye of the Astrarch himself, to repair the damaged atomic converters.

They had crossed the orbit of Venus, when the autosight came back to humming life. The Astrarch was standing beside Brek, at the curved control table. The shadow of doubt had returned to his reddened, sleepless eyes. "Now," he demanded, "what can you do about the battle?"

"Nothing, directly," Brek admitted. "First we must search the past. We must find the factor that caused Tony Grimm to invent a better autosight than mine. With the high-frequency field—and the full power of the ship's converters, if need be—we must reverse that factor. Then the battle should have a different outcome."

The achron-integrators whirred, as Brek manipulated the controls, and the huge black cube began to flicker with the passage of ghostly images. Symbols of colored fire flashed and vanished within it.

"Well?" anxiously rasped the Astrarch.

"It works!" Brek assured him. "The tracer fields are following all the world lines that intersected at the battle, back across the months and years. The analyzers will isolate the smallest—and hence most easily altered—essential factor."

The Astrarch gripped his shoulder. "There—in the cube—yourself!"

The ghostly shape of the Earthman flickered out, and came again. A hundred times, Brek Veronar glimpsed himself in the cube. Usually the scene was the great arsenal laboratory, at Astrophon. Always he was differently garbed, always younger.

Then the background shifted. Brek caught his breath as he recognized glimpses of barren, stony, ocher-colored hills, and low, yellow adobe buildings. He gasped to see a

freckled, red-haired youth and a slim, tanned, dark-eyed
girl.

"That's on Mars!" he whispered. "At Toran. He's Tony
Grimm. And she's Elora Ronee—the Martian girl we
loved."

The racing flicker abruptly stopped, upon one frozen
tableau. A bench on the dusty campus, against a low adobe
wall. Elora Ronee, with a pile of books propped on her
knees to support pen and paper. Her dark eyes were staring
away across the campus, and her sun-brown face looked
tense and troubled.

In the huge dim room aboard the wrecked warship, a
gong throbbed softly. A red arrow flamed in the cube,
pointing down at the note on the girl's knee. Cryptic
symbols flashed above it. And Brek realized that the
humming of the achron-integrators had stopped.

"What's this?" rasped the anxious Astrarch. "A schoolgirl writing a note—what has she to do with a space battle?"

Brek scanned the fiery symbols. "She was deciding the
battle—that day twenty years ago!" His voice rang with
elation. "You see, she had a date to go dancing in Toran
with Tony Grimm that night. But her father was giving a
special lecture on the new theories of achronic force. Tony
broke the date, to attend the lecture."

As Brek watched the motionless image in the cube, his
voice turned a little husky. "Elora was angry—that was
before she knew Tony very well. I had asked her for a date.
And, at the moment you see, she has just written a note, to
say that she would go dancing with me."

Brek gulped. "But she is undecided, you see. Because
she loves Tony. A very little would make her tear up the
note to me, and write another to Tony, to say that she would
go to the lecture with him."

The Astrarch stared cadaverously. "But how could that
decide the battle?"

"In the past that we have lived," Brek told him, "Elora
sent the note to me. I went dancing with her, and missed the
lecture. Tony attended it—and got the germ idea that finally
caused his autosight to be better than mine.

"But, if she had written to Tony instead, he would have offered, out of contrition, to cut the lecture—so the analyzers indicate. I should have attended the lecture in Tony's place, and my autosight would have been superior in the end."

The Astrarch's waxen head nodded slowly. "But—can you really change the past?"

Brek paused for a moment, solemnly. "We have all the power of the ship's converters," he said at last. "We have the high-frequency achronic field, as a lever through which to apply it. Surely, with the millions of kilowatts to spend, we can stimulate a few cells in a schoolgirl's brain. We shall see."

His long, pale fingers moved swiftly over the control keys. At last, deliberately, he touched a green button. The converters whispered again through the silent ship. The achron-integrators whirred again. Beyond, giant transformers began to whine.

And that still tableau came to sudden life.

Elora Ronee tore up the note that began, "Dear Bill—" Brek and the Astrarch leaned forward, as her trembling fingers swiftly wrote: "Dear Tony—I'm so sorry that I was angry. May I come with you to father's lecture? Tonight—"

The image faded.

"Minus four—"

The metallic rasp of the speaker brought Brek Veronar to himself with a start. Could he have been dozing—with contact just four minutes away? He shook himself. He had a queer, unpleasant feeling—as if he had forgotten a nightmare dream in which the battle was fought and lost.

He rubbed his eyes, scanned the control board. The autosight was set, the pick-ups were tuned, the director relays tested. His part was done. He tried to relax the puzzling tension in him.

"Minus three—"

Sodium bombs filled the void ahead with vast silver plumes and streamers. Staring into the black cube of the screen, Brek found once more the six tiny black motes o

Tony Grimm's ships. He couldn't help an uneasy shake of his head.

Was Tony mad? Why didn't he veer aside, delay the contact? Scattered in space, his ships could harry the Astrarchy's commerce, and interrupt bombardment of the Earth. But, in a head-on battle, they were doomed.

Brek listened to the quiet hum of the achron-integrators. Under these conditions, the new autosight gave an accuracy of fire of forty percent. Even if Tony's gunnery was perfect, the odds were still two to one against him.

"Minus two—"

Two minutes! Brek looked down at the jeweled chronometer on his wrist. For a moment he had an odd feeling that the design was unfamiliar. Strange, when he had worn it for twenty years.

The dial blurred a little. He remembered the day that Tony and Elora gave it to him—the day he left the university to come to Astrophon. It was too nice a gift. Neither of them had much money.

He wondered if Tony had ever guessed his love for Elora. Probably it was better that she had always declined his attentions. No shadow of jealousy had ever come over their friendship.

"Minus one—"

This wouldn't do! Half angrily, Brek jerked his eyes back to the screen. Still, however, in the silvery sodium clouds, he saw the faces of Tony and Elora. Still he couldn't forget the oddly unfamiliar pressure of the chronometer on his wrist—it was like the soft touch of Elora's fingers, when she had fastened it there.

Suddenly the black flecks in the screen were not targets any more. Brek caught a long gasping breath. After all, he was an Earthman. After twenty years in the Astrarch's generous pay, this timepiece was still his most precious possession.

His gray eyes narrowed grimly. Without the autosight, the Astrarch's fleet would be utterly blind in the sodium clouds. Given any sort of achronic range finder, Tony Grimm could wipe it out.

Brek's gaunt body trembled. Death, he knew, would be the sure penalty. In the battle or afterward—it didn't matter. He knew that he would accept it without regret.

"Zero!"

The achron-integrators were whirring busily, and the *Warrior Queen* quivered to the first salvo of her guns. Then Brek's clenched fists came down on the carefully set keyboard. The autosight stopped humming. The guns ceased to fire.

Brek picked up the Astrarch's telephone. "I've stopped the autosight." His voice was quiet and low. "It is quite impossible to set it again in two minutes."

The telephone clicked and was dead.

The vessel shuddered and the lights went out. Sirens wailed. Air valves clanged. The lights came on, went off again. Presently, there were no more hits. Smothered in darkness, the great room remained very silent.

The tiny racing tick of the chronometer was the only sound.

After an eternal time, feeble emergency lights came on. The Astrarch came stumbling into the room, looking dazed and pale.

A group of spacemen followed him. Their stricken, angry faces made an odd contrast with their gay uniforms. Before their vengeful hatred, Brek felt cold and ill. But the Astrarch stopped their ominous advance.

"The Earthman has doomed himself as well," the shaken ruler told them. "There's not much more that you can do. And certainly no haste about it."

He left them muttering at the door and came slowly to Brek.

"Crushed," he whispered. "You destroyed me, Veronar." A trembling hand wiped at the pale waxen mask of his face. "Everything is lost. The *Queen* disabled. None of our ships able to undertake rescue. We'll be baked alive."

His hollow eyes stared dully at Brek. "In those two minutes, you destroyed the Astrarchy." His voice seemed merely tired, strangely without bitterness. "Just two minutes," he murmured wearily. "If time could be recaptured—"

"Yes," Brek said, "I stopped the autosight." He lifted his gaunt shoulders defiantly, and met the menacing stares of the spacemen. "And they can do nothing about it?"

"Can you?" Hope flickered in the Astrarch's eyes. "Once you told me, Veronar, that the past could be changed. Then I wouldn't listen. But now—try anything you can. You might be able to save yourself from the unpleasantness that my men are planning."

Looking at the muttering men, Brek shook his head. "I was mistaken," he said deliberately. "I failed to take account of the two-way nature of time. But the future, I see now, is as real as the past. Aside from the direction of entropy change and the flow of consciousness, future and past cannot be distinguished.

"The future determines the past, as much as the past does the future. It is possible to trace out the determiner factors, and even, with sufficient power, to cause a local deflection of the geodesics. But world lines are fixed in the future, as rigidly as in the past. However the factors are rearranged, the end result will always be the same."

The Astrarch's waxen face was ruthless. "Then, Veronar, you are doomed."

Slowly, Brek smiled. "Don't call me Veronar," he said softly. "I remembered, just in time, that I am William Webster, Earthman. You can kill me in any way you please. But the defeat of the Astrarchy and the new freedom of Earth are fixed in time—forever."

THE LAST BATTALION

David Drake

"Well, I'm sorry it stopped working," Senator Stone answered irritably over his shoulder, "but since the late news was one of the things I got a mountain cabin to avoid . . ."

"Well, it is strange," his wife repeated. She was as trim-bodied at fifty as she had been when he married her just after VD Day, the first time he could think of a future after three years of flying Mustangs into hostile skies. She was still as stubborn as the WAAF he had married, too. "It was fine and then the color went off in flashes and everything got blurry. And it's getting worse, Hershal."

Stone sighed, closing a file that was long, confidential, and involved the potential expenditure of $73,000,000. The cabin's oak flooring had an unexpected tingle as he walked across it in slippers to the small TV. His feet were asleep, he thought; but could they both be? Not that it mattered. He slapped the set while Miriam waited expectantly. The screen continued to match colored pulses to the bursts of raw noise coming from the speaker. Occasionally an intelligible word or a glimpse of Dan Rather slipped through.

"Some kind of interference," Stone said. He was six feet tall, with a plumpness that his well-cut suits concealed from the public but was evident in pajamas. His hair had grayed early, but it was still thick and smooth after sixty-one years, no small political asset. Stone was no charmer, but he had learned years before that a man who is honest and has the physical presence to be called forthright will be respected even if he is wrong—and there are never many candidates the voters can respect. Shrugging, he clicked the set off. "If you needed somebody to fix your TV, you should have married some tech boy," he added.

"Instead of my hotshot pilot?" Miriam laughed, stretching out an arm to her husband. She paused as she stood, and at the same moment both realized that the high-pitched keening they had associated with the television was now louder. The hardwood floor carried more of a buzz than a trembling. Miriam's smile froze into a part of her human architecture, like the ferrous curls of hair framing her face.

Earthquake? thought Stone as two strides carried him to the south door. Not in the Smokies, surely; but politics had taught him even more emphatically than combat that there were always going to be facts that surprised you, and that survivors were people who didn't pretend otherwise. He threw the door open. Whipsnake Ridge dropped southward, a sheer medley of grays formed by mist and distance. The sky should have been clear and colorless since the Moon had not yet risen, but an auroral glow was flooding from behind the cabin to paint the night with a score of strange pastels. The whine was louder, but none of the nearby trees were moving.

"Miriam," Stone began, "you'd—"

The rap of knuckles on the north door cut him off.

"I'll get it," Miriam said quickly.

"You'll stay right here!" the senator insisted, striding past her; but her swift heels rapped down the hallway just behind him.

Stone snapped on the entryway light before unlatching the door. The cabin had no windows to the north as the only view would have been the access road and a small clearing in the second-growth pine of the Ridge, a poor exchange for the vicious storms that ripped down in winter. The outside door opened into an anteroom to further insulate the cabin, and that alcove, four feet square in floor plan, was filled by two men in black uniforms.

"You will forgive the intrusion, Senator and Madame Stone," stated the foremost in a rusty voice more used to commands, "but we could not very well contact you in more normal fashion in our haste." The speaker was as tall as Stone, a slim ramrod of a man whose iron-gray hair was cropped so short as to almost be shaven beneath the band of his service hat. The dull cloth of his uniform bagged into jackboots as highly polished as his waist-belt and pistol holster. It was not the pistol, nor the long-magazined rifle the other visitor bore that struck the first real fear into Stone, though: both men wore collar insignia, the twin silver lightning-bolt runes Stone thought he had seen the last of thirty years before. They were the badge of Hitler's SS.

"May we enter?"

"You go straight to Hell!" Stone snarled. His left hand knotted itself in the nearer black shirt while reflex cocked his right for as much of a punch as desks and the poisonous atmosphere of Washington had left him. The second Nazi was as gray as the first and was built like a tank besides, but there was nothing slow about his reactions. The barrel of his rifle slammed down across Stone's forearm. Almost as part of the same motion the stock pivoted into the senator's stomach, throwing him back in a sprawl over Miriam's legs. The entranceway light haloed the huge gunman as he swung his weapon to bear on the tangle of victims almost at its muzzle.

"Lothar!" the slim German shouted.

His subordinate relaxed, "Ja, mein Oberführer," he said as he again ported his rifle.

With a smile that was not wholly one of satisfaction, the black-shirted officer said, "Senator, I am Colonel Ernst Riedel. My companion—what would you say—Master-Sergeant Lothar Mueller and I have reached a respectable age without inflicting our presence on you. I assure you that only necessity causes us to do so now."

Stone rose to his feet. Riedel did not offer a hand he knew would be refused. Miriam remained silent behind her husband, but her right arm encircled his waist. Stone looked from the men to the rifle used to club him down. It was crude, a thing of enameled metal and green-black plastic: an MP-44, built in the final days of the Third Reich. "You're real, aren't you!" the senator said. "You aren't just American slime who wanted something different from white sheets to parade in. Where do you hide, Nazi? Do you sell cars in Rio during the week and take out your uniform Sundays to look at yourself in the mirror?"

"We are real, Senator Stone," Riedel said through his tight smile. He raised his left cuff so that the motto worked on the band there showed. It read "Die Letze" in old-style letters. "We are the Last Battalion, Senator. And as for where we hide—that you will know very shortly, for we were sent to bring you there.

"Madame Stone," he went on formally, "we will have your husband back to you in days if that is possible. I assure you, on my honor as a true Aryan and before the good God and my Leader, that we mean no harm to either of you."

"Oh, I'll trust your honor," Miriam blazed. Fifteen years as a senator's wife had taught her the use of tact, but nothing would ever convince her that every situation should be borne in silence. "How many prisoners did *you* shoot in the back at Malmedy?"

For the first time, Riedel's chalky face pinched up. "It is well for you both, Madame, that Mueller does not speak English." He added, "You may trust my honor or not, as you will. But it is not in our interests alone that we have been sent to you, nor in those alone of the country you represent. If we fail, Senator, there may well in a short time be no Aryan life remaining on Earth."

His hand gestured Stone toward the door. "You will please precede us."

Without hesitation or a backward glance, Stone brushed past the two Germans. Had he looked back he would have called attention to his wife, erect and dry-eyed in the hall. He had known enough killers while he was in service to realize that Mueller's bloodlust was no pretense. The big man had been a finger's pressure away from double murder, and they would not have been his first.

The outside door opened and dragged a gasp from Stone in the rush of warmed air. Instead of the clear night sky, a convex lens of metal roofed the clearing a dozen feet over Stone's head. The size of the clearing gave the object dimension: it was a two-hundred-foot saucer resting on a central gondola and three pillarlike legs spaced halfway between the center and the rim. Through the windows of the gondola could be seen other men, both seated and standing. An incandescent light flooded stairs which extended from the gondola to the ground, but the whole scene was lighted by the burnished iridescence of the saucer itself.

Behind Stone, the Nazi officer laughed. "It is not heat so much as the eddy currents from the electromagnetic motors that make the hull plates glow so handsomely. But walk ahead, please, Senator. She glows as much on the upper side as well and we—we do not wish to attract close attention while we are grounded."

Stone's carpet slippers brushed crisply through the ankle-high grass. The dew that should have gemmed the blades had evaporated under the hot metal lid. Stone always wore slippers and pajamas when he did not expect company, but it was one hell of an outfit in which to take the surrender of a batch of Nazi holdouts in a flying saucer.

Except that Stone knew inside him that men like Riedel were not about to surrender.

"This is Dora, the largest of our experimental models," Riedel said with pride. "She is sheathed with impervium—chromium-vanadium alloy, you perhaps know. There is no limit, nearly, to the speeds at which she may be driven without losing the strength of her hull, even in the thickest of atmospheres."

Closer to the gondola, Stone could see that it rested not on wheels but on inflated rubber cushions that must have been heavily reinforced to bear the weight of the craft.

There were small signs of age visible at a nearer glance, too—if Dora was experimental, it was an old experiment. The rectangular windows whose plane surfaces suggested glass or quartz instead of nonrefractive Plexiglas were fogged by tiny pits, and the stair runners appeared to be of several different materials as if there had been replacements over the years. All the men in the gondola were bald or as gray-haired as Mueller and Riedel. The colonel noticed Stone's surprise and said, "Everyone volunteered for the mission, but we Old Fighters, of course, had preference. Everyone here was of my original crew."

The man who reached through the hatch to hasten Stone up the last high step wore gray coveralls from which any insignia had long been removed, though his air of authority was evident. He was not even middle-aged. His hands were thin and gnarled, their hairs gleaming silvery against the age-dappled skin, and the bright lights within the gondola shadowed his wrinkles into a road map through eighty years. His exchange in German with Riedel was quick and querulous. The colonel did not translate for Stone's benefit, but tones and the flash of irritation in the eyes of both men explained more than the bland, "Over-Engineer Tannenberg is anxious that we be under weigh. You will please come with me to the control room. We will have time to discuss matters fully after we have lifted off."

All ice and darkness, the Nazi strode to one of the pair of latticework elevators in the center of the gondola. Flipping one of a bank of switches, toggles instead of buttons, he set the cage in smooth but squealing upward motion. Wholly fascinated, the senator stared around him.

A bell pinged each time the cage rose to another level. Through the sides, Stone saw identical masses of copper and silicon iron, suggesting the inside of a transformer rather than the computer room the craft's gleaming exterior had left him to expect. Narrow gangways threaded into the mass, and twice Stone glimpsed aged men in stained coveralls intent on their hand-held meters. There was nothing subtle in the vessel's layout. It reeked of enormous power as surely as it did of ozone and lubricant. There were eight levels above the gondola, each of them nearly identical to the others, before the cage pinged a ninth time and grated to a stop.

"Sit there, please," Riedel directed, gesturing toward a frame-backed couch that looked unpleasantly like a catafalque. Stone obeyed without comment, his eyes working quickly. They had entered a circular room fifty feet across. Its eight-foot ceiling was soundproofed metal, but the whole circumference was open to the world through crystalline panels like those of the gondola. The saucer, domed with more of a curve on the upper side than the lower, was a fountain of pale iridescence against which the grim SS runes stood out like toppling tombstones.

A dozen preoccupied men shared the control room with Stone and Riedel. Sgt. Mueller was one of them, looking no less dangerous for having put aside his rifle. The others appeared to be officers or gray-suited engineers like Tannenberg. Three of the latter clustered in front of a console far more complex than those sprouting from the deck beside the other benches. One of the men spoke urgently into a throat mike while his companions followed the quivering motions of a hundred dials apiece.

Riedel stood, arms akimbo, and snapped out a brief series of orders. The heavyset man nearest him nodded and began flipping toggles. All three of the engineers were now speaking intently in low voices. Lights dimmed in the control room, and the air began to sing above the range of audibility.

Stone felt his weight shift. Trees climbing into the night slanted and suddenly shrank downward. Stone's cabin was below, now, visible past the glowing dome of the saucer. Lone in the pool of the yard light stood Miriam, waving her clenched right fist. Then the disk tilted again and Stone was driven flat onto his bench by a vertical acceleration not experienced since he had reached the age limit and could no longer zoom-climb a Phantom during Reserve training. The sensation lasted for longer than Stone would have believed possible, and by the time it settled into the queasiness of steady forward motion, the sky had changed. It was black, but less from the absence of light than the utter lack of anything to reflect light.

Riedel was returning. "Not bad," Stone said with a trace of false condescension, "but can you outrun a Nike Zeus?"

"The Russian equivalent, yes indeed, Senator," replied the German, capping Stone's gibe. "Each couch"—his gesture disclosed rubber lips edging the top of the bench—"can enfold a man like an oyster's shell and hold him in a water suspension. For the strongest accelerations we use even a fluid breathing medium, though of course"—and Riedel frowned in concentration at the thought—"that requires time for preparation that we do not always have."

He seated himself beside Stone. The American blinked, more incredulous than angry at what seemed an obvious lie. "You expect me to believe that this—my God, it must weigh a thousand tons! *This* could outaccelerate an anti-missile missile?"

Riedel nodded, delighted with the effect he had made. "Yes, yes, the power is here—is it not obvious? That was Schauberger's work, almost entirely. But to make it usable for human beings took our Engineer Tannenberg." The colonel chuckled before adding, "Have you noticed that when men of genius grow old, they become more like old women than even old women do? Tannenberg is afraid every moment we are not aloft that the Russians will catch us."

The earlier name had snagged Stone's attention. "Schauberger?" he repeated. "Sure, I remember him. In the fifties he was touting an implosion motor or some damned thing. I remember a major from Wright-Patterson telling me about it. But then nothing came of it."

"But then your FBI questioned poor Viktor with, shall we say, a little too much enthusiasm," Riedel corrected with a tolerant smile, "and he was reported beaten to death by Chicago hoodlums. The implosion motor was only a smokescreen, though, for the electromagnetic engine he had already developed for his Führer. Think of it, this craft and these mighty engines that you see filling it—able to draw fuel from the Earth, from the very fabric of space itself!"

"If that were true," Stone said carefully, "I frankly don't see why you would need me." He chose his words to deny what he feared, that the story was as solid as the steel floor beneath his feet. To admit that aloud would gratify this colonel whose arrogance only slightly increased the disgust Stone already felt for his uniform.

The implied question reminded the Nazi sickeningly of his mission. He sighed, wondering how much to tell the fellow now. Stone was the only man short of his unapproachable president who had enough power with military and political leaders to act with the necessary swiftness. Without his willing cooperation, more than the whole Plan was a ruin. "At first we were based at Kertl," Riedel began, "where the airframe had been fabricated." He was avoiding a direct answer partly in hope that it would somehow become unnecessary if he explained the background. Riedel owned to few superiors, but there was One—and of late, with age and the pressure He bore most of all of them, that One had displayed an ever-lowering acceptance of failure. "The engines arrived by train, at last, from Obersalzberg, and we worked all night to unload them before the bombers came."

Riedel laid his service cap beside him and scrabbled the fingers of his left hand through hair that for thirty-seven years had been cropped to between five and ten millimeters' length. While everything else had changed, that precision had not. "There was no time to do what was required—you have seen the engines—but we did it anyway. It was like shifting mountains with a spoon to emplace them in the airframe using the equipment we had, and all the work underground as well. But in those days the impossible was normal, and we were Waffen-SS. The time that we had was being bought for us with the lives of our comrades on the front lines, fighting tanks with hand grenades."

Of the men in the control room, only Sgt. Mueller was openly watching Stone and Riedel; but the inattention of the others was the studied sort, that of jackals waiting for lions to end their meal. All of the crew understood the importance of their mission.

"The final order came by courier from Berlin, an SS major with an attaché case in the sidecar of his motorcycle. It had been chained to his right wrist, he told us, but the shell that killed his driver had taken that arm off at the elbow. With teeth and one hand he had tourniqueted himself before retrieving the case. The orders were not those we expected, but in the face of such dedication we could not have refused them."

"You ran," Stone interjected flatly, knowing that truth would twist the edged words deeper than any emphasis he could give them.

"We took off in three hours," the German said, his face a block of gray iron. "It was the first time, as soon as final engine hookups had been made. All of us were aboard, even the kitchen staff. Everything worked. I could not believe it—five years of design and construction, and then no flaws. But again, there was no choice. From the air we could see British tanks already within three kilometers and nothing but the forest itself to slow them. Had we left fifteen minutes later, they might have captured our base before the demolition charges exploded."

"What you seem to be afraid to admit," Stone pressed, "is that a single plane—saucer, whatever—isn't worth a damn no matter how advanced it is." He stood, a commanding presence again now that he had recovered his poise. The mass and smooth power of the vessel made its speed a matter of only conscious awareness. "It's only a bargaining chip, to be sold to one side or the other since you can't develop it yourself. And we and the Russians both will soon have equipment in the air that will match it, so you're running out of time to deal."

"You are incorrect to assume we are alone," Riedel said, as careful as the American to avoid theatrical emphasis that would only give truth a false patina. "We escaped alone, but there were fifty-three submarines of Type XXI—no, I do not exaggerate—that could run submerged all around the world with their snorkels. They carried above 3,000 persons, couples and young people, out before the Russians captured Danzig; and in Norway they picked up . . . some who had flown by jet out of Tempelhof just at the end."

Stone licked dry lips but his voice was firm as he insisted, "Even then they couldn't go anywhere. I've heard about the money Himmler was spreading around in South America, but even so there wasn't a country there that could have hidden such a fleet without word leaking out. A fleet needs a base."

"It has one." It was time for the final hammerblow of truth. "In New Swabia, where we met them."

"Huh?" grunted Stone, surprised and uncomprehending.

"Imbecile!" snarled the Nazi, seeing all his preparation threatened by his listener's ignorance. "In Antarctica, Queen Maud Land as you and your Allies call it! Kapitan Ritscher explored it in 1937 and we have held the interior since, no matter what color the coast is painted on a pretty map. And there is one other place we have been for twenty years, my good Senator," Riedel said, loudly now and wagging his finger like a pedant's pointer, "though others seem to believe they were the first there."

He paused, breathing very rapidly. "This vessel is not limited to the atmosphere, Senator; indeed, we are above it now to all intents and purposes. We have a base on the Moon where we have manufactured a hundred ships of this design!"

But as Stone's jaw worked in stunned silence, Riedel's pride too dissolved in despair. "We had a hundred, yes," he repeated, "but the Russians have a thousand, and they are destroying us. You must help us fight them, or Aryan man is doomed."

The sky was an emptiness that would have been violet if it had color. Pits on the crystal windows prevented the stars from gaining any real body, but a slight course correction brought the Moon in sight to port. It was gibbous and the gray of fresh-cut lead. "I don't believe that," Stone insisted. "I've made it my business over the years to know about Russian strength. Our intelligence people trust me. They aren't lying to me, and notwithstanding all the nonsense my colleagues and the media like to spout, the Russians aren't fooling our people either. Besides, if the Reds had a whole fleet like this, we'd have learned about it the hard way long since. Unless there's more to détente than *I've* ever believed."

Riedel shrugged. " 'When one has eliminated the impossible . . . ,' " he quoted, then paused to consider how he should continue. Stone's logic was impeccable, its only flaw being Russia's unfathomable, senseless subtlety in not showing an apparently pat hand. Riedel had not believed it at first, either, but facts were facts. "At the first report in 1947, we thought rumors of our Dora, here, were being retailed in garbled form," he explained. "At that time, we had only the one ship—no others had been completed before the final holocaust, and the Antarctic base was not suitable for manufactures this major. It was not until we could process aluminum on the Moon that we could expand, and that was five years later.

"There were too many reports. We were very careful with Dora, you must understand; and though we had our contacts with the world outside, no one beyond the Battalion knew anything except our Plan, to control the balance when at last East and West joined in Götterdämmerung." Riedel's face gleamed with the sweat of earnestness. He brushed at his face and extended both thin hands toward Stone. "Our rocket scientists, you and the Russians had captured; but we thought all but the least word of the Diskus Projekt had been hidden. Now we began to fear that the other sightings were more than imagination, and that our secret had escaped."

"You never saw them yourselves?" Stone asked. "The other UFOs, I mean?"

"I did," Riedel said, pride warming his words. "We had completed the first disk to be built on the Moon and I was flight-testing it. Because we expected fleet maneuvers in the future, Engineer Tannenberg had coupled a locator to the engines to display other users of the spectrum—our own vessels, we intended. But as we began our first atmospheric approach—" and Riedel lived again the moments as he described them to Stone.

• • •

In a voice as wizened as his face, Tannenberg had announced, "Colonel, there is another ship within a kilometer, at five degrees to our heading and a little lower."

"Nonsense!" Riedel snapped. At thirty kilometers altitude their test craft could have encountered only Dora, and she would have been a bright dot on their radar screen.

A bead glared suddenly against the screen's green background. It was near them, much closer than it should have been before being picked up in the radar's fifteen-second sweep. "Navigation!" he called, his temper that of a wounded bear looking for a victim. First trial of the new hull in the pressures and powerful magnetic fields of Earth was a tense enough business without having unknown vessels slip through undetected.

"S-sir," said the white-faced technician at the main radar display, "it just now appeared."

"Colonel," Sgt. Mueller said, his hair-spined forefinger pointing downward into the blue-white haze into which their craft was descending. Metal winked, a reflection with no definable color.

"It's off the screen again!" the fearful radarman was bleating, but Riedel's voice cut through his junior's without hesitation: "Attention! All crewmen to acceleration couches! Sergeant Mueller, arm the rockets and stand by." Disconnecting his throat mike, for he spoke to himself rather than his men, Riedel added, "They think to play with us, do they? Well then, we will play with them."

Only Sgt. Mueller heard, and he grinned a wolf's grin as he ran his hands over the switches of his console.

At 300 meters, the black, portless hull of the foreign disk was stark against the sky-curve beyond. It bore no marking. Both craft were steady at a little over 1800 kph, far below the capacity of Riedel's engines. This was not his Dora, though, he thought with rage. Impervium hulls were beyond their ability to forge on the Moon—or on Earth without arousing the interest of the nations who had to be lulled into forgetfulness. Aluminum was cheap, given lunar ores and abundant power, but the new hulls could not stand the friction heating of 4,000 kph or more in the atmosphere.

"Unknown craft, identify yourself," Riedel ordered in German. He was broadcasting only on eleven meters, but with a 10 kw transmitter driving his beam, even the light bulbs on the other craft would be repeating his words.

There was no response. He tried again in English, for they were over northern Canada. All his subordinates but Mueller had slipped into their clamshell couches, taking their information from the gauges slaved into the panels over their faces. Riedel started to rebuke the sergeant, then realized that with the enemy able to evade radar, only visual control could be used for the rockets.

And there seemed little doubt that the black disk was an enemy. "Does anyone aboard speak Russian?" No one answered. Besides, what did they have to discuss with the conquerors of Berlin? "Fire one, sergeant," Riedel said evenly.

Mueller's finger stroked a 20 cm rocket from the ventral weapons bay. Its hundred kilos of explosive could be wire-guided 5,000 meters, but the gap between the two ships was point-blank range.

The charge went off scarcely halfway to the black vessel.

The spurt of red on black smoke, half a second early, was a greater surprise to Riedel than the howl of air through the fragment-riddled panels before him. The missile's own fuse should not have armed at so short a distance. Something invisible surrounding the other craft had detonated the weapon while it was almost as dangerous to its user as its target, and the target was diving away. Riedel followed, ignoring for the moment the stresses to which he was subjecting his ship and his own unshielded body. Sgt. Mueller had yanked down a whole handful of switches and four guidance flares leaped together after the black craft. It wobbled under the multiple shockwave, but a beam as pale as an icteric sclera needled back from its dome. Riedel saw the hull directly in front of him boil away as the laser struck it. His instant course change bagged his cheeks and flattened his eyeballs. The black vessel did not attempt pursuit.

The executive officer in his acceleration couch had taken over when Riedel regained full consciousness. They had resumed their planned course toward Antarctica, flying below 2,500 meters because of the gashed hull. Sgt. Mueller was clenching his hands in fierce frustration. "We need something better to kill them with," he kept repeating.

"And we got it," Riedel concluded, affect raining out of his voice. "Tannenberg said his detector could easily be modified to cause a surge in other electromagnetic engines, to cause them to vaporize. For twenty-three years he was right and we hunted the Russians throughout space. There were losses, since their lasers could very quickly slit the hulls of the ships we built—not a bad weapon, lasers; we might have fitted our bases with them sooner had not Tannenberg's induced overloads left so little of their targets." He paused in an aura of satisfaction, looking out over the clean, black sky but seeing something very different. "From a pip of light the disks we destroy become great expanding balls that are all the colors of the rainbow. In atmosphere even the copper burns, so intense is the energy released."

"You bastards," Stone said with utter conviction. "I wonder if you'll find it so pretty when *they* come up with your gadget?"

"Colonel, we are closing with another vessel," broke in one of the crewmen.

"It may be ours. We were to have an escort when we reached open sea, if the situation permitted it," Riedel replied on his throat mike. To Stone he continued, "The Russians are an ignorant people, able only to steal from their betters. In all that time they have not duplicated the weapon."

He took a deep breath, adding, "But six months ago, they found a defense against it. And since then only the few lasers for which we have been able to buy components have kept them from our bases."

"You can't be serious," Stone said. But Riedel's mind was like his body—gray and honed and rigid. He could no more accept the superiority of an "under race" than could a computer which had been misprogrammed to deny it. That quirk has caused Riedel and his men to ignore the obvious.

"Look, lasers—I don't know how long we've had them, but they weren't weapons back in 1950. And this detonator screen or whatever, *we* damned well don't have it now. If—"

"Colonel! The ship is not one of ours. It is closing!"

"Couches!" Riedel ordered. He stood, pressing as he did the switch that turned Stone's bench into an enveloping cushion. "Raise your legs and lie down, Senator. The television will show you what occurs, and we will release you as soon as possible."

The hull curve, a smooth violet as Riedel strode to his station, suddenly blazed white in a meter-long knife edge. The impervium alloy held, but Dora's evasive action in response to the laser thrust hurled the slender officer to the deck. He gripped a chart table, then let skewed acceleration fling him in the direction he wanted to go. He was safely within his couch before the third zigzag snatched at him.

"Riedel," he announced, "taking command." His fingers caressed switches they knew by touch. The enemy craft was an eddy in the frozen blue swirls of Earth's magnetic fields pictured on the detector screen. Riedel set the television cameras to track the detector anomaly, though he would not need the picture. By the time Dora had been retrofitted with television, he was used to being guided to battle by the detector alone. And even with their surge weapon ineffective, there would still be a battle with Riedel at the controls. He knew his Dora.

The other craft was within two kilometers now. It fingered Dora's hull with another short burst, probably unaware that its target was more refractory than earlier victims. The Nazi commander's face was a grinning death's head within his couch as he cut forward thrust and flipped Dora to spin like a coin toward the icecap twenty kilometers below. The blue eddy danced around the center of the detector screen and the TV began to flash images of a black disk seeming to approach at a thousand angles. Fluid-filled membranes clamped down on every surface of Riedel's body, but still the maddening spin worked on his ear canals and the colloid of his brain itself.

The eddy was almost in the center of the detector. Riedel's fingers acted more through instinct than by conscious calculation. On the television, the spinning edge of the black vessel froze and expanded. There was a terrible, rending crash as Dora's impervium edge buzz sawed into the unknown material of her enemy's hull. A sheet of white fire enveloped both craft as the chrome-van alloy proved tougher than what it impacted. Objects vomited from the spiraling gash in the hostile craft. One of them tumbled almost against Dora, now motionless as her enemy fell away from her. The thing was momentarily alive and quite visible on the television screens. It was about nine feet tall, with four limbs that looked like ropes knotted over a thin framework. Its mouth was working and its eyes glittered fear of death through each of their facets.

"You butchers," a voice rasped through Riedel's earphones. His anger awakened him to the fact that he still had Dora to pilot, and the anger faded when he realized it was the American who had spoken and not one of his crewmen. "It wasn't enough to fight the whole rest of the world. You Nazis had to start an interstellar war."

There was an air leak between compartments F-87 and F-88; a bulkhead had crumpled but the outer skin, though indented, was not seriously torn. Riedel touched switches. As his acceleration couch withdrew into itself, Dora plunged down as smoothly as an elevator and swiftly enough that her passengers neared the weightlessness of free fall.

"Murderers! Criminals!"

Riedel ripped out the jack of his headset. In two steps he had snapped the outside latch on Stone's couch, effectively silencing and isolating the senator. "Lieutenant Wittvogel," he ordered, "raise the base. Secrecy is no longer necessary."

"No reply, sir," the tall communications officer called across the room. "Not even to the emergency signal."

"We're within fifty kilometers," Riedel said, but he spoke under his breath. "Keep trying," he ordered.

With an atmosphere to scatter it, sunlight and its reflection from the ice below blazed through the windows. The computer installed three years earlier—a massive thing, not a sophisticated "black box"; but Dora was not a volume-starved turbojet—was guiding them back at 3,000 kph and there was no need for Riedel to stare tensely into the rippling whiteness they skimmed. Beside him stood Sgt. Mueller, as silent as a bored sentry. He had been out of his couch before his commander. When Stone had been locked in, Mueller's responsibility had ended and he had relaxed with a grin. Even so, it was his ease rather than Riedel's stark anticipation that caught the first sight of the base.

"Sir, there's something ahead there that glows!"

Riedel took instant manual control, cutting speed and raising Dora to a kilometer's altitude. They circled the glow, banked inward for observation rather than flight necessity. A hole had been blasted in the ice, four kilometers across and of a depth obscured by the boiling lake that snarled at its rim.

"The Führer," Sgt. Mueller whispered. He jackknifed and vomited across the deck plates. Lt. Wittvogel had hurled away his microphone and, like several of his fellow crewmen, was openly weeping. Riedel himself was the least visibly affected, but as he unlatched Stone's prison he muttered, "I wonder if we taught them about the Bomb, too. They were such bad fighters, no instinct for it at all . . ."

Riedel was back at the controls, following at full speed and a kilometer's altitude the brown rim of beach against gray-green water, when Stone touched his shoulder. "You're done now, aren't you?" the American said softly.

"He could have escaped. He could be at the Moon base now—perhaps they had only one bomb. He—" Riedel's throat choked him into sudden silence.

"He?" Stone echoed. His face went as white and cold as the ice below. "I fought three years for a chance to kill—that one. If these others have done that, they have my thanks. Whatever else they intend."

On the horizon was a small freighter static in the shadow of shear, snow-browed cliffs. Inshore of it were a huddle of

Quonset huts set in a splotch of snow dirtied by human habitation. "I swore an oath to your wife," Riedel forced out through tight lips, "and I would prefer to keep it. But if you say another word, Senator, you will go out at a thousand meters."

The landing legs squealed while Riedel's practiced fingers brought the disk to a hover over the Quonsets. "Wohlman," the colonel ordered abruptly, and his executive officer took the controls with a nod.

"What will you do now?" Stone asked as he stepped to the elevator in anticipation of a command.

"The Moon base will need us," Riedel said, his black and silver chest separated from the American's by an invisible wall of grief.

"If it's still there. They would have hit it first, wouldn't they?"

The cage ground to a halt in the observation gondola. The four men there were tense, hands close to their sidearms. "Inform your people, Senator," Riedel said. He riffled a worn, mimeographed book, then handed it to Stone. "Our maintenance manual. Perhaps your experts can construct their down disks from it. I have nothing better to offer you here."

Men in furs were running out of the huts. A blast of dry, chill air hammered the compartment as the hatch opened and the stairway extended. "These are Argentinians. At this time of year you should have no trouble getting a swift return to your country."

"But what are you going to do?" Stone insisted, the rubberized treads warm under his feet though the wind was a knife across the rest of his body.

Riedel's eyes, colder than the ice, thrust the American down the gangway. "Do?" he repeated. "We are SS, Senator. We will continue to fight."

Dora was rising again even before the stairs had fully retracted. A dozen startled Argentinians clustered around Stone, their parka fringes blending indistinguishably with their bushy facial hair. Around them all a huge disk had been etched in the powdered snow by the radiant metal above it.

The Antarctic sky was clear, except for a speck that vanished even as Stone's eyes followed it upward.

SHADOW ON THE STARS

Algis Budrys

At the barren heart of midnight, at the precise stroke of twelve, the Farlan Empire—Henlo's empire—would be dying.

Henlo looked forward to death with distaste. But being a realist, he accepted personal extinction as he accepted the death of his entire, tremendous creation. And there was no longer anything he could do to stop the Earthman.

At midnight, the implacable statistics of his birth would shunt him aside, forever stripped of his leadership. Worse, the Earthmen would have a free hand while he lived along uselessly, somewhere, with his books and courtesy guards. And the guards would be fiercely single-minded young men with no ears for anything he might say, dedicated to nothing but the continuance of his life at the new ruler's whim.

He doubted very much that the fierce young men could save the empire that had once been his pride and his glory.

He was senile. No one would talk to him, or listen to him, though everyone would be most respectful. How ironic that he could still be respected and accorded every courtesy despite his statistical senility.

It did not matter that only he was equipped, and that by luck, to recognize the deadly, never-ceasing danger and take steps to prevent it. No matter how brilliant his successor—no doubt long-since picked and impatiently waiting—he could not understand about the Earthmen. And Henlo could not tell him. They would never even see each other, and any memoranda Henlo left behind would be discarded without being read. What purpose could there be in listening to a replaced Empire Builder, or reading his words? He was senile and the verdict could not be reversed.

He watched the shadows sweep along the avenues of Farla City, and reflected with bitterness on the laws and customs of Farla. They determined inexorably that a man, on reaching the age of one hundred, became automatically senile. Well, the rule had doubtless served its purposes in the past.

Farla turned, and the years followed. There were customs which were honored in the breach, and his personal list of these was longer than most. But not even he could prevent Farla from revolving only two hundred and seven times before it went once around the sun. He was trapped by the unalterable fact of his birthdate.

Laws. Customs. Only once in his life had he met a man who understood their basis completely.

Henlo looked out in complete frustration at the city that was no longer his. And even more vividly than before the years began to unroll backwards in his mind's eye vision, coalescing into patterns of long ago. It seemed only yesterday somehow . . .

I

Captain D' Henlo of the Farlan Starfleet sat in the cabin of his first fleet command, trying desperately to sleep. Around him, echoing through the companionways and vibrating from the plates, were the thousand and one sounds of fitting-out.

Hurried footsteps bounded through the companionways, and auxiliary motors throughout the ship rumbled with overload or howled at sudden slack as supplies were hoisted aboard and dispersed into bunkers and loading chutes. At intervals, the open circuit of the ship's Intervoice rattled the cabin speaker's grille with tinny messages.

A small part of Henlo's mind monitored this babble, precisely as a musician's ear studies the notes of a tuning orchestra. But only a small part—and only the sudden emergence of a false note brought the constant noise to the full attention of his thoughts. Ship's noises had long since ceased to interfere with Henlo's natural ability to snatch a few moments of sleep from the rigors of his routine.

It was the thought of death and defeat—of the destruction of his fleet, and of the inevitable end of the Farlan Union—which now kept him in a state of constant, chill apprehension, and denied him all repose.

The Vilkai controlled the Galaxy. They had driven the Earthmen back to the Rim before that pale, furless race had even fairly begun the burgeoning rush of expansion which seemed its sure, remorseless destiny. They had scoured the universe clean of opposition, controlled its commerce, and levied their supplies from the shadowy remnants of a dozen lesser empires which were now mere puppet districts in the greater domain. Only Farla stood in their way, and that only for as long as it suited their predatory plans.

Theoretically, they were not all-powerful. They were over-extended, and they were barbarians. The over-extended barbarian invariably tends to go home and return at a later date, when he has seen to the conception of a new generation of barbarians and filled out his lean ribs. He is, moreover, given to quarrelling and dissension within his own ranks, and the pursuit of loot in preference to the more exacting demands of strategy.

The primary objective of a barbarian is not the conquest of territory for its own sake, or the prosecution of some political dogma. It is individual power and individual glory. That is his weakness, and a well-led, well-disciplined professional military force can cut him to ribbons, no matter what the size of his horde.

Unfortunately Farla, unlike Earth, which had simply been unprepared, was not well-led, or well-organized.

Captain D' Henlo's short, almost vestigial tail lashed nervously. He had no desire to see his career cruelly interrupted by the sawing of a Vilk trophy-knife. Possibly, had he been a few years farther along in the ranks, he might have attempted to engineer some pressure at the capital. It was barely possible that he might gain something there, knowing as he did that the admirals of war are rarely the same men as the admirals of peace.

But the possibility was only an improbability. He knew his own worth and talents, and his contacts at the capital were rightly suspicious of his political ability. There were certain things beyond the pale of custom, and promotion over the heads of half the Fleet priority list was one of them. It might very well have caused a general mutiny.

Not in the ranks, perhaps, for the ranks no longer cared who led them. But the officers would be furious, and the officers could smash the government immediately. Governments being covetous of governing, it followed as a logical premise that D' Henlo, genius or not, was doomed to be just another ship commander involved in the last, gasping flicker of life in the race of Farlans.

He bared his teeth in a snarl at the inevitable, but he recognized that inevitable for what it was.

Grimly, he tried to bore himself to sleep by recounting the various incompetencies of his staff-level superiors, the ministers of state, and the ruler himself. He reasoned, with absolute assurance, that this amusement could easily still be incomplete at the time when his fur would be flapping from some Vilk rooftree.

The Intervoice put a sudden, loud quietus on his hopes of sleep.

"With the Captain's pardon, a Fleet Messenger requests permission to call and deliver."

"Granted," Henlo said, and, scratching his thigh with annoyance, unlatched his door.

II

The messenger handed him the usual sealed letter, saluted, and withdrew to the companionway. The message was brief—a few lines directing Henlo to report immediately to the Port Director's office for transportation.

Henlo looked at it with narrowed, speculative eyes. Tapping its folded length against his hip, he paced softly back and forth.

It meant something important, certainly. The bare word 'transportation,' without further amplification, conveyed as much. But what, precisely, *did* it mean? A secret conference of some kind, apparently—too secret to be entrusted to a Fleet Messenger.

He throttled the impulsive thought that it might, against all logic and reason, be his promotion to admiralty. He had not achieved his present status by acting against logic. It followed, then, that he was either being court martialed for some unknown offense, or was being entrusted with a special mission. Of the two possibilities, the latter seemed the more likely. His last intelligences from the capital had indicated only growing strength among his contacts.

Still, he hated uncertainty. He called for his personal vehicle with a rasp in his voice, and stalked up the companionway at a pace that forced the messenger to bound.

Ten minutes later he sprang from his vehicle, the messenger having peeled off to go it afoot, and marched into the Port Director's office, whence, shortly, he emerged by way of the rooftop platform. There he stepped into an official flyer, and was blasted across the sky at a screaming pace which almost, but not quite, matched the janglings galloping through his nerves. By the time he arrived at the capital he was still outwardly cool, as befitted his position, but he would have attacked mountain sajaks barehanded.

From its very beginning, the conference strained his nerves even more intolerably. It soon became evident that he was to be interviewed by the complete cabinet, and, when he finally entered the presence of the twelve men, he found himself confronted by a long table behind which they stood and stared at him silently.

He sat down and waited, his eyes slowly traveling up and down the table, his mental catalogues spinning as he tried to determine what course of conduct to pursue from his information about each man individually.

Finally, the Minister for Preparedness picked up a file—Henlo's own Fleet dossier—opened it, studied it for a moment, and put it down. With that formal signal that the hearing had begun, the Minister for the Fleet began to speak.

"You are Captain D' Henlo," he stated.

Henlo nodded. "I am."

"In command of *Torener*, City-Class sub-battleship, Fleet, currently fitting out at Port Terag."

"Yes."

The Minister for the Fleet nodded, and turned D' Henlo over to the Minister for Preparedness.

"Captain Henlo," the minister said, "we'll begin by assuming that only the passage of time lies between you and important commands. Your record indicates as much, and your decorations bear it out."

Henlo could see no advantage to himself in permitting the Minister to continue to believe that flattery could in any way alter his ingrained habits of caution and reserve.

"That is correct," he said coldly and matter-of-factly. The Minister for Preparedness grinned with one corner of his mouth, and nodded a brief acknowledgment of the situation.

"Let us, then, proceed in accordance with that appraisal," he said, this time sounding far more sincere.

"Captain Henlo," he continued, "I am sure you realize that the Fleet is totally incapable of prosecuting a successful defense of the Farlan Union against the Vilkai hordes. I believe, too, that you are perfectly aware of the factors which create that incapability. But I shall not compromise you—or ourselves—by asking you to confirm this belief. Let it suffice for me to tell you that we are about to appoint a new Admiral-in-Chief."

Inasmuch as Henlo had been keeping his features and bodily posture carefully inexpressive, he did not betray himself. But the tension of his nerves very nearly touched the danger point.

And still, something—some firmly-rooted, stubborn belief in his own thought processes—did not permit him to hope that the impossible gift was about to be given.

"Moreover," the Minister for Preparedness went on, "we are about to appoint to this high position a man who is a completely unknown and obscure officer in the Reserve."

Henlo's tail jumped once, quivered, and lashed out again in a vicious blow at the unheeding air. Then he had control of himself once more.

"Allow me to congratulate you on your composure," the minister said. "I hope it is indicative of the attitude with which other officers will greet the news."

Inwardly, Henlo was a riot of triggered emotions and flashing thought. He, too, congratulated himself on having lost control where it would not be noticed. But that was the only crumb of comfort he could offer himself.

A Reserve officer! Well, perhaps—just perhaps—that might not be the mortal insult a line officer's jump would have been. Paradoxically, Reserve officers were so far beyond the pale that most line men considered them incapable of affecting a regular fleet man enough to insult him. It remained to be seen how they'd react to following a pariah's orders.

But to have that as yet unnamed man do the very thing that Henlo had decided was impossible for himself! Henlo could not, honestly, decide whether to chuckle at such audacity or be overwhelmed with resentment. In either case, his emotional attitude would have no effect on the plan which he was already beginning to formulate for the man's eventual removal.

He returned his full attention to the Minister of Preparedness.

"The officer," the minister resumed, "is L' Miranid, and I assure you that he is a military genius. We are fully confident that, under his command, the Fleet will be able to defeat the Vilkai hordes."

Ah? And where had they found this paragon? But that was relatively unimportant. Probably he'd been instructing in tactics at some insignificant school. Offhand, Henlo could recall no one named Miranid, but it was a likely-enough name. He pried at its etymology and decided that it probably derived from the occupational cognomen "ranis," or metalworker. Which, of course, meant smith, and was at least of some use as an insight on the man's hereditary character. Most descendants of smiths called themselves by the plain 'Kalvit.'

There was the faint possibility that Miranid might suffer from the fatal weakness of pretentiousness. With that theory as a tentative start, Henlo was able to give part of his mind something with which to occupy itself while he outwardly devoted all his attention to the minister.

"Therefore," the minister was saying, "we have assigned your ship, *Torener*, to his flag. You will make the requisite preparations to quarter him in accordance with his station."

Henlo nodded.

"And, you will serve not only as ship commander under his direction, but will be his aide for the duration of hostilities."

Henlo nodded again, inwardly glowing with satisfaction. He'd have the man where he could observe his character—and learn from him.

The Minister for Preparedness picked up Henlo's dossier again, leafed to the very last page, and extracted the flimsy.

"I will now read the following officer's dossier copy of orders as issued by the Minister for the Fleet and endorsed by the Minister for Preparedness:

"Subject: Elevation in rank.

"A vacancy for the position of Admiral-in-Chief of the Grand Farlan Starfleet exists due to the death in battle of Admiral L' Miranid.

"Vice-Admiral D' Henlo is therefore directed to assume command of the Grand Farlan Starfleet with the title and permanent rank of Admiral-in-Chief.

"As signed, endorsed and executed this day . . ."

The Minister for Preparedness stopped reading at that point, and returned the flimsy to its place in the file.

"The date, unfortunately, is yet to be determined," he

said, staring fixedly at Henlo. "It will coincide with the date of that battle which, in your judgment, determines the issue beyond doubt in Farla's favor. Have I made myself clear?"

Henlo nodded. "Yes, sir, very clear." As Henlo spoke he sent a quick look up and down the ministerial ranks. The thought struck him that the ministers might be incapable of educating good line officers, but that they were certainly nonpareils at picking assassins.

"I may assume," he said, "that my elevation to the rank of Vice-Admiral will come at some convenient time during the next year?"

"We had thought," the Minister for the Fleet said, "to implement it as of this date."

"I would respectfully suggest that it be withheld until I have furnished a convenient pretext in the form of significant battle action," Henlo replied.

The Minister for Preparedness nodded slowly. "An excellent suggestion." He looked at Henlo shrewdly. "May I say, Captain Henlo, that you are an even more remarkable man than your record would indicate."

Henlo accepted the compliment gracefully. He hated equivocal situations. Now he could be sure that he would also have to guard against the Ministry's attempts to assassinate *him*.

All in all, it had been a nerve-wracking but remarkable and satisfying session.

III

Henlo returned to *Torener* with his nerves in the fine, whetted condition which had always produced his best thinking. He called in his Executive Officer immediately, and issued orders for the provision of admiral's facilities aboard ship.

"Are we going to carry Rahoul's flag, sir?" the exec asked.

"That's right," Henlo said, and grinned nastily at his subordinate's disconcerted expression. He had fully expected the story of Miranid's promotion to become current almost immediately. It only remained for him to discover just what, in the exec's estimation, constituted subtle probing.

"Ah—I meant Admiral Miranid, of course, rather than the late Commander," the man said hastily. "A mistake of the tongue."

"Undoubtedly. A bit character revealing, wouldn't you say?"

The exec departed in hasty confusion. Nevertheless, Henlo reflected, he would have used exactly the same approach himself, three years earlier. In about six years, that officer might require judicious attention.

Every carefully analyzed little fragment of psychological data helped keep a man's fur on.

But all this was merely automatic routine. What mattered now was Miranid. What manner of man was he? Henlo had no intention of following his carefully implied orders until he'd had a chance to suck the ephemeral admiral dry of any useful political techniques he might have developed.

And, for that matter, precisely *why* did Miranid have to be removed?

Miranid did not arrive before *Torener* was completely fitted-out and ready to take her place with the fleet. In that interval, Henlo managed to keep his own tensions from showing, and was also able to get a fair idea of the reactions his subordinate officers would manifest.

Heaven only knew what the regular officers in the remainder of the fleet were thinking. Aboard *Torener*, Henlo awaited his arrival with a mixture of curiosity and amusement. The admiral would find it rough going.

Miranid arrived at night. A thin, close-packed man with thick but dull fur, he marched up the lowered ship's ramp with a lithe grace and quickness to his movements that reminded Henlo of something wild.

The formalities were short, as usual, since the admiral was presumed competent until proved otherwise. As a matter of fact, Henlo had arranged it nicely, with the ship's officers lined up in order of rank and with himself at their head, of course. The required minimal exchange of salutes finished the entire ceremony in a quarter of an hour.

Rahoul, who had set something of a standard for incapability, had been welcomed to the Ministerial Office Building with three full hours of music, saluting, and drill, during the progress of which he had grown increasingly restive. At the conclusion, he had taken the un-subtle hint, and not even presented himself at the Ministry before going home and suiciding.

"My compliments on your evident good health," Miranid said, in the usual formula.

"And mine on yours," Henlo replied neutrally enough.

They exchanged no further amenities. Miranid assumed command immediately, and, with a startling familiarity for the more esoteric flight characteristics of the City Class, had *Torener* blasted up to spearhead the formation in which the remainder of the fleet lay.

Henlo wondered, briefly, whether he was going to make his command address to the fleet immediately, or wait until all ships had acknowledged *Torener's* arrival. Apparently, some of them were being deliberately laggard in so doing.

Miranid threw a quick glance at the Admiral's Plot board which had been installed in one of the control room bulkheads. The white lights marking the positions of friendly ships were only sparsely modified to pink by the brilliant red "Your Position Determined and Acknowledged" lights.

He grunted, and for a moment Henlo thought he was going to turn the ship back to Captain's command and make the bold stroke of beginning the customary address immediately, regardless of whether those ships pretended not to know of his presence.

Miranid was across the compartment in three strides, and in the Master Navigator's chair. "Grab holds," he lashed out, and Henlo got a palm around a stanchion just as *Torener* spurted ahead.

The Plot board went crazy. His head spinning, his free arm busy fending off loose equipment that came flying at him, Henlo realized dimly, and with horror, that Miranid had interlocked all of the fleet's navigators with his own controls.

It was over in a third of an hour. Unspeaking, his hands flashing over the navigation board, and with the same highly unexpected familiarity with the capacities of even the most inconsequential Fleet vessels, the new admiral had the entire armada whipped into a compact group along unfamiliar but, to Henlo, brilliant organizational lines. And the entire Grand Farlan Starfleet was leaving the home system rapidly behind, pursuing a course which Henlo recognized as being the most deceptive possible while still permitting rapid diversion toward the very part of the Vilkai territories which Henlo had long decided was ripest for attack.

So much for Miranid's first move. When he flicked the switch that unlocked the other ships' navigating computers, the second began almost instantly.

The admiral threw a look over his shoulder at the Plot chart. In the same motion, he scooped up an Intervoice microphone.

"Gunnery."

"Gunnery here."

"Coordinates as indicated—" He punched out a position for the gun computers. "Fire!"

And *Regra*, an off-screen destroyer that had instantly attempted to go into turnover and return to the home system, burst apart.

Then, at last, Miranid switched over to General Comm and made his command address to the fleet. It was this:

"Have I made myself clear?"

He switched off, got out of the chair, and stalked by Henlo.

"Your ship, Captain," he said.

"Thank you, sir," Henlo said unsteadily, and Miranid clanged the airtight hatch behind him as he strode away toward his cabin. In the control compartment, officers and men with anomalous expressions began picking up the loose gear they had assumed it was safe to unlatch once *Torener* had rendezvoused with the fleet.

IV

Once again, Henlo sat in his cabin, trying to sleep. And again, it was not the innumerable creakings and drummings of a ship running under constant acceleration that kept him from succeeding. His thoughts were in a hopeless muddle.

Where had they found Miranid—or, rather, and with much more apparent logic—where had Miranid been before he chose to reveal himself?

Point Number One: No officer in the fleet—and Henlo had checked thoroughly—had ever heard of any officer, Reserve or no, named L' Miranid. Most of them had simply shrugged their ignorance off, and none of them were actively curious. This despite the fact that Henlo would have wagered heavily on the fleet's containing so thorough a cross-section of all Fleet officers that, between them, they must have met or heard of everyone who had ever held a relatively minor post.

Point Number Two: The Fleet was Miranid's, pin, stock, and barrel. Not one of the line Fleet officers would now dream of challenging his authority. Apparently, Henlo was the only one who still questioned its validity.

Point Number Three: The reason behind the sudden switch in the officers' attitudes was painfully apparent—painfully because Henlo had to admit that it was also the cause of his own unaccustomed confusion. Miranid had over-awed them all.

In a society based on the supremacy of the strong over the weak, that had been an audacious maneuver. And Miranid had carried it off without a flaw.

What hurt was that Henlo was himself over-awed, a totally unfamiliar sensation, and one which sat badly on his stomach.

In the first place, Miranid had followed what was, in retrospect, the most logical and effective plan. He had acted in a manner so dramatically ruthless that he had made the Fleet understand that he was capable of besting it single-handed.

Now that he had seen the triumph demonstrated, and felt its effect, Henlo had to admire it. But he could never have initiated it, or, having thought of it, dared take the risk.

Miranid *was* a genius!

Well, he'd planned to learn from the man, hadn't he? Apparently, Miranid was going to be his post-graduate course.

Henlo felt a surge of returning confidence. Of all the Fleet officers, only he had a powerful shield against Miranid's awe-inspiring strength.

The strong man dies as easily as the weak, and Miranid's life was in Henlo's hand.

That, above all other things, was Henlo's source of hidden—and therefore even stronger—strength.

Once again, D' Henlo was not given his sleep. Once again, the Intervoice called him.

"Admiral's request and wish: Captain D' Henlo to report at once to Admiral's cabin."

Henlo stood up, grunted, "Complying," and, his tail not quite bar-steady, walked down the companionway to Miranid's cabin.

When he knocked, he heard Miranid pushing back a chair before his voice came through the door. "Will you enter?"

"With your permission," Henlo replied, according to formula. Apparently, Miranid was going to maintain his advantage by standing in Henlo's presence—which would, most probably, be a seated one.

"Granted," came from beyond the door.

Henlo shrugged. He felt no qualms about the traditional position of inferiority. It meant nothing. But it might be advantageous to pretend otherwise.

He stepped in, and Miranid turned away from his desk. "Please stand," he said briefly, spreading a star chart on the desk. "I'd like you to know my plans for the next few days."

"Of course, Admiral," Henlo said, moving forward to the chart and grimacing briefly behind Miranid's back. The man was thoroughly unpredictable.

He comforted himself with the thought that persistent unpredictability was predictable.

"I assume, Captain, that you've had time to decide against opposing me," Miranid said casually, touching the fleet's present position with one point of his dividers.

Henlo's whiskers quivered in the general ripple that crossed his facial fur.

"Therefore," Miranid went on in the same tone, "here's our plan for the time being." The dividers twirled from point to point, like a dancer describing an involuted spiral, and one point sank into the chart at Ceroii, a Vilkan holding some light-years within their ragged frontier. "So. Three days under acceleration, two in braking. We come out of hyperspace three Standard hours before we reach there. Can you tell me why I'm giving them that much warning?"

Henlo had recovered by a considerable application of will. He decided to play Miranid's game for the time being.

Moreover, the admiral was using substantially the same tactics he had himself planned, but never, of course, hoped to see executed.

"I would say, sir, that your plan is to make Ceroii a diversion. Three hours' warning will permit them to call for help, but not to mount a substantial defense. I suggest, respectfully, that you then intend to move rapidly to some other sector—Ganelash, or Dira, either of which is liable to be left open by the Vilkan rush to defend at Ceroii—or perhaps even to split the fleet and attack both. Your subsequent maneuvers would depend on what sector would next be left vulnerable by the inevitable rushing-about which these tactics will produce among the enraged barbarians."

Miranid nodded. "Quite correct, Captain. I congratulate you as an apt strategist. A quality which," he added dryly, "seems to be rare in the Grand Farlan Starfleet."

Henlo could not decide exactly how the remark was meant—whether as an observation that it was remarkable for anyone to be as good as Miranid, or simply as the normal Reserve officer's opportunity to make some pointed observations.

Miranid held up a finger. "One correction. I *will* split the fleet after Ceoii—but into three parts. Some Vilkan sub-chief may just keep his head sufficiently to launch direct retaliation at Farla. We'll need some ships to delay any such move until we can catch him from behind. I plan to use Vice-Admiral Y' Gern. Does this agree with your estimation of him?"

"Your grasp of the characters of your officers is remarkable," Henlo managed to say.

It was quite true. Gern was perhaps the one Vice-Admiral in the fleet who had any stomach to him, together with the strength to command such an action. But the important part of that last announcement had been Miranid's revelation of his intention of attacking Ganelash and Dira with only one-third of a fleet at each vital point. It just might be done, but it would be hot work. And the casual manner in which the man had provided for the englobement of any possible retaliators was an even more astonishing indication of just how Miranid's tactical mind worked.

It was the same basic principle which had given him the fleet within an hour of his first setting foot on his flagship. He out-thought his opponents completely, and then let their own efforts provide him with the means for unfolding his tactics.

Where, *where* had they found Miranid?

"I'll ask you, as my aide, to draw up the detailed battle plan, Captain Henlo," Miranid said.

"Yes, sir," Henlo replied. It was a plain indication that their conference had ended. "With your permission?"

"You may leave."

Henlo returned to his own cabin, and once more tried to find an hour's time in which to sleep.

V

Ceroii was, effectively speaking, dust, and Ganelash flamed under Henlo's guns. Four parsecs away, he knew, *Larharis*, temporarily carrying Miranid's flag, was giving Dira the same breakfast.

Henlo's original thesis—and Miranid's, obviously—was

being proved correct. The Vilkan horde was not a homogenous body, and the Vilk forces, though numerous, were not organized. They could roll up empires like a pack of sajaks stampeding cattle, but they were highly vulnerable to the rush-and-slash tactics that Miranid was using.

Particularly were they vulnerable when inter-tribal jealousies did more to help than another fleetful of guns. A half-day's travel from Ganelash, for instance, was a numerous force of Vilks. If Henlo knew of them, they assuredly knew of Henlo and what he was doing. But those ships were busy idling, waiting until the Farlans were through. The Vilk commander was a sworn blood-enemy of Ganelash's defender, and he preferred to wait and then move in to finish the job—and pick up the loot. Whether he would even bother to swipe at the Farlans was problematical.

And as far as Henlo knew, Vice-Admiral Gern's detachment had yet to detect even one Vilkan ship blazing toward Farla.

Henlo surveyed the ruined planet below and signaled for the action to be broken off. It might be just as well to leave those hungry Vilks some unbroken loot to occupy them.

The fleet rendezvoused around Gern, and Henlo noticed that there had been few casualties—fewer even than he'd anticipated. Once he'd listened to his brother officers, he discovered the reason. They were almost unanimous in their nearly un-Farlan admiration for Miranid, and were working with a coordination no previous Admiral-in-Chief had been able to beg out of them.

Henlo scratched the side of his nose, telling himself that if he were the Minister for Preparedness, he would most certainly have the man killed the instant victory was assured.

But how could anyone have anticipated this development? It had so come about that the man had been wise beyond his knowledge. However, the final battle was still a good time away and might never come. He had leisure in which to investigate—and meanwhile there was a war to prosecute . . .

The war continued in much the same pattern as before, at

least in its early months. Miranid was continually nipping at soft spots, then gouging away the even softer areas which their defense would expose. It was Miranid's initiative at every battle, and he carried it off well.

He persistently refused to close with Vilkan fleets in space, where the only available loot and glory would be in the destruction of his own fleet, and thus he avoided overwhelming opposition. Instead, he attacked planetary bases, which were difficult to defend but easy to destroy. He attacked with utter ruthlessness, devoting no thought, apparently, to the fact that the bases were almost completely inhabited by subject nationals of former independent empires, and only garrisoned by Vilks.

There was logic behind that, too. Each planet constituted the loot and physical embodiment of glory belonging to some Vilkan war-prince. His cousin princes were invariably only too glad to assign that loot to their own coffers after the Farlans had left. Then, with their ships crammed, they would retreat to their faraway home planets to celebrate before returning to the now perceptibly diminishing frontier. If they returned at all, for, after all, they had anxious heirs at home.

The Farlan power was not in their guns—it was in Miranid's phenomenal mind.

VI

Once again, the fleet rendezvoused, and once again Miranid conferred with Vice-Admiral Henlo. Henlo had his own flagship now, for the fleet had been reinforced to almost half-again its original strength, and functioned as a loose group of semi-autonomous units.

Henlo's old executive officer had *Torener* now, and Henlo occasionally wondered what inspirations the man drew from pacing the same bridge that Miranid had trod. Grandiose ones, probably, for he noticed that *Torener* was constantly being crippled in over-audacious actions. Well, so much the better. Perhaps, someday, *Torener* might not rendezvous at all.

His Vice-Admiralty, Henlo reflected, together with the

fleet's strength being so augmented as to give him a substantial command, was strongly indicative of sentiments in the ministries. They looked for a speedy end to the fabulously successful war—and to L' Miranid. To hasten the day, Henlo's own position was being strengthened.

That reckless gamble with the unpredictable might yet prove the costliest mistake their august ministerial ambitions could make. The over-paid assassin might sometimes thus be provided with the price of empire.

But that was for another, albeit hastened, day, he reminded himself as his aide knocked on Miranid's door.

There was the usual exchange of formulas, and then Henlo, leaving his aide in the companionway, entered Miranid's cabin.

"Henlo, I compliment you on your evident good health."

"And I you on yours, Admiral," Henlo replied. Miranid, as usual, was alone in his quarters, and the chart in his hand, and the desk on which he laid it, might have been the same as those aboard the now-forgotten *Torener*.

But the situation, Admiral, Henlo commented to himself, is not precisely the same.

Miranid had not changed. The thick fur was just as thick—and just as lifeless in sheen—and the tail was as stiff and rigidly unmoving as ever. It was Henlo who had changed—Henlo, whose horizons became more glowingly attainable with every planet that marked the smoking, death-blazoned track into Vilkai.

"Well, Henlo, it seems we constantly meet in situations which are superficially the same, but fundamentally different," Miranid remarked, and for a moment Henlo's heart stood still. He'd been away from the admiral too long. He had forgotten the man's almost terrifying perception of mind.

Not for the first time—but for the first time so strongly— Henlo wondered if that perception could possibly be so limited as not to fully comprehend what the ministries had in mind for him—and whom they had chosen to supplant him.

But Miranid, apparently at least, was referring to something else.

"As you've no doubt realized," he said, "we can no longer hope to capitalize so successfully on the inherent barbarian weaknesses of our enemies. Up to now, we have been operating entirely outside their actual borders. But the day the first Vilkan females and pups die will be the day the entire horde forgets everything but the preservation of the communal hearth.

"We shall then see," he added drily, "which among all our heroes of the Grand Farlan Starfleet are merely men."

"I've been thinking along much the same lines," Henlo agreed.

Miranid nodded. "A happy faculty."

And again, Henlo could not determine within himself just how the admiral had intended the comment to be taken.

"Did you know, Henlo, that certain eminent military tacticians have proved to my satisfaction that war in space is impossible?"

Henlo arched the fur over his eyes. "I haven't heard the theory."

"No, I didn't think you had," Miranid said in a rambling tone of voice. "However, our present situation is a splendid example.

"Consider. If you picture the present Vilkan holdings as a solid sphere in space, bristling with weapons pointed outward, and our own fleet as a hollow sphere designed to contain and crush it, then you must allow that all Farla with half the Galaxy to help it could not supply us with enough strength to keep our sphere impenetrable from the inside at all points. With the further problem of uncertain ship detection in hyperspace we could not prevent repeated breakthroughs from the inside.

"Once our hollow sphere is broken it is caught between two fires, and gradually decimated if it does not withdraw into a larger, and even more porous, sphere—which can again be broken. Thus, stalemate, eventual disgust, and, finally inconclusive peace at an inconclusive price.

"Now, since we are not going to be foolish enough to form such a sphere the only alternative is to attempt an attack by a knife-like method. We can spit, split, slice, or whittle.

"Spitting is out of the question. If we try to drive through, we expose ourselves to attack from all sides. The splitting procedure gives rise to the same objections. This leaves slicing or whittling—and since a whittle is only a small slice, or a slice a large whittle, let us discuss them simultaneously."

Miranid looked steadily at Henlo.

"I will not whittle if I can slice, but I cannot slice, and for the same reason, I cannot whittle. For this is not a clay sphere, Henlo, but a steel ball—and red-hot, to boot. With every stroke I make, I will lose a greater percentage of my available ships than the enemy will.

"His supply lines are short—I've shortened them for him. His ships can land, be repaired, refueled, and re-armed, their crews replaced by fresh men, and sent back into battle a hundred times for each new ship that can reach me from Farla. I have a limited supply of men, equipment, and food. With every stroke, I wear down my sharpness a little more."

He paused an instant, then went on, "Until, finally, I attack the sphere for one last time and my dull, worn knife slips off the surface without leaving an impression. So, again, stalemate, eventual disgust, and no true peace—that is, no peace which will not leave conditions immediately ripe for another useless war.

"I would say, as a matter of fact, that this same theory makes true peace impossible so long as any wars are attempted."

Miranid grinned at Henlo, his professorial mood abruptly ended. "Fortunately, in this special case, we can do the impossible on both counts."

Henlo granted that it all seemed to make sense—and that Miranid was holding some effective strategy between his ears. It was less easy, however, to understand why the lecture had been launched in the first place. After all, if Miranid had his strategy carefully planned, all the situation required was for him to simply lay that strategy out, and have Henlo execute it.

It could only mean that Miranid's purposes extended far beyond the mere winning of a war—a fact which Henlo naturally assumed in connection with anyone engaged in any sort of activity. But this was the first time that Miranid had ever revealed his thoughts so candidly.

Was Miranid, too, conscious that things might come to an unexpectedly large head at that last battle?

Henlo noticed with a start that Miranid had deliberately been giving him time to arrive at his conclusions. The admiral grinned again, but now resumed the thread of the discussion without making any comment.

"Our barbarian friends have another weakness, which we have up to this point not been able to utilize without compromising its existence. I've carefully saved it until now, and they have considerately not discovered it within themselves.

"The Vilks, of course, were able to make war quite successfully. Since they were operating as a horde of mobile independent principalities, and since they were after loot and glory only, they were never forced to gain what civilized nations would term 'victory,' or 'conquest.'

"They were reapers, harvesting the same field again and again, and gradually extending their borders. They had no time for the re-education of subject peoples to their own ideals or patriotic causes—a fact further implemented by their total lack of such civilized appurtenances. They merely informed their vassals that they had become the property of whatever Vilk it happened to be, and levied tribute accordingly. They left it to the natural fertility of the Vilk soldier to gradually erase all traces of independent nationality among such nations as could interbreed, and to the natural inertia of generations of slavery among such as could not.

"The result has been the gradual accumulation, in Vilk ranks, of a number of Vilks who are not Vilks."

Miranid seemed anxious to stress the point.

"And these Vilks may be good, barbarian Vilks like all

the rest of them. But some of them inevitably feel that their *particular* kind of Vilk is better fitted to rule the communal roost.

"A situation, you will agree, which does not apply among such civilized communities as Farla, which may have its internal dissensions, but no special uniforms of hide-color, limb-distribution, or digital anomalies around which infra-nationalistic sentiments may be rallied."

Miranid stabbed the chart with his dividers. "We will slice here, here, and here, with most of our lighter units supported by some heavier groups. You and I, Henlo, will take the remainder of the main fleet and spit right through to Vilkai, where we will crown some highly un-Vilkish Vilk king of the Vilks, and then leave him to perish.

"The entire sorry mess will slash itself to suicide in the petty nationalistic squabbles which are sure to follow the precedent we set them. We will be enabled to do so quite easily by the allies which our housewifely intelligence corps has neatly suborned for us."

Miranid stared down at the chart, his weight on his spread arms.

"Henlo," he said thoughtfully, "I think we may have come, finally, to our last battle."

VII

The deceleration of apparent time had begun for Henlo a few moments before, when he had reached that same conclusion. He realized, on the level of cold reason, that it was not time which was slowing. It was his own thoughts which were speeding, driving through his brain so fast that they tricked the time-sense geared to his normal thinking pace. But, nevertheless, it seemed to him that the world was drowned in glue through which only he moved with ease and fluidity.

It was a phenomenon of mind that came to him in battles and conspiracies, and he enjoyed it, in one special part of his mind, whenever it came. And it was a paradox of the situation that he thereby enjoyed it less, for he arrived at his inevitable conclusion sooner, and thus ended the moment stolen from mortality.

"It would certainly seem so," he said calmly, in agreement with Miranid's conviction. "But we can still lose the war. Something can go wrong. And if it does, every other battle will have been wasted."

Miranid nodded. "You're quite right. But I don't think anything disastrous will happen. So plan this battle as though it were the last, definitely."

He grinned. The lopsided expression was known throughout the fleet, and the men—officers and crew—had long ago nicknamed him "The Laughing Genius."

"Because," he said, "even if it isn't, we'll never plan another."

No, thought Henlo, we never will. Even if it is.

"Your permission?"

"Granted."

Henlo turned to go, and was at the door when Miranid called him back. The admiral was looking at him cautiously, as if trying to decide how far he might go. Finally he seemed to come to a conclusion, for he spoke abruptly.

"Henlo," he said, "you're a first-class phenomenon, for Farla. Somehow, you got by the System, probably by being infinitely superior in your special kind of politics to the people who administer it. But are you phenomenon enough to have figured out what your rapid promotions are leading up to?"

"Admiral?" Henlo looked puzzled. He was not, but he looked it, which, among Farlans, amounted to the same thing for conversational purposes.

Miranid looked at him shrewdly. "I thought so." He shook his head, his eyes enigmatical with an emotional shading which just might have been admiration.

"One favor, Henlo."

"Surely, sir. What is it?"

"Would you repeat, for what you may classify as my whimsical amusement, the standard Farlan textbook definition of paranoia?"

"Paranoia, sir? Why, I believe paranoia is that form of

psychosis which is characterized by delusions in the subject of benevolence toward the world in general and of his almost certain inferiority to all other individuals. It's accompanied by an irrational persistence in believing only good of others.

"It is most easily detected by the manifestation of the following symptoms: incurable addiction to literal truth in the transmission of information, and an unshakable conviction that the method of success is the commission of as many genuinely altruistic favors as possible to as many individuals as possible. The altruism is coupled with the expectation of genuinely reciprocal action on the part of other individuals."

"Thank you, Henlo," Miranid said, as if chuckling at some secret joke. "I just wanted to hear it again."

Henlo ended the conversation with a few neutral conclusion-formula phrases, and left to plan his battle.

His battle, not Miranid's. It was obvious, now, that Miranid knew that there was something strong and sinister upwind. But he only knew it in the same manner that Henlo was cognizant of something similar planned for himself. Logic dictated that no man as powerful as either of them had become could be permitted to live.

But while Henlo could be almost certain that none of his subordinates would dare take the risk, Miranid must, this near the end of his extraordinary appointment, be trying desperately to determine who it was that had been given the orders for his assassination.

Come to think of it, Miranid had just as many reasons—just as many *identical* reasons—for believing that none of *his* subordinates would dare . . . Including Henlo . . .

Including Henlo!

Suddenly, Henlo found himself wondering desperately who *his* unobtrusive executioner might be. And very shortly thereafter realized just how shrewd and sharp a parallel Miranid had drawn between them. For there could be no doubt that Miranid understood completely that his own sudden promotion could only result in assassination, once his usefulness had come to an end.

He realized, too, the significance of Miranid's request for the definition of paranoia. Only the insane could expect anything else. And both he and Miranid were eminently sane men. Too sane, perhaps, to let themselves be murdered and murdered murderer in turn?

Miranid had wondered how close to death he had stepped, and then had stepped safely away, by expressing his conclusion that this might not be the last battle.

And he had been right. It would be the last against the Vilks, perhaps, but not their last. Not their last together.

Cold logic drove Henlo to the conclusion that he could not let Miranid die, if he himself hoped to live.

He began to reason accordingly. Once more he spent his alloted nap-time in thought, but the sacrifice was worth the price. By the time he was ready to begin particularizing Miranid's general plan for the conquest of Vilkai, the far more important plan was carefully drawn up and filed safely in his brain.

VIII

The lesser plan worked perfectly. While the lighter part of the Farlan fleet chopped at one side of the tight Vilk sphere, Miranid, with Henlo on his bridge, led the stabbing force that hissed toward Vilkai.

They met no serious opposition. With every solar system their forces left behind them, their fleet grew in groups of eight ships, twelve, or twenty, each led by a fierce-visaged nominal Vilk who was actually a Ganelash, or Diran, or Tylhean, or whatever other kind of Vilk by adoption he might racially be.

A few of them stayed with their ships, but most of them turned command over to the fleet's general control, and came to Miranid's flagship. There they and the admiral and Henlo stood and plotted out each new contact with each successive race of 'Vilks,' each of whom, of course, were convinced that in their people rested true Vilk destiny.

Still, they got along well enough together aboard the ship. They and the Farlan admiral seemed to understand each other, despite the language barriers. Henlo appraised them all for first-class fighting men, as good as anything Farla was likely to turn up, and in far greater numbers.

He suspected strongly that Miranid's quoted theory might well have proven correct in the case of the Vilks, at least. And he made the first move of the greater battle. Somehow, in the course of an otherwise unimpressive battle, *Torener*, still fighting with Henlo's old executive officer still commanding, was "accidentally" caught in the flagship's gunfire and completely destroyed.

Henlo felt easier in his stomach. But, of course, it had only been a move directed by the logic of probabilities, which had never yet in the history of man been so acted upon as to produce more than a probable certainty.

"Most regrettable," Miranid had commented when Henlo reported the accident to him. His whiskers had twitched, and Henlo felt sure that, though there had been no actual exchange of plans between them, Miranid's own moves would mesh neatly with his own, once they had been decided on.

To guard against the outside contingency that they might, at this point, mesh too neatly, he took every possible precaution against being so far physically from Miranid as the battle progressed that any accident to himself might not be mutual.

More and more, Henlo realized, the pressure of events and actions was welding them together into a tacit alliance—an alliance that was not so much the product of mutual desire as the result of their sharing a common, deadly danger.

They were well-matched, but they were, nevertheless, peculiar bedfellows.

"Odd people, these, to be working together," Miranid commented casually one day when he and Henlo were standing some distance away from the allied chiefs. Henlo, of course, saw the actual meaning behind the parallel, and nodded.

"And yet, similar," Miranid went on. "Nature seems to have chosen the symmetrical quadruped as the basic form with which to supplement most of her intelligences. Some of them she has turned into bipeds by making them walk erect, and others she has tilted onto their forelimbs. But they are all basically the same, and one intelligence is basically capable of understanding another."

"I see your meaning exactly, sir," Henlo replied, and Miranid grinned his trademark laugh . . .

Vilkai was almost an anti-climax. It fell without serious opposition to half the spearheading segment, while the remainder of the heavy fleet formed a sphere around the system and then expanded outward, relentlessly crushing Vilk ships against the bottom of the hollow globe which the lighter ships had formed from outside.

The formation was, of course, extremely porous. But the surviving Vilks were successfully scattered and thus broken up into the small tribes which Miranid desired—to trouble whatever king sat on the sham throne at Vilkai.

Now, Henlo knew, he and Miranid had been set free to fight their personal war with the Farlan ministries. Taut, keyed-up to fighting pitch, he hurried down the companionway to Miranid's quarters.

IX

"Well, Henlo, the fleet celebrates," the admiral said drily while the sounds of men savagely drunk with joy and victory, glory and alcohol, according to their weaknesses, echoed through the ship's gaping metal corridors.

Henlo smiled. "Sir, I compliment you on your evident and *continued* good health," he said.

"And I you on yours," Miranid replied. "So it *was* you they detailed." He grinned. "A poor choice, as they'll find out." He took a small flask of amber fluid out of a cabinet, poured it into a cup, and stood looking at it thoughtfully.

"I'd offer you some of this, Henlo, but I don't think you'd like it. It's an acquired taste, for all the merchants say. For that matter, I don't even know if I'll like it, with these taste buds."

He raised the cup to his mouth, and took a sip. Then he threw his head back and said something with a ritual ring to it, but in a language so foreign that even Henlo could understand that his tongue and vocal cords had difficulty in forming the sounds properly. Then he drained the cup and shook himself with pleasure. It was the first time Henlo had ever seen him display normal gratification at some appealing vice.

He set the cup down and grinned at Henlo. "That's my genuine trademark, Admiral-in-Chief D' Henlo. One toast in skaatch to the Agency when I finish a job. But you wouldn't know."

Henlo looked at him with complete mystification, and Miranid widened his grin. "You *were* going to suggest your announcing to Farla that I had died in battle, weren't you. In accordance with the orders handed you by the Minister for Preparedness. A most engaging rascal. But he should have done something about his inability to recognize superior talent—meaning yours, not mine."

"Substantially, that was my plan, yes," Henlo said, still trying to glean all of Miranid's implications from his almost incomprehensible remarks. "The next step, of course, would have been to play on your remarkable popularity with the fleet. We would have jointly revealed the entire plot to them, declared that no such government was fit to rule, and staged a coup."

"Thereafter ruling together in prosperous harmony, eh, my *Machiavellian* comrade?"

Henlo tried to find some meaning for the exotic word, as he had tried for *skaatch*, and similarly failed.

"Well, that's precisely what we shall do, up to a point," Miranid assured him. "But with one modification. Just before we reach Farla, I shall die most convincingly—and most, to remove all doubts from the minds of the fleet, naturally. My dying wish shall be to be buried in space, in a lifeboat. That lifeboat, conveniently enough for me, shall be pointed toward Earth.

"I might hastily add, at this point, Henlo, that my fur may be grafted and my tail false, but the weapons built into me are far from imitations. I should not advise your indulging your natural instincts when I tell you, as I tell you now, that I am an Earthman."

Henlo's tail lashed violently, and his eyes dilated. He had not lost control of himself so thoroughly since his youth. He stared at Miranid for several silent moments, then moved his hand slowly toward his sidearm.

Miranid chuckled. "I didn't think you'd bluff." He flexed his shoulders and something small and glittering pushed its nose out of the thick, dead fur at the base of his heavy pectorals. "That's one of them, Henlo. Just one, and don't make me stretch any farther, or it will go off." The glittering thing was pointed directly at Henlo's skull. "Besides, you need me. You need me right up to the last, when I chug off valiantly in my steel mausoleum. You'll never get the fleet to accept your succession to leadership unless I pass it to you."

Henlo stared malevolently at the Earthman, and his lipless mouth compressed until it almost disappeared. But he took his hand away from the sidearm.

"I am, as I've said, an Earthman—a hired soldier, if you'll believe there are such people. And believe me, the Minister for Preparedness was only too glad to get me—neglecting to realize that I had his little schemes figured out before he even conceived them.

"After all," he said depreciatingly, "We've got paranoids on Earth, too."

Henlo failed to understand the reference.

"And, for what it's worth as a compliment—a genuine, sincere, altruistic compliment, Henlo—even if I could, I wouldn't take my chances with you, on Farla. After all, I'm getting old, and you're bound to improve over even the remarkable standard you now maintain."

Miranid *really* smiled then, with the mellow warmth of an undefeated soldier-philosopher cheered by wine.

"Can an entire society be psychotic and not realize it? Apparently it can. All of you Farlans have passed over the borderline. You are all paranoids. You are all twice as mad as March hares. But you have a beautiful way of rationalizing it—exemplified in the Farlan definition of paranoia. So long as you hold fast to that definition, which is the exact

pposite of the truth in all respects, you will continue to
elieve that black is white, and white black!"

X

Ienlo walked slowly away from the window.

The years he had bought so painfully were gone, dribbled
way in hours here and half-hours there, and now suddenly
t was as though that half-century had never been, except in
he memory of a senile old man.

Slowly, through the spinning of the years, he had put the
tructure together, guessing what he must and confirming
vhen he could, until he could see it, looming over Farla,
asting shadows deeper than the night.

For one man—even the Laughing Genius the fleet still
emembered so fondly and so erroneously—could never
ave arranged so complicated a negotiation, or had himself
o well disguised and indoctrinated. And Miranid—the
:arthman, rather, an Earthman named Smith—had just
nce, in one cryptic phrase, mentioned an agency. *The
Agency*.

There were agencies of various kinds on Farla, dealing in
ervices and commodities, and collecting their percentages.
A pity, he thought, that none of them dealt in years. But it
vas The Agency which would have the necessary facilities
or locating, offering, and indoctrinating the required talent.

Smith. Smith, and how many more like him? The leaders
f the Vilk tribes that had allied themselves with the fleet?
'es . . . and the others. The others he *knew* were agents.
"he great leaders of the hundred empires that had sprung
emarkably to life from the blasted ashes of the Vilk's
:aptive nations, all squabbling among themselves, all fight-
ng stalemate wars—and all hating Farla, for it had been
'arlan ships and Farlan guns that had systematically
coured their planets.

The barbarian empire was gone, collapsed in its own
lood, as Smith had predicted. In its place were a hundred
ivilizations, pressing close to Farla's borders.

Bit by bit, he had given his frontiers away to them, rather
han fight. Piece by piece, they had tattered Farla's hide.

For he did not dare leave Farla to lead the fleet—he had too
many heirs at home. And the fleet, in any case, was weaker
than ever. He had not dared leave it intact, or permit it to
have able officers.

Governments were covetous of governing, he had once
told himself.

He laughed bitterly. Here, in this impregnable fortress
dungeon that was his capitol, *he* was the government. And
his heirs had waited patiently, once he'd taught them its
impregnability. But now it was over. They'd waited pa
tiently, as the Earthmen were waiting.

Wars in space were impossible. But the strength of
Farla's fleet had not been in her guns, but in Smith's mind.
An Earthman's mind.

And he wondered now, as the darkest shadows fell, how
much was in the minds of the Earthmen. Had they, as he
himself once had, chosen the definite situation in preference
to the equivocal? Had they deliberately given him all these
hints, knowing that he must act as he had, stripping Farla's
strength in exchange for her life, rather than ever hire an
Agency hero to give Farla another poison dose of treacher
ous strength?

Certainly, they had never even attempted to contact him.
But were they waiting now, only until his successor took his
place, to offer pat salvation to the bleeding Farlan Empire?
Waiting for this new opportunity?

They had used Farla to destroy Vilkai, and Farla to
destroy Farla. Would they use Farla again, to sub-divide
space into smaller and smaller empires until there were no
longer any foes to throw their ships back to the piddling
solar system from whence they came?

He did not know. But he suspected.

He suspected. But he did not know.

And there had been nothing for him to do but follow
either one track or the other, and both roads led to Earth.

Soon, he suspected, all roads, all over the Galaxy, would
lead to Earth. To wily, scheming Earth.

The die had been cast.

TIME LAG

Poul Anderson

522 *Anno Coloniae Conditae:*

Elva was on her way back, within sight of home, when the raid came.

For nineteen thirty-hour days, riding in high forests where sunlight slanted through leaves, across ridges where grass and the first red lampflowers rippled under springtime winds, sleeping by night beneath the sky or in the hut of some woodsdweller—once, even, in a nest of Alfavala, where the wild little folk twittered in the dark and their eyes glowed at her—she had been gone. Her original departure was reluctant. Her husband of two years, her child of one, the lake and fields and chimney smoke at dusk which were now hers also, these were still too marvelous to leave.

But the Freeholder of Tervola had duties as well as rights. Once each season, he or his representative must ride circuit. Up into the mountains, through woods and deep dales, across the Lakeland as far as The Troll and then following the Swiftsmoke River south again, ran the route which Karlavi's fathers had traveled for nearly two centuries. Whether on hailu-back in spring and summer, through the scarlet and gold of fall, or by motorsled when snow had covered all trails, the Freeholder went out into his lands. Isolated farm clans, forest rangers on patrol duty, hunters and trappers and timber cruisers, brought their disputes to him as magistrate, their troubles to him as leader. Even the flitting Alfavala had learned to wait by the paths, the sick and injured trusting he could heal them, those with more complex problems struggling to put them into human words.

This year, however, Karlavi and his bailiffs were much preoccupied with a new dam across the Oulu. The old one had broken last spring, after a winter of unusually heavy snowfall, and 5000 hectares of bottom land were drowned. The engineers at Yuvaskula, the only city on Vaynamo, had developed a new construction process well adapted to such situations. Karlavi wanted to use this.

"But blast it all," he said, "I'll need every skilled man I have, including myself. The job has got to be finished before the ground dries, so the ferroplast can bond with the soil. And you know what the labor shortage is like around here."

"Who will ride circuit, then?" asked Elva.

"That's what I don't know." Karlavi ran a hand through his straight brown hair. He was a typical Vaynamoan, tall, light-complexioned, with high cheekbones and oblique blue eyes. He wore the working clothes usual to the Tervola district, leather breeches ending in mukluks, a mackinaw in the tartan of his family. There was nothing romantic about his appearance. Nonetheless, Elva's heart turned over when he looked at her. Even after two years.

He got out his pipe and tamped it with nervous motions. "Somebody must," he said. "Somebody with enough technical education to use a medikit and discuss people's difficulties intelligently. And with authority. We're more tradition-minded hereabouts than they are at Ruuyalka, dear. Our people wouldn't accept the judgment of just anyone. How could a servant or tenant dare settle an argument between two pioneers? It must be me, or a bailiff, or—" His voice trailed off.

Elva caught the implication. "No!" she exclaimed. "I can't! I mean . . . that is—"

"You're my wife," said Karlavi slowly. "That alone gives you the right, by well-established custom. Especially since you're the daughter of the Magnate of Ruuyalka. Almost equivalent to me in prestige, even if you do come from the other end of the continent, where they're fishers and marine farmers instead of woodsfolk." His grin flashed. "I doubt if you've yet learned what awful snobs the free yeomen of Tervola are!"

"But Hauki, I can't leave him."

"Hauki will be spoiled rotten in your absence, by an adoring nanny and a villageful of ten wives. Otherwise he'll do fine." Karlavi dismissed the thought of their son with a wry gesture. "I'm the one who'll get lonesome. Abominably so."

"Oh, darling," said Elva, utterly melted.

A few days later she rode forth.

And it had been an experience to remember. The easy, rocking motion of the six-legged hailu, the mindless leisure of kilometer after kilometer—where however the body, skin and muscle and blood and all ancient instinct, gained an aliveness such as she had never before felt; the silence of mountains with sunlit ice on their shoulders, then birdsong in the woods and a river brawling; the rough warm hospitality when she stayed overnight with some pioneer, the eldritch welcome at the Alfa nest—she was now glad she had encountered those things, and she hoped to know them again, often.

There had been no danger. The last violence between humans on Vaynamo (apart from occasional fist fights, caused mostly by sheer exuberance and rarely doing any harm) lay a hundred years in the past. As for storms, landslides, flood, wild animals, she had the unobtrusive attendance of Huiva and a dozen other "tame" Alfavala. Even these, the intellectual pick of their species, who had chosen to serve man in a doglike fashion rather than keep to the forests, could speak only a few words and handle only the simplest tools. But their long ears, flat nostrils, feathery antennae, every fine green hair on every small body, were always aquiver. This was their planet, they had evolved here, and they were more animal than rational beings. Their senses and reflexes kept her safer than an armored aircraft might.

All the same, the absence of Karlavi and Hauki grew sharper each day. When finally she came to the edge of cleared land, high on the slopes of Hornback Fell, and saw Tervola below, a momentary blindness stung her eyes.

Huiva guided his hailu alongside hers. He pointed down the mountain with his tail. "Home," he chattered. "Food tonight. Snug bed."

"Yes." Elva blinked hard. *What sort of crybaby am I, anyhow?* she asked herself, half in anger. *I'm the Magnate's daughter and the Freeholder's wife, I have a University degree and a pistol-shooting medal, as a girl I sailed through hurricanes and skindove into grottos where fang-fish laired, as a woman I brought a son into the world . . . I will* not *bawl!*

"Yes," she said. "Let's hurry."

She thumped heels on the hailu's ribs and started downhill at a gallop. Her long yellow hair was braided, but a lock of it broke loose, fluttering behind her. Hoofs rang on stone. Ahead stretched grainfields and pastures, still wet from winter but their shy green deepening toward summer hues, on down to the great metallic sheet of Lake Rovaniemi and then across the valley to the opposite horizon, where the High Mikkela reared into a sky as tall and blue as itself. Down by the lake clustered the village, the dear red tile of roofs, the whale shape of a processing plant, a road lined with trees leading to the Freeholder's mansion. There, old handhewn timbers glowed with sun; the many windows flung the light dazzlingly back to her.

She was halfway down the slope when Huiva screamed. She had learned to react fast. Thinly scattered across all Vaynamo, men could easily die from the unforeseen. Reining in, Elva snatched loose the gun at her waist. "What is it?"

Huiva cowered on his mount. One hand pointed skyward.

At first Elva could not understand. An aircraft descending above the lake . . . what was so odd about that? How else did Huiva expect the inhabitants of settlements hundreds of kilometers apart to visit each other?—And then she registered the shape. And then, realizing the distance, she knew the size of the thing.

It came down swiftly, quiet in its shimmer of antigrav fields, a cigar shape which gleamed. Elva holstered her pistol again and took forth her binoculars. Now she could see how the sleekness was interrupted with turrets and boat housings, cargo locks, viewports. An emblem was set into the armored prow, a gauntleted hand grasping a planetary orb. Nothing she had ever heard of. But—

Her heart thumped, so loudly that she could almost not hear the Alfavala's squeals of terror. "A spaceship," she breathed. "A spaceship, do you know that word? Like the ships my ancestors came here in, long ago. . . . Oh, bother! A big aircraft, Huiva. Come on!"

She whipped her hailu back into gallop. The first spaceship to arrive at Vaynamo in, in, how long? More than a hundred years. And it was landing here! At her own Tervola!

The vessel grounded just beyond the village. Its enormous mass settled deeply into the plowland. Housings opened and auxiliary aircraft darted forth, to hover and swoop. They were of a curious design, larger and blunter than the fliers built on Vaynamo. The people, running toward the marvel, surged back as hatches gaped, gangways extruded, armored cars beetled down to the ground.

Elva had not yet reached the village when the strangers opened fire.

There were no hostile ships, not even an orbital fortress. To depart, the seven craft from Chertkoi simply made rendezvous beyond the atmosphere, held a short gleeful conference by radio, and accelerated outward. Captain Bors Golyev, commanding the flotilla, stood on the bridge of the *Askol* and watched the others. The light of the yellow sun was incandescent on their flanks. Beyond lay blackness and the many stars.

His gaze wandered off among constellations which the parallax of fifteen light-years had not much altered. The galaxy was so big, he thought, so unimaginably enormous. . . . Sedes Regis was an L scrawled across heaven. Tradition claimed Old Sol lay in that direction, a thousand parsecs away. But no one on Chertkoi was certain any longer. Golyev shrugged. Who cared?

"Gravitational field suitable for agoric drive, sir," intoned the pilot.

Golyev looked in the sternward screen. The planet called Vaynamo had dwindled, but remained a vivid shield, barred with cloud and blazoned with continents, the overall color a cool blue-green. He thought of ocherous Chertkoi, and the other planets of its system, which were not even habitable. Vaynamo was the most beautiful color he had ever seen. The two moons were also visible, like drops of liquid gold.

Automatically, his astronaut's eye checked the claims of the instruments. Was Vaynamo really far enough away for the ships to go safely into agoric? Not quite, he thought— no, wait, he'd forgotten that the planet had a five percent greater diameter than Chertkoi. "Very good," he said, and gave the necessary orders to his subordinate captains. A deep hum filled air and metal and human bones. There was a momentary sense of falling, as the agoratron went into action. And then the stars began to change color and crawl weirdly across the visual field.

"All's well, sir," said the pilot. The chief engineer confirmed it over the intercom.

"Very good," repeated Golyev. He yawned and stretched elaborately. "I'm tired! That was quite a little fight we had at that last village, and I've gotten no sleep since. I'll be in my cabin. Call me if anything seems amiss."

"Yes, sir." The pilot smothered a knowing leer.

Golyev walked down the corridor, his feet slamming its metal under internal pseudogravity. Once or twice he met a crewman and accepted a salute as casually as it was given. The men of the Interplanetary Corporation didn't need to stand on ceremony. They were tried spacemen and fighters, every one of them. If they chose to wear sloppy uniforms, to lounge about off-duty cracking jokes or cracking a bottle, to treat their officers as friends rather than tyrants—so much the better. This wasn't the nice-nelly Surface Transport Corporation, or the spit-and-polish Chemical Synthesis trust, but IP, explorer and conqueror. The ship was clean and the guns were ready. What more did you want?

Pravoyats, the captain's batman, stood outside the cabin door. He nursed a scratched cheek and a black eye. One hand rested broodingly on his sidearm. "Trouble?" inquired Golyev.

"Trouble ain't the word, sir."

"You didn't hurt her, did you?" asked Golyev sharply.

"No, sir. I heard your orders all right. Never laid a finger on her in anger. But she sure did on me. Finally I wrassled her down and gave her a whiff of sleepy gas. She'd'a torn the cabin apart otherwise. She's probably come out of it by now, but I'd rather not go in again to see, captain."

Golyev laughed. He was a big man, looming over Pravoyats, who was no midget. Otherwise he was a normal patron-class Chertkoian, powerfully built, with comparatively short legs and strutting gait, his features dark, snubnosed, bearded, carrying more than his share of old scars. He wore a plain green tunic, pants tucked into soft boots, gun at hip, his only sign of rank a crimson star at his throat. "I'll take care of all that from here on," he said.

"Yes, sir." Despite his wounds, the batman looked a shade envious. "Uh, you want the prod? I tell you, she's a troublemaker."

"No."

"Electric shocks don't leave any scars, captain."

"I know. But on your way, Pravoyats." Golyev opened the door, went through, and closed it behind him again.

The girl had been seated on his bunk. She stood up with a gasp. A looker, for certain. The Vaynamoan women generally seemed handsome; this one was beautiful, tall and slim, delicate face and straight nose lightly dusted with freckles. But her mouth was wide and strong, her skin suntanned, and she wore a coarse, colorful riding habit. Her exoticism was the most exciting thing: yellow hair, slant blue eyes, who'd ever heard of the like?

The tranquilizing after-effects of the gas—or else plain nervous exhaustion—kept her from attacking him. She backed against the wall and shivered. Her misery touched Golyev a little. He'd seen unhappiness elsewhere, on Imfan and Novagal and Chertkoi itself, and hadn't been bothered thereby. People who were too weak to defend themselves must expect to be made booty of. It was different, though, when someone as good-looking as this was so woebegone.

He paused on the opposite side of his desk from her, gave a soft salute, and smiled. "What's your name, my dear?"

She drew a shaken breath. After trying several times, she managed to speak. "I didn't think . . . anyone . . . understood my language."

"A few of us do. The hypnopede, you know." Evidently she did not. He thought a short, dry lecture might soothe her. "An invention made a few decades ago on our planet. Suppose another person and I have no language in common. We can be given a drug to accelerate our nervous systems, and then the machine flashes images on a screen and analyzes the sounds uttered by the other person. What it hears is transferred to me and impressed on the speech center of my brain, electronically. As the vocabulary grows, a computer in the machine figures out the structure of the whole language—semantics, grammar, and so on—and orders my own learning accordingly. That way, a few short, daily sessions make me fluent."

She touched her lips with a tongue that seemed equally parched. "I heard once . . . of some experiments at the University," she whispered. "They never got far. No reason for such a machine. Only one language on Vaynamo."

"And on Chertkoi. But we've already subjugated two other planets, one of 'em divided into hundreds of language groups. And we expect there'll be others." Golyev opened a drawer, took out a bottle and two glasses. "Care for brandy?"

He poured. "I'm Bors Golyev, an astronautical executive

of the Interplanetary Corporation, commanding this scout force," he said. "Who are you?"

She didn't answer. He reached a glass toward her. "Come, now," he said, "I'm not such a bad fellow. Here, drink. To our better acquaintance."

With a convulsive movement, she struck the glass from his hand. It bounced on the floor. "Almighty Creator! No!" she yelled. "You murdered my husband!"

She stumbled to a chair, fell down in it, rested head in arms on the desk and began to weep. The spilled brandy crept across the floor toward her.

Golyev groaned. Why did he always get cases like this? Glebs Narov, now, had clapped hands on the jolliest twany wench you could imagine, when they conquered Marsya on Imfan: delighted to be liberated from her own drab culture.

Well, he could kick this female back down among the other prisoners. But he didn't want to. He seated himself across from her, lit a cigar out of the box on his desk, and held his own glass to the light. Ruby smoldered within.

"I'm sorry," he said. "How was I to know? What's done is done. There wouldn't have been so many casualties if they'd been sensible and given up. We shot a few to prove we meant business, but then called on the rest over a loudspeaker, to yield. They didn't. For that matter, you were riding a six-legged animal out of the fields, I'm told. You came busting right *into* the fight. Why didn't you ride the other way and hid out till we left?"

"My husband was there," she said after a silence. When she raised her face, he saw it gone cold and stiff. "And our child."

"Oh? Uh, maybe we picked up the kid, at least. If you'd like to go see—"

"No," she said, toneless and yet somehow with a dim returning pride. "I got Hauki away. I rode straight to the mansion and got him. Then one of your fire-guns hit the roof and the house began to burn. I told Huiva to take the baby—never mind where. I said I'd follow if I could. But Karlavi was out there, fighting. I went back to the barricade. He had been killed just a few seconds before. His face was all bloody. Then your cars broke through the barricade and someone caught me. But you don't have Hauki. Or Karlavi!"

As if drained by the effort of speech, she slumped and stared into a corner, empty-eyed.

"Well," said Golyev, not quite comfortably, "your people had been warned." She didn't seem to hear him. "You never got the message? But it was telecast over your whole planet. After our first non-secret landing. That was several days ago. Where were you? Out in the woods?—Yes, we scouted telescopically, and made clandestine landings, and caught a few citizens to interrogate. But when we understood the situation, more or less, we landed openly in, uh, your city. Yuvaskula, is that the name? We seized it without too much damage, captured some officials of the planetary government, claimed the planet for IP and called on all citizens to cooperate. But they wouldn't! Why, one ambush alone cost us fifty good men. What could we do? We had to teach a lesson. We announced we'd punish a few random villages. That's more humane than bombarding from space with cobalt missiles. Isn't it? But I suppose your people didn't really believe us, the way they came swarming when we landed. Trying to parley with us first, and then trying to resist us with hunting rifles! What would you expect to happen?"

His voice seemed to fall into an echo-less well.

He loosened his collar, which felt a trifle tight, took a deep drag on his cigar and refilled his glass. "Of course, I don't expect you to see our side of it at once," he said reasonably. "You've been jogging along, isolated, for centuries, haven't you? Hardly a spaceship has touched at your planet since it was first colonized. You have none of your own, except a couple of interplanetary boats which hardly ever get used. That's what your President told me, and I believe him. Why should you go outsystem? You have everything you can use, right on your own world. The nearest sun to yours with an oxygen atmosphere planet is three parsecs off. Even with a very high-powered agoratron, you'd need ten years to get there, another decade to get back. A whole generation! Sure, the time-contraction effect would keep you young—ship's time for the voyage would only be a few weeks, or less—but all your friends would be middle-aged when you came home. Believe me, it's lonely being a spaceman."

He drank. A pleasant burning went down his throat. "No wonder man spread so slowly into space, and each colony is so isolated," he said. "Chertkoi is a mere name in your archives. And yet it's only fifteen light-years from Vaynamo. You can see our sun on any clear night. A reddish one. You call it Gamma Navarchi. Fifteen little light-years, and yet there's been no contact between our two planets for four centuries or more!

"So why now? Well, that's a long story. Let's just say Chertkoi isn't as friendly a world as Vaynamo. You'll see that for yourself. We, our ancestors, we came up the hard way, we had to struggle for everything. And now there are four billion of us! That was the census figure when I left. It'll probably be five billion when I get home. We have to have more resources. Our economy is grinding to a halt. And we can't afford economic dislocation. Not on as thin a margin as Chertkoi allows us. First we went back to the other planets of our system and worked them as much as practicable. Then we started re-exploring the nearer stars. So far we've found two useful planets. Yours is the third. You know what your population is? Ten million, your President claimed. Ten million people for a whole world of forests, plains, hills, oceans . . . why, your least continent has more natural resources than all Chertkoi. And you've stabilized at that population. You don't want more people!"

Golyev struck the desk with a thump. "If you think ten million stagnant agriculturists have a right to monopolize all that room and wealth, when four billion Chertkoians live on the verge of starvation," he said indignantly, "you can think again."

She stirred. Not looking at him, her tone small and very distant, she said, "It's our planet, to do with as we please.

If you want to breed like maggots, you must take the consequences."

Anger flushed the last sympathy from Golyev. He ground out his cigar in the ashwell and tossed off his brandy. "Never mind moralizing," he said. "I'm no martyr. I became a spaceman because it's fun!"

He got up and walked around the desk to her.

538 A.C.C.:

When she couldn't stand the apartment any more, Elva went out on the balcony and looked across Dirzh until that view became unendurable in its turn.

From this height, the city had a certain grandeur. On every side it stretched horizonward, immense gray blocks among which rose an occasional spire shining with steel and glass. Eastward at the very edge of vision it ended before some mine pits, whose scaffolding and chimneys did not entirely cage off a glimpse of primordial painted desert. Between the buildings went a network of elevated trafficways, some carrying robofreight, others pullulating with gray-clad clients on foot. Overhead, against a purple-black sky and the planet's single huge moon, nearly full tonight, flitted the firefly aircars of executives, engineers, military techs, and others in the patron class. A few stars were visible, but the fever-flash of neon drowned most of them. Even by full red-tinged daylight, Elva could never see all the way downward. A fog of dust, smoke, fumes and vapors, hid the bottom of the artificial mountains. She could only imagine the underground, caves and tunnels where workers of the lowest category were bred to spend their lives tending machines, and where a criminal class slunk about in armed packs.

It was rarely warm on Chertkoi, summer or winter. As the night wind gusted, Elva drew more tightly around her a mantle of genuine fur from Novagal. Bors wasn't stingy about clothes or jewels. But then, he liked to take her out in public places, where she could be admired and he envied. For the first few months she had refused to leave the apartment. He hadn't made an issue of it, only waited. In

the end she gave in. Nowadays she looked forward eagerly
to such times; they took her away from these walls. But of
late there had been no celebrations. Bors was working too
hard.

The moon Drogoi climbed higher, reddened by the
hidden sun and the lower atmosphere of the city. At the
zenith it would be pale copper. Once Elva had fancied
the markings on it formed a death's head. They didn't
really; that had just been her horror of everything Chertkoian. But she had never shaken off the impression.

She hunted among the constellations, knowing that if she
found Vaynamo's sun it would hurt, but unable to stop. The
air was too thick tonight, though, with an odor of acid and
rotten eggs. She remembered riding out along Lake Rovaniemi, soon after her marriage. Karlavi was along: no one
else, for you didn't need a bodyguard on Vaynamo. The two
moons climbed fast. Their light made a trembling double
bridge on the water. Trees rustled, the air smelled green,
something sang with a liquid plangency, far off among
moon-dappled shadows.

"But that's beautiful!" she had whispered. "Yonder
songbird. We haven't anything like it in Ruuyalka."

Karlavi chuckled. "No bird at all. The Alfavala name—
well, who can pronounce that? We humans say 'yanno.' A
little pseudomammal, a terrible pest. Roots up tubers. For a
while we thought we'd have to wipe out the species."

"But they sing so sweetly."

"True. Also, the Alfavala would be hurt. Insofar as they
have anything like a religion, the yanno seems to be part of
it, locally. Important somehow, to them, at least." Unspo-
ken was the law under which she and he had both been
raised: the green dwarfs are barely where man was, two or
three million years ago on Old Earth, but they are the real
natives of Vaynamo, and if we share their planet, we're
bound to respect them and help them.

Once Elva had tried to explain the idea to Bors Golyev.
He couldn't understand at all. If the abos occupied land men
might use, why not hunt them off it? They'd make good,
crafty game, wouldn't they?

"Can anything be done about the yanno?" she had asked Karlavi.

"For several generations, we fooled around with electric fences and so on. But just a few years ago, I consulted Paaska Ecological Institute and found they'd developed a wholly new approach to such problems. They can now tailor a dominant mutant gene which produces a strong distaste for Vitamin C. I suppose you know Vitamin C isn't part of native biochemistry, but occurs only in plants of Terrestrial origin. We released the mutants to breed, and every season there are fewer yanno that'll touch our crops. In another five years there'll be too few to matter."

"And they'll still sing for us." She edged her hailu closer to his. Their knees touched. He leaned over and kissed her.

Elva shivered. *I'd better go in,* she thought.

The light switched on automatically as she re-entered the living room. At least artificial illumination on Chertkoi was like home. Dwelling under different suns had not yet changed human eyes. Though in other respects, man's colonies had drifted far apart indeed. . . . The apartment had three cramped rooms, which was considered luxurious. When five billion people, more every day, grubbed their living from a planet as bleak as this, even the wealthy must do without things that were the natural right of the poorest Vaynamoan. Spaciousness, trees, grass beneath bare feet, your own house and an open sky. Of course, Chertkoi had very sophisticated amusements to offer in exchange, everything from multisensory films to live combats.

Belgoya pattered in from her offside cubicle. Elva wondered if the maidservant ever slept. "Does the mistress wish anything, please?"

"No." Elva sat down. She ought to be used to the gravity by now, she thought. How long had she been here? A year, more or less. She hadn't kept track of time, especially when they used an unfamiliar calendar. Denser than Vaynamo, Chertkoi exerted a ten percent greater surface pull; but that wasn't enough to matter, when you were in good physical condition. Yet she was always tired.

"No, I don't want anything." She leaned back on the

couch and rubbed her eyes. The haze outside had made them sting.

"A cup of stim, perhaps, if the mistress please?" The girl bowed some more, absurdly doll-like in her uniform.

"No!" Elva shouted. "Go away!"

"I beg your pardon. I am a worm. I implore your magnanimity." Terrified, the maid crawled backward out of the room on her belly.

Elva lit a cigaret. She hadn't smoked on Vaynamo, but since coming here she'd taken it up, become a chainsmoker like most Chertkoians who could afford it. You needed something to do with your hands. The servility of clients toward patrons no longer shocked her, but rather made her think of them as faintly slimy. To be sure, one could see the reasons. Belgoya, for instance, could be fired any time and sent back to street level. Down there were a million eager applicants for her position. Elva forgot her and reached after the teleshow dials. There must be something on, something loud and full of action, something to watch, something to do with her evening.

The door opened. Elva turned about, tense with expectation. So Bors was home. And alone. If he'd brought a friend along, she would have had to go into the sleeping cubicle and merely listen. Upper-class Chertkoians didn't like women intruding on their conversation. But Bors alone meant she would have someone to talk to.

He came in, his tread showing he was also tired. He skimmed his hat into a corner and dropped his cloak on the floor. Belgoya crept forth to pick them up. As he sat down, she was there with a drink and a cigar.

Elva waited. She knew his moods. When the blunt, bearded face had lost some of its hardness, she donned a smile and stretched herself along the couch, leaning on one elbow. "You've been working yourself to death," she scolded.

He sighed. "Yeh. But the end's in view. Another week, and all the obscenity paperwork will be cleared up."

"You hope. One of your bureaucrats will probably invent nineteen more forms to fill out in quadruplicate."

"Probably."

"We never had that trouble at home. The planetary government was only a coordinating body with strictly limited powers. Why won't you people even consider establishing something similar?"

"You know the reasons. Five billion of them. You've got room to be an individual on Vaynamo." Golyev finished his drink and held the glass out for a refill. "By all chaos! I'm tempted to desert when we get there."

Elva lifted her brows. "That's a thought," she purred.

"Oh, you know it's impossible," he said, returning to his usual humorlessness. "Quite apart from the fact I'd be one enemy alien on an entire planet—"

"Not necessarily."

"—All right, even if I got naturalized (and who wants to become a clodhopper?) I'd have only thirty years till the Third Expedition came. I don't want to be a client in my old age. Or worse, see my children made clients."

Elva lit a second cigaret from the stub of the first. She drew in the smoke hard enough to hollow her cheeks.

But it's all right to be launching the Second Expedition and make clients of others, she thought. *The First, that captured me and a thousand more (What's become of them? How many are dead, how many found useless and sent lobotomized to the mines, how many are still being pumped dry of information?) . . . that was a mere scouting trip. The Second will have fifty warships, and try to force surrender. At the very least, it will flatten all possible defenses, destroy all imaginable war potential, bring back a whole herd of slaves. And then the Third, a thousand ships or more, will bring the final conquests, the garrisons, the overseers and entrepreneurs and colonists. But that won't be for forty-five Vaynamo years or better from tonight. A man on Vaynamo . . . Hauki . . . a man who survives the coming of the Second Expedition will have thirty-odd years left in which to be free. But will he dare have children?*

"I'll settle down there after the Third Expedition, I think," Golyev admitted. "From what I saw of the planet last time, I believe I'd like it. And the opportunities are unlimited. A whole world waiting to be properly developed!"

"I could show you a great many chances you'd otherwise overlook," insinuated Elva.

Golyev shifted position. "Let's not go into that again," he said. "You know I can't take you along."

"You're the fleet commander, aren't you?"

"Yes, I will be, but curse it, can't you understand? The IP is not like any other corporation. We use men who think and act on their own, not planet-hugging morons like what's-her-name—" He jerked a thumb at Belgoya, who lowered her eyes meekly and continued mixing him a third drink. "Men of patron status, younger sons of executives and engineers. The officers can't have special privileges. It'd ruin morale."

Elva fluttered her lashes. "Not that much. Really."

"My oldest boy's promised to take care of you. He's not such a bad fellow as you seem to think. You only have to go along with his whims. I'll see you again, in thirty years."

"When I'm gray and wrinkled. Why not kick me out in the streets and be done?"

"You know why!" he said ferociously. "You're the first woman I could ever talk to. No, I'm not bored with you! But—"

"If you really cared for me—"

"What kind of idiot do you take me for? I know you're planning to sneak away to your own people, once we've landed."

Elva tossed her head, haughtily. "Well! If you believe that of me, there's nothing more to say."

"Aw, now, sweetling, don't take that attitude." He reached out a hand to lay on her arm. She withdrew to the far end of the couch. He looked baffled.

"Another thing," he argued. "If you care about your planet at all, as I suppose you do, even if you've now seen what a bunch of petrified mudsuckers they are . . . remember, what we'll have to do there won't be pretty."

"First you call me a traitor," she flared, "and now you say I'm gutless!"

"Hoy, wait a minute—"

"Go on, beat me. I can't stop you. You're brave enough for that."

"I never—"

In the end, he yielded.

553 A.C.C.:

The missile which landed on Yuvaskula had a ten-kilometer radius of total destruction. Thus most of the city went up in one radioactive fire-gout. In a way, the thought of men and women and little children with pet kittens, incinerated, made a trifle less pain in Elva than knowing the Old Town was gone: the cabin raised by the first men to land on Vaynamo, the ancient church of St. Yarvi with its stained glass windows and gilded belltower, the Museum of Art where she went as a girl on entranced visits, the University where she studied and where she met Karlavi— *I'm a true daughter of Vaynamo,* she thought with remorse. *Whatever is traditional, full of memories, whatever has been looked at and been done by all the generations before me, I hold dear. The Chertkoians don't care. They haven't any past worth remembering.*

Flames painted the northern sky red, even at this distance, as she walked among the plastishelters of the advanced base. She had flown within a hundred kilometers, using an aircar borrowed from the flagship, then landed to avoid possible missiles and hitched a ride here on a supply truck. The Chertkoian enlisted men aboard had been delighted until she showed them her pass, signed by Commander Golyev himself. Then they became cringingly respectful.

The pass was supposed to let her move freely about only in the rear areas, and she'd had enough trouble wheeling it from Bors. But no one thereafter looked closely at it. She herself was so unused to the concept of war that she didn't stop to wonder at such lax security measures. Had she done so, she would have realized Chertkoi had never developed anything better, never having faced an enemy of comparable strength. Vaynamo certainly wasn't, even though the planet was proving a hard-shelled opponent, with every farmhouse a potential arsenal and every forest road a possible death trap. Guerrilla fighters hindered the movements of an invader with armor, atomic artillery, complete control of air and space; they could not stop him.

Elva drew her dark mantle more tightly about her and crouched under a gun emplacement. A sentry went by, his helmet square against the beloved familiar face of a moon, his rifle aslant across the stars. She didn't want needless questioning. For a moment the distant blaze sprang higher, unrestful ruddy light touched her, she was afraid she had been observed. But the man continued his round.

From the air she had seen that the fire was mostly a burning forest, kindled from Yuvaskula. Those wooden houses not blown apart by the missile stood unharmed in whitest glow. Some process must have been developed at one of the research institutes for indurating timber, since she left. . . . How Bors would laugh if she told him! An industry which turned out a bare minimum of vehicles, farm machinery, tools, chemicals; a science which developed fireproofing techniques and traced out ecological chains; a population which deliberately held itself static, so as to preserve its old customs and laws—presuming to make war on Chertkoi!

Even so, he was too experienced a fighter to dismiss any foe as weak without careful examination. He had been excited enough about one thing to mention it to Elva—a prisoner taken in a skirmish near Yuvaskula, when he still hoped to capture the city intact: an officer, who cracked just enough under interrogation to indicate he knew something important. But Golyev couldn't wait around for the inquisitors to finish their work. He must go out the very next day to oversee the battle for Lempo Machine Tool Works, and Elva knew he wouldn't return soon. The plant had been constructed underground as an economy measure, and to preserve the green parkscape above. Now its concrete warrens proved highly defensible, and were being bitterly contested. The Chertkoians meant to seize it, so they could be sure of demolishing everything. They would not leave Vaynamo any nucleus of industry. After all, the planet would have thirty-odd years to recover and rearm itself against the Third Expedition.

Left alone by Bors, Elva took an aircar and slipped off to the advanced base.

She recognized the plastishelter she wanted by its Intelligence insignia. The guard outside aimed a rifle at her. "Halt!" His boyish voice cracked over with nervousness. More than one sentry had been found in the morning with his throat cut.

"It's all right," she told him. "I'm to see the prisoner Ivalo."

"The gooze officer?" He flashed a pencil-thin beam across her face. "But, you're a—uh–"

"A Vaynamoan myself. Of course. There are a few of us along, you know. Prisoners taken last time, who've enlisted in your cause as guides and spies. You must have heard of me. I'm Elva, Commander Golyev's lady."

"Oh. Yes, mistress. Sure I have."

"Here's my pass."

He squinted at it uneasily. "But, uh, may I ask what, uh, what *you* figure to do? I've got strict orders—"

Elva gave him her most confidential smile. "My own patron had the idea. The prisoner is withholding valuable information. He has been treated roughly, but resisted. Now, all at once, we'll take the pressure off. An attractive woman of his own race. . . ."

"I get it. Maybe he will crack. I dunno, though, mistress. These slant-eyed towheads are mean animals—begging your pardon! Go right on in. Holler if he gets rough or, or anything."

The door was unlocked for her. Elva went on through, into a hemicylindrical room so low that she must stoop. A lighting tube switched on, showing a pallet laid across the floor.

Captain Ivalo was gray at the temples, but still tough and supple. His face had gone haggard, sunken eyes and a stubble of beard; his garments were torn and filthy. When he looked up, coming awake, he was too exhausted to show much surprise. "What now?" he said in dull Chertkoian. "What are you going to try next?"

Elva answered in Vaynamoan (Oh, God, it was a year and a half, her own time, nearly seventeen years cosmic time, since she had uttered a word to anyone from her planet!): "Be quiet. I beg you. We mustn't be suspected."

He sat up. "Who are you?" he snapped. His own Vaynamoan accent was faintly pedantic; he must be a teacher or scientist in that peacetime life which now seems so distant. "A collaborator? I understand there are some. Every barrel must hold a few rotten apples, I suppose."

She sat down on the floor near him, hugged her knees and stared at the curving wall. "I don't know what to call myself," she said tonelessly. "I'm with them, yes. But they captured me the last time."

He whistled, a soft note. One hand reached out, not altogether steady and stopping short of touching her. "I was young then," he said. "But I remember. Do I know your family?"

"Maybe. I'm Elva, daughter of Byarmo, the Magnate of Ruuyalka. My husband was Karlavi, the Freeholder of Tervola." Suddenly she couldn't stay controlled. She grasped his arm so hard that her nails drew blood. "Do you know what became of my son? His name was Hauki. I got him away, in care of an Alfa servant. Hauki, Karlavi's son, Freeholder of Tervola. Do you know?"

He disengaged himself as gently as possible and shook his head. "I'm sorry. I've heard of both places, but only as names. I'm from the Aakinen Islands myself."

Her head dropped.

"Ivalo is my name," he said clumsily.

"I know."

"What?"

"Listen." She raised her eyes to his. They were quite dry. "I've been told you have important information."

He bridled. "If you think—"

"No. Please listen. Here." She fumbled in a pocket of her

gown. At last her fingers closed on the vial. She held it out
to him. "An antiseptic. But the labels says it's very
poisonous if taken internally. I brought it for you."

He stared at her for a long while.

"It's all I can do," she mumbled, looking away again.

He took the bottle and turned it over and over in his
hands. The night grew silent around them.

Finally he asked, "Won't you suffer for this?"

"Not too much."

"Wait . . . If you could get in here, you can surely
escape completely. Our troops can't be far off. Or any
farmer hereabouts will hide you."

She shook her head. "No. I'll stay with them. Maybe I
can help in some other small way. What else has there been
to keep me alive, but the hope of—It wouldn't be any better,
living here, if we're all conquered. There's to be a final
attack, three decades hence. Do you know that?"

"Yes. Our side takes prisoners too, and quizzes them.
The first episode puzzled us. Many thought it had only been
a raid by—what's the word?—by pirates. But now we know
they really do intend to take our planet away."

"You must have developed some good linguists," she
said, seeking impersonality. "To be able to talk with your
prisoners. Of course, you yourself, after capture, could be
educated by the hypnopede."

"The what?"

"The language-teaching machine."

"Oh, yes, the enemy do have them, don't they? But we
do too. After the first raid, those who thought there was a
danger the aliens might come back set about developing
such machines. I knew Chertkoian weeks before my own
capture."

"I wish I could help you escape," she said desolately.
"But I don't see how. That bottle is all I can do. Isn't it?"

"Yes." He regarded the thing with a fascination.

"My patron . . . Golyev himself—said his men would
rip you open to get your knowledge. So I thought—"

"You're very kind." Ivalo grimaced, as if he had tasted
something foul. "But your act may turn out pointless. I

don't know anything useful. I wasn't even sworn to secrecy about what I do know. Why've I held out, then? Don't ask me. Stubbornness. Anger. Or just hating to admit my people—our people, damn it!—that they could be so weak and foolish."

"What?"

"They could win the war at a stroke," he said. "They won't. They'd rather die, and let their children be enslaved by the Third Expedition."

"What do you *mean?*" She crouched to hands and knees.

He shrugged. "I told you, a number of people on Vaynamo took the previous invasion at its word, that it was the vanguard of a conquering army. There was no official action. How could there be, with a government as feeble as ours? But some of the research biologists—"

"Not a plague!"

"Yes. Mutated from the local paracoryzoid virus. Incubation period, approximately one month, during which time it's contagious. Vaccination is still effective two weeks after exposure, so all our population could be safeguarded. But the Cherokoians would take the disease back with them. Estimated deaths, ninety percent of the race."

"But—"

"That's where the government did step in," he said with bitterness. "The information was suppressed. The virus cultures were destroyed. The theory was, even to save ourselves we couldn't do such a thing."

Elva felt the tautness leave her. She sagged. She had seen small children on Chertkoi too.

"They're right, of course," she said wearily.

"Perhaps. Perhaps. And yet we'll be overrun and butchered, or reduced to serfdom. Won't we? Our forests will be cut down, our mines gutted, our poor Alfavala exterminated . . . To hell with it." Ivalo gazed at the poison vial. "I don't have any scientific data, I'm not a virologist. It can't do any military harm to tell the Chertkoians. But I've seen what they've done to us. I would give them the sickness."

"I wouldn't." Elva bit her lip.

He regarded her for a long time. "Won't you escape? Never mind being a planetary heroine. There's nothing you can do. The invaders will go home when they've wrecked all our industry. They won't come again for thirty years. You can be free most of your life."

"You forget," she said, "that if I leave with them, and come back, the time for me will only have been one or two years." She sighed. "I can't help make ready for the next battle. I'm just a woman. Untrained. While maybe . . . oh, if nothing else, there'll be more Vaynamoan prisoners brought to Chertkoi. I have a tiny bit of influence. Maybe I can help them."

Ivalo considered the poison. "I was about to use this anyway," he muttered. "I didn't think staying alive was worth the trouble. But now—if you can—No." He gave the vial back to her. "I thank you, my lady."

"I have an idea," she said, with a hint of vigor in her voice. "Go ahead and tell them what you know. Pretend I talked you into it. Then I might be able to get you exchanged. It's barely possible."

"Oh, perhaps," he said.

She rose to go. "If you are set free," she stammered, "will you make a visit to Tervola? Will you find Hauki, Karvali's son, and tell him you saw me? If he's alive."

569 A.C.C.:

Dirzh had changed while the ships were away. The evolution continued after their return. The city grew bigger, smokier, uglier. More people each year dropped from client status, went underground and joined the gangs. Occasionally, these days, the noise and vibration of pitched battles down in the tunnels could be detected up on patron level. The desert could no longer be seen, even from the highest towers, only the abandoned mine and the slag mountains, in process of conversion to tenements. The carcinogenic murkiness crept upward until it could be smelled on the most elite balconies. Teleshows got noisier and nakeder, to compete with live performances, which were now offering more elaborate bloodlettings than old-fashioned combats.

The news from space was of a revolt suppressed on Novagal, resulting in such an acute labor shortage that workers were drafted from Imfan and shipped thither.

Only when you looked at the zenith was there no apparent change. The daylit sky was still cold purplish-blue, with an occasional yellow dustcloud. At night there were still the stars, and a skull.

And yet, thought Elva, you wouldn't need a large telescope to see the Third Expedition fleet in orbit—eleven hundred spacecraft, the unarmed ones loaded with troops and equipment, nearly the whole strength of Chertkoi marshalling to conquer Vaynamo. Campaigning across interstellar distances wasn't easy. You couldn't send home for supplies or reinforcements. You broke the enemy or he broke you. Fleet Admiral Bors Golyev did not intend to be broken.

He did not even plan to go home with news of a successful probing operation or a successful raid. The Third Expedition was to be final. And he must allow for the Vaynamoans having had a generation in which to recuperate. He'd smashed their industry, but if they were really determined, they could have rebuilt. No doubt a space fleet of some kind would be waiting to oppose him.

He knew it couldn't be of comparable power. Ten million people, forced to recreate all their mines and furnaces and factories before they could lay the keel of a single boat, had no possibility of matching the concerted efforts of six-and-a-half billion whose world had been continuously industrialized for centuries, and who could draw on the resources of two subject planets. Sheer mathematics ruled it out. But the ten million could accomplish something; and nuclear-fusion missiles were to some degree an equalizer. Therefore Bors Golyev asked for so much strength that the greatest conceivable enemy force would be swamped. And he got it.

Elva leaned on the balcony rail. A chill wind fluttered her gown about her, so that the rainbow hues rippled and ran into each other. She had to admit the fabric was lovely. Bors tried hard to please her. (Though why must he mention the price?) He was so childishly happy himself, in his accomplishments, at his new eminence, at the eight-room apartment which he now rated on the very heights of the Lebedan Tower.

"Not thát we'll be here long," he had said, after they first explored its mechanized intricacies. "My son Nivko has done good work in the home office. That's how come I got this command; experience alone wasn't enough. Of course, he'll expect me to help along his sons. . . . But anyhow, the Third Expedition can go even sooner than I'd hoped. Just a few months, and we're on our way!"

"We?" murmured Elva.

"You do want to come?"

"The last voyage, you weren't so eager."

"Uh, yes. I did have a deuce of a time, too, getting you aboard. But this'll be different. First, I've got so much rank I'm beyond criticism, even beyond jealousy. And second— well, you count too. You're not any picked-up native female. You're Elva! The girl who on her own hook got that fellow Ivalo to confess."

She turned her head slightly, regarding him sideways from droop-lidded blue eyes. Under the ruddy sun, her yellow hair turned to raw gold. "I should think the news would have alarmed them, here on Chertkoi," she said. "Being told that they nearly brought about their own extinction. I wonder that they dare launch another attack."

Golyev grinned. "You should have heard the ruckus. Some Directors did vote to keep hands off Vaynamo. Others wanted to sterilize the whole planet with cobalt missiles. But I talked 'em around. Once we've beaten the fleet and occupied the planet, its whole population will be hostage for good behavior. We'll make examples of the first few goozes who give us trouble of any sort. Then they'll know we mean what we say when we announce our policy. At the first suspicion of plague among us, we'll lay waste a continent. If the suspicion is confirmed, we'll bombard the whole works. No, there will not be any bug warfare."

"I know. I've heard your line of reasoning before. About five hundred times, in fact."

"Destruction! Am I really that much of a bore?" He came up behind her and laid his hands on her shoulders. "I don't mean to be. Honest. I'm not used to talking to women, that's all."

"And I'm not used to being shut away like a prize goldfish, except when you want to exhibit me," she said sharply.

He kissed her neck. His whiskers tickled. "It'll be different on Vaynamo. When we're settled down. I'll be governor of the planet. The Directorate has as good as promised me. Then I can do as I want. And so can you."

"I doubt that! Why should I believe anything you say? When I told you I'd made Ivalo talk by promising you would exchange him, you wouldn't keep the promise." She tried to wriggle free, but his grip was too strong. She contented herself with going rigid. "Now, when I tell you the prisoners we brought back this time are to be treated like human beings, you whine about your damned Directorate—"

"But the Directorate makes policy!"

"You're the Fleet Admiral, as you never lose a chance to remind me. You can certainly bring pressure to bear. You can insist the Vaynamoans be taken out of those kennels and given honorable detention—"

"Awww, now." His lips nibbled along her cheek. She turned her head away and continued:

"—and you can get what you insist on. They're your own prisoners, aren't they? I've listened enough to you, and your dreary officers, when you brought them home. I've read books, hundreds of books. What else is there for me to do, day after day and week after week?"

"But I'm busy! I'd like to take you out, honest, but—"

"So I understand the power structure on Chertkoi just as well as you do, Bors Golyev. If not better. If you don't know how to use your own influence, then slough off some of the conceit, sit down and listen while I tell you how!"

"Well, uh, I never denied, sweetling, you've given me some useful advice from time to time."

"So listen to me! I say all the Vaynamoans you hold are

to be given decent quarters, recreation, and respect. What did you capture them for, if not to get some use out of them? And the proper use is not to titillate yourself by kicking them around. A dog would serve that purpose better.

"Furthermore, the fleet has to carry them all back to Vaynamo."

"What? You don't know what you're talking about! The logistics is tough enough without—"

"I do so know what I'm talking about. Which is more than I can say for you. You want guides, intermediaries, puppet leaders, don't you? Not by the score, a few cowards and traitors, as you have hitherto. You need hundreds. Well, there they are, right in your hands."

"And hating my guts," Golyev pointed out.

"Give them reasonable living conditions and they won't. Not quite so much, anyhow. Then bring them back home—a generation after they left, all their friends aged or dead, everything altered once you've conquered the planet. And let me deal with them. You'll get helpers!"

"Uh, well, uh, I'll think about it."

"You'll do something about it!" She eased her body, leaning back against the hard rubbery muscles of his chest. Her face turned upward, with a slow smile. "You're good at doing things, Bors," she said languidly.

"Oh, Elva—"

Later: "You know one thing I want to do? As soon as I'm well established in the governorship? I want to marry you. Properly and openly. Let 'em be shocked. I won't care. I want to be your husband, and the father of your kids, Elva. How's that sound? Mistress Governor General Elva Golyev of Vaynamo Planetary Province. Never thought you'd get that far in life, did you?"

584 A.C.C.:

As they neared the end of the journey, he sent her to his cabin. An escape suit—an armored cylinder with gravity propulsors, air regenerator, food and water supplies, which she could enter in sixty seconds—occupied most of the room. "Not that I expect any trouble," he said. "But if something should happen . . . I hope you can make it down to the surface." He paused. The officers on the bridge moved quietly about their tasks; the engines droned; the distorted stars of near-light velocity framed his hard brown face. There was a thin sheen of sweat on his skin.

"I love you, you know," he finished. Quickly, he turned back to his duties. Elva went below.

Clad in a spaceman's uniform, seated on the bunk, enclosed in toning metal, she felt the inward wrench as the agoratron went off and speed was converted back to atomic mass. The cabin's private viewscreen showed stars in their proper constellations again, needle-sharp against blackness. Vaynamo was tiny and blue, still several hundred thousand kilometers remote. Elva ran fingers through her hair. The scalp beneath felt tight, and her lips were dry. A person could not help being afraid, she thought. Just a little afraid.

She called up the memory of Karlavi's land, where he had now lain for sixty-two years. Reeds whispered along the shores of Rovaniemi, the wind made a rippling in long grass, and it was time again for the lampflowers to blow, all down the valley. Dream-like at the edge of vision, the snowpeaks of the High Mikkela floated in an utter blue.

I'm coming back, Karlavi, she thought.

In her screen, the nearer vessels were glinting toys, plunging through enormous emptiness. The further ones were not visible at this low magnification. Only the sense of radar, gravpulse, and less familiar creations, analyzed by whirling electrons in a computer bank, gave any approach to reality. But she could listen in on the main intercom line to the bridge if she chose, and hear those data spoken. She flipped the switch. Nothing yet, only routine reports. Had the planet's disc grown a trifle?

Have I been wrong all the time? she thought. Her heart stopped for a second.

Then: "Alert! Condition red! Alert! Condition red! Objects detected, approaching nine-thirty o'clock, fifteen degrees high. Neutrino emissions indicate nuclear engines."

"Alert! Condition yellow! Quiescent object detected in orbit about target planet, two-thirty o'clock, ten degrees low, circa 75,000 kilometers distant. Extremely massive. Repeat, quiescent. Low level of nuclear activity, but at bolometric temperature of ambient space. Possibly an abandoned space fortress, except for being so massive."

"Detected objects identified as space craft. Approaching with average radial velocity of 25° KPS. No evident deceleration. Number very large, estimated at five thousand. All units small, about the mass of our scoutboats."

The gabble went on until Golyev's voice cut through: "Attention! Fleet Admiral to bridge of all units. Now hear this." Sardonically: "The opposition is making a good try. Instead of building any real ships—they could have constructed only a few at best—they've turned out thousands of manned warboats. Their plan is obviously to cut through our formation, relying on speed, and release tracking torps in quantity. Stand by to repel. We have enough detectors, anti-missiles, negafields, to overwhelm them in this department too! Once past us, the boats will need hours to decelerate and come back within decent shooting range. By that time we should be in orbit around the planet. Be alert for possible emergencies, of course. But I expect only standard operations to be necessary. Good shooting!"

Elva strained close to her screen. All at once she saw the Vaynamoan fleet, mere sparks, but a horde of them twinkling among the stars. Closer! Her fingers strained against each other. *They* must *have some plan,* she told herself. *If I'm blown up in five minutes—I was hoping I'd get down to you, Karlavi. But if I don't, goodbye, goodbye.*

The fleets neared each other: on the one side, ponderous dreadnoughts, cruisers, auxiliary warcraft, escorting swarms of transport and engineer ships; on the opposite side, needle-thin boats whose sole armor was velocity. The guns of Chertkoi swung about, hoping for a lucky hit. At such speeds it was improbable. The fleets would interpenetrate and pass in a fractional second. The Vaynamoans could not be blasted until they came to grips near their home world. However, if a nuclear shell should find its mark now—what a blaze in heaven!

The flagship staggered.

"Engine room to bridge! What's happened?"

"Bridge to engine room! Gimme some power there! What in all destruction—?"

"*Sharyats* to *Askol!* *Sharyats* to *Askol!* Am thrown off course! Accelerating! What's going on?"

"Look out!"

"*Fodorev* to *Zuevots!* Look alive, you bloody fool! You'll ram us!"

Cushioned by the internal field, Elva felt only the minutest fraction of that immense velocity change. Even so, a wave of sickness went through her. She clutched at the bunk stanchion. The desk ripped from a loose mooring and crashed into the wall, which buckled. The deck split open underfoot. A roar went through the entire hull, ribs groaned as they bent, plates screamed as they sheared. A girder snapped in twain and spat sharp fragments among a gun turret crew. A section broke apart, air gushed out, a hundred men died before the sealing bulkheads could close.

After a moment, the stabilizing energies regained interior control. The images on Elva's screen steadied. She drew a shaken lungful of air and watched. Out of formation, the *Askol* plunged within a kilometer of her sister ship the *Zuevots*—just when that cyclopean hull smashed into the cruiser *Fodorev*. Fire sheeted as accumulator banks were shorted. The two giants crumpled, glowing white at the point of impact, fused, and spun off in a lunatic waltz. Men and supplies were pinwheeled from the cracks gaping in them. Two gun turrets wrapped their long barrels around each other like intertwining snakes. Then the whole mass struck a third vessel with shattering impact. Steel chunks exploded into space.

Through the noise and the human screaming, Golyev's voice blasted. "Pipe down there! Belay that! By Creation, I'll shoot the next man who whimpers! The enemy will be here in a minute. All stations, by the numbers, report."

A measure of discipline returned. These were fighting men. Instruments fingered outward, the remaining computers whirred, minds made deductive leaps, gunners returned to their posts. The Vaynamoan fleet passed through, and the universe exploded in brief pyrotechnics. Many a Chertkoian ship died then, its defenses too battered, its defenders too stunned to ward off the tracking torpedoes. But others fought back, saved themselves, and saw their enemies vanish in the distance.

Still they tumbled off course, their engines helpless to free them. Elva heard a physicist's clipped tones give the deduction from his readings. The entire fleet had been caught in a cone of gravitational force emanating from that massive object detected in orbit. Like a maelstrom of astronomical dimensions, it had snatched them from their paths. Those closest and in the most intense field strength— a fourth of the armada—had been wrecked by sheer deceleration. Now the force was drawing them down the vortex of itself.

"But that's impossible!" wailed the *Askol*'s chief engineer. "A gravity attractor beam of that magnitude. . . . Admiral, it can't be done! The power requirements would burn out any generator in a microsecond!"

"It's being done," said Golyev harshly. "Maybe they figured out a new way to feed energy into a space distorter. Now, where are those figures on intensity? And my slide rule. . . . Yeh. The whole fleet will soon be in a field so powerful that—Well, we won't let it happen. Stand by to hit that generator with everything we've got."

"But sir . . . we must have—I don't know how many ships—close enough to it now to be within total destruction radius."

"Tough on them. Stand by. Gunnery Control, fire when ready."

And then, whispered, even though that particular line was private and none else in the ship would hear: "Elva! Are you all right down there? Elva!"

Her hands had eased their trembling enough for her to light a cigaret. She didn't speak. Let him worry. It might reduce his efficiency.

Her screen did not happen to face the vortex source, and thus did not show its destruction by the nuclear barrage. Not that that could have been registered. The instant explosion of sun-center ferocity transcended any sense, human or electronic. Down on Vaynamo surface, in broad daylight, they must have turned dazzled eyes from that brilliance. Anyone within a thousand kilometers of those warheads died, no matter how much steel and force field he had interposed. Two score Chertkoian ships were suddenly manned by corpses. Those further in were fused to lumps. Still further in, they ceased to exist, save as gas at millions of degrees temperature. The vessels already crashed on the giant station were turned into unstable isotopes, their very atoms dying.

But the station itself vanished. And Vaynamo had had the capacity to build only one such monster. The Chertkoian ships were free again.

"Admiral to all captains!" cried Golyev's lion voice. "Admiral to all captains. Let the reports wait. Clear the lines. I want every man in the fleet to hear me. Stand by for message.

"Now hear this! This is Supreme Commander Bors Golyev. We just took a rough blow, boys. The enemy had an unsuspected weapon, and cost us a lot of casualties. But we've destroyed the thing. I repeat, we blew it out of the cosmos. And I say, well done! I say also, we still have a hundred times the strength of the enemy, and he's shot his bolt. We're going on in! We're going to—"

"Alert! Condition red! Enemy boats returning. Enemy boats returning. Radial velocity circa 50 KPS, but acceleration circa 100 G."

"*What?*"

Elva herself saw the Vaynamoan shooting stars come back into sight.

Golyev tried hard to shout down the panic of his officers. Would they stop running around like old women? The enemy had developed something else, some method of accelerating at unheard-of rates under gravitational thrust. But not by witchcraft! It could be an internal-stress compensator developed to ultimate efficiency, plus an adaptation of whatever principle was used in the attractor vortex. Or it could be a breakthrough, a totally new principle,

maybe something intermediate between the agoratron and
the ordinary interplanetary drive. . . . "Never mind what,
you morons! They're only flocks of splinters! Kill them!"

But the armada was roiling about in blind confusion. The
detectors had given mere seconds of warning, which were
lost in understanding that the warning was correct and in
frantically seeking to rally men already shaken. Then the
splinter fleet was in among the Chertkoians. It braked its
furious relative velocity with a near-instantaneous quickness for which the Chertkoian gunners and gun computers
had never been prepared. However, the Vaynamoan gunners were ready. And even a boat can carry torpedoes which
will annihilate a battleship.

In a thousand fiery bursts, the armada died.

Not all of it. Unarmed craft were spared, if they would
surrender. Vaynamoan boarding parties freed such of their
countrymen as they found. The *Askol*, under Golyev's
personal command, stood off its attackers and moved
doggedly outward, toward regions where it could use the
agoratron to escape. The captain of a prize revealed that
over a hundred Vaynamoans were aboard the flagship. So
the attempt to blow it up was abandoned. Instead, a large
number of boats shot dummy missiles, which kept the
defense full occupied. Meanwhile, a companion force lay
alongside, cut its way through the armor, and sent men in.

The Chertkoian crew resisted. But they were grossly
outnumbered and outgunned. Most died, under bullets and
grenades, gas and flamethrowers. Certain holdouts, who
fortified a compartment, were welded in from the outside
and left to starve or capitulate, whichever they chose. Even
so, the *Askol* was so big that the boarding party took several
hours to gain full possession.

The door opened. Elva stood up.

At first the half-dozen men who entered seemed foreign.
In a minute—she was too tired and dazed to think clearly—
she understood why. They were all in blue jackets and
trousers, a uniform. She had never before seen two Vaynamoans dressed exactly alike. *But of course they would be,*

she thought in a vague fashion. *We had to build a navy, didn't we?*

And they remained her own people. Fair skin, straight hair, high cheekbones, tilted light eyes which gleamed all the brighter through the soot of battle. And, yes, they still walked like Vaynamoans, the swinging freeman's gait and the head held high, such as she had not seen for . . . for how long? So their clothes didn't matter, nor even the guns in their hands.

Slowly, through the ringing in her ears, she realized that the combat noise had stopped.

A young man in the lead took a step in her direction. "My lady—" he began.

"Is that her for certain?" asked someone else, less gently. "Not a collaborator?"

A new man pushed his way through the squad. He was grizzled, pale from lack of sun, wearing a sleazy prisoner's coverall. But a smile touched his lips, and his bow to Elva was deep.

"This is indeed my lady of Tervola," he said. To her: "When these men released me, up in Section Fourteen, I told them we'd probably find you here. I am so glad."

She needed a while to recognize him. "Oh. Yes." Her head felt heavy. It was all she could do to nod. "Captain Ivalo. I hope you're all right."

"I am, thanks to you, my lady. Someday we'll know how many hundreds of us are alive and sane—and here!— because of you."

The squad leader made another step forward, sheathed his machine pistol and lifted both hands toward her. He was a well-knit, good-looking man, blond of hair, a little older than she: in his mid-thirties, perhaps. He tried to speak, but no words came out, and then Ivalo drew him back.

"In a moment," said the ex-captive. "Let's first take care of the unpleasant business."

The leader hesitated, then, with a grimace, agreed. Two men shoved Bors Golyev. The admiral dripped blood from a dozen wounds and stumbled in his weariness. But when he saw Elva, he seemed to regain himself. "You weren't hurt," he breathed. "I was so afraid . . ."

Ivalo said like steel: "I've explained the facts of this case to the squad officer here, as well as his immediate superior. I'm sure you'll join us in our wish not to be inhumane, my lady. And yet a criminal trial in the regular courts would publicize matters best forgotten and could give this man only a limited punishment. So we, here and now, under the conditions of war and in view of your high services—"

The squad officer interrupted. He was white about the nostrils. "Anything you order, my lady," he said. "You pass the sentence. We'll execute it at once."

"Elva," whispered Golyev.

She stared at him, remembering fire and enslavement and a certain man dead on a barricade. Everything seemed distant, not quite real.

"There's been too much suffering already," she said.

She pondered a few seconds.

"Just take him out and shoot him."

The officer looked relieved. He led his men forth. Golyev started to speak, but was hustled away too fast.

Ivalo remained in the cabin. "My lady—" he began, slow and awkward.

"Yes?" As her weariness overwhelmed her, Elva sat down again on the bunk. She fumbled for a cigaret. There was no emotion in her, only a dull wish for sleep.

"I've wondered. . . . Don't answer this if you don't want to. You've been through so much."

"That's all right," she said mechanically. "The trouble is over now, isn't it? I mean, we mustn't let the past obsess us."

"Of course. Uh, they tell me Vaynamo hasn't changed much. The defense effort was bound to affect society somewhat, but they've tried to minimize that, and succeeded. Our culture has a built-in stability, you know, a negative feedback. To be sure, we must still take action about the home planet of those devils. Liberate their slave worlds and make certain they can't ever try afresh. But that shouldn't be difficult.

"As for you, I inquired very carefully on your behalf. Tervola remains in your family. The land and the people are as you remember."

She closed her eyes, feeling the first thaw within herself. "Now I can sleep," she told him.

Remembering, she looked up with a touch of startlement. "But you had a question for me, Ivalo?"

"Yes. All this time, I couldn't help wondering. Why you stayed with the enemy. You could have escaped. Did you know all the while how great a service you were going to do?"

Her own smile was astonishing to her. "Well, I knew I couldn't be much use on Vaynamo," she said. "Could I? There was a chance I could help on Chertkoi. But I wasn't being brave. The worst had already happened to me. Now I need only wait . . . a matter of months, only, my time . . . and everything bad would be over. Whereas— well, if I'd escaped from the Second Expedition, I'd have lived most of my life in the shadow of the Third. Please don't make a fuss about me. I was actually an awful coward."

His jaw dropped. "You mean you knew we'd win? But you couldn't have. Everything pointed the other way!"

The nightmare was fading more rapidly than she had dared hope. She shook her head, still smiling, not triumphant but glad to speak the knowledge which had kept her alive. "You're being unfair to our people. As unfair as the Chertkoians were. They thought that because we preferred social stability and room to breathe, we must be stagnant. They forgot you can have bigger adventures in, in the spirit, than in all the physical universe. We really did have a very powerful science and technology. It was oriented toward life, toward beautifying and improving instead of exploiting nature. But it wasn't less virile for that. Was it?"

"But we had no industry to speak of. We don't even now."

"I wasn't counting on our factories, I said, but on our science. When you told me about that horrible virus weapon being suppressed, you confirmed my hopes. We aren't

saints. Our government wouldn't have been quite so quick
to get rid of those plagues—would at least have tried to bluff
with them—if there weren't something better in prospect.
Wouldn't it?

"I couldn't even guess what our scientists might develop,
given two generations which the enemy did not have. I did
think they would probably have to use physics rather than
biology. And why not? You can't have an advanced chemical, medical, genetic, ecological technology without knowing all the physics there is to know. Can you? Quantum
theory explains mutations. But it also explains atomic
reactions, or whatever they used in those new machines.

"Oh, yes, Ivalo, I felt sure we'd win. All I had to do
myself was work to get us prisoners—especially me, to be
quite honest—get us all there at the victory."

He looked at her with awe. Somehow that brought back
the heaviness in her. *After all*, she thought . . . *sixty-two
years. Tervola abides. But who will know me? I am going to
be so much alone.*

Boots rang on metal. The young squad leader stepped
forward again. "That's that," he said. His bleakness vanished and he edged closer to Elva, softly, almost timidly.

"I trust," said Ivalo with a rich, growing pleasure in his
voice, "that my lady will permit me to visit her from time
to time."

"I hope you will!" she murmured.

"We temporal castaways are bound to be disoriented for
a while," he said. "We must help each other. You, for
example, may have some trouble adjusting to the fact that
your son Hauki, the Freeholder of Tervola—"

"Hauki!" She sprang to her feet. The cabin blurred
around her.

"—is now a vigorous elderly man who looks back on a
most successful life," said Ivalo. "Which includes the
begetting of Karlavi here." Her grandson's strong hands
closed about her own. "Who in turn," finished Ivalo, "is
the recent father of a bouncing baby boy named Hauki. And
all your people are waiting to welcome you home!"